OVERLORD

Volume 5: The Men of the Kingdom PART I

Kugane Maruyama | Illustration by so-bin

YEN ON
NEW YORK

OVERLORD

VOLUME 5

KUGANE MARUYAMA

Translation by Emily Balistrieri
Cover art by so-bin

©2014 KUGANE MARUYAMA
All rights reserved.

First published in Japan in 2014 by KADOKAWA CORPORATION ENTERBRAIN.
English translation rights arranged with KADOKAWA CORPORATION ENTERBRAIN, through Tuttle-Mori Agency, Inc., Tokyo.

English translation © 2017 by Yen Press, LLC

Yen On
1290 Avenue of the Americas
New York, NY 10104

Visit us at yenpress.com
facebook.com/yenpress
twitter.com/yenpress
yenpress.tumblr.com
instagram.com/yenpress

First Yen On Edition: September 2017

Yen On is an imprint of Yen Press, LLC.
The Yen On name and logo are trademarks of Yen Press, LLC.

The publisher is not responsible for websites (or their content) that are not owned by the publisher.

Library of Congress Cataloging-in-Publication Data
Names: Maruyama, Kugane, author. | So-bin, illustrator. | Balistrieri, Emily, translator.
Title: Overlord / Kugane Maruyama ; illustration by So-bin ; translation by Emily Balistrieri.
Other titles: Ōbārōdo. English
Description: First Yen On edition. | New York, NY : Yen On, 2016-
Identifiers: LCCN 2016000142 | ISBN 9780316272247 (v. 1 : hardback) |
ISBN 9780316363914 (v. 2 : hardback) | ISBN 9780316363938 (v. 3 : hardback) |
ISBN 9780316397599 (v. 4 : hardback) | ISBN 9780316397612 (v. 5 : hardback)
Subjects: LCSH: Alternate reality games—Fiction. | Internet games—Fiction. | Science fiction. |
BISAC: FICTION / Science Fiction / Adventure.
Classification: LCC PL873.A37 O2313 2016 | DDC 895.63/6—dc23
LC record available at http://lccn.loc.gov/2016000142

ISBNs: 978-0-316-39761-2 (hardcover)
978-0-316-39762-9 (ebook)

3 5 7 9 10 8 6 4

LSC-C

Printed in the United States of America

Contents

OVERLORD

Prologue

1 *Late Fire Moon* (September) 2:15 PM

Looking up, he saw the dark clouds, which had covered the sky since early morning, begin spitting a light rain as if unable to resist the urge any longer. The captain of the Royal Select, Gazef Stronoff, clicked his tongue at the hazy world before him.

A little earlier and he would have been able to reach home without getting soaked.

He peered out across the sky but couldn't see any breaks in the dark clouds that completely enveloped Re-Estize, the royal capital sharing a name with the wider Re-Estize Kingdom. Even if he waited, it didn't seem like the rain would stop.

Abandoning the idea of lingering inside the castle, he pulled his cloak's hood over his head and stepped into the rain.

The guards at the gate knew him, and he passed freely onto the city's main street.

Normally this street would have been full of activity, but now there were hardly any people to be seen. Only a few were out, picking their paths carefully so as not to slip and fall on the road that looked almost black, it was so drenched.

From the lack of crowds, he figured the rain must have started some time ago. *Then maybe it wouldn't have mattered if I had left earlier.*

As his cloak grew gradually heavier in the shower, he walked in silence, passing by a few people similarly outfitted with rain gear. His cloak was serving as a rain jacket for now, but when wet, the way it clung to his skin was uncomfortable. Gazef picked up his pace to hurry home.

He was nearing his house and sighed with relief, knowing he would soon be free of his sopping wet cloak, when suddenly his attention was almost magnetically drawn down an alley off to the right where, in this thinly veiled world, a shabby-looking man sat letting the drizzle soak him as it pleased.

The wet hair plastered to the man's forehead, dripping raindrops, was a different color at the roots. Perhaps it was a half-hearted dye job? Since the man was looking down, Gazef couldn't make out his face.

The reason Gazef's eyes had stopped on him was not because he wondered why the man had no weather-appropriate clothing and was steadily becoming drenched. Instead, he had the feeling something was off about this stranger. Something inconsistent. The man's right hand in particular caught his attention.

The weapon gripped there, tightly like the way a child holds their mother's hand, didn't match the grimy man at all. It was an extremely rare weapon, a katana, made in a city that was said to lie far to the south in a desert.

Did he steal it…? No. I don't get that feeling from him. He seems familiar somehow… Gazef felt a bizarre sensation, like he'd buttoned his shirt one hole off.

The moment Gazef halted and saw the man's profile, memories came flooding back to him.

"Could it be…U-Unglaus?" The minute he'd said it, the thought *Not a chance* flashed across his mind.

Brain Unglaus was the man he'd once fought in the final match of the royal tournament.

The image of the man he'd had such a close battle with was seared into his brain. He couldn't forget the face of the strongest warrior he'd dueled since picking up a sword, the one he still considered a rival—even if the feeling was one-sided.

Yes, the man's hollow cheeks resembled his rival's face.

But—it couldn't be him.

Certainly, his appearance was similar. Despite the changes that accompanied time's passage, his features were clearly recognizable. But the man Gazef remembered would never wear such a pathetic expression. He had been a man overflowing with confidence in his sword and enveloped in an intense, burning will to fight. He wasn't an old, wet dog like this.

Gazef approached the man, footsteps splashing.

Reacting to the noise, the man sluggishly raised his head.

Gazef gasped. Seeing the man's face head-on confirmed it. He was Brain Unglaus, the brilliant swordsman.

But he had none of his former radiance. The Brain who Gazef looked upon now had been completely broken, like a beaten animal.

Brain staggered to his feet. His slow, or perhaps listless, movements were not those of a warrior, nor even an old soldier. He dropped his eyes and turned around without saying a word. Then he set off, dejectedly walking away.

As that back receded into the rain, Gazef had the feeling if they parted like this they would never meet again, so he closed the distance and shouted. "…Unglaus! Brain Unglaus!"

If the man said he was wrong, Gazef would tell himself it was a coincidental resemblance. But the very quiet voice that reached his ears did not contradict him.

"…Stronoff?"

There was no soul in that voice. Gazef never would have thought it was the same Brain he had clashed swords with. "What…what happened to you?" he asked in shock.

What in the world could have happened to him?

It's possible for anyone to ruin themselves. Gazef had known a few who had done it. When people were always seeking out easier ways to live, one failure could cause them to lose everything.

But he couldn't imagine that genius swordsman, Brain Unglaus, having anything to do with those people. Was it because he didn't want to acknowledge that his greatest opponent ever had fallen so far?

Their eyes met.

What a face…

Brain's cheeks were hollow, and there were dark patches under his eyes. The eyes themselves contained no energy, and his skin was pale. He looked almost like a corpse.

No, a dead person would look better… Unglaus is dead on his feet.

"…Stronoff, it's broken."

"What?"

The first thing Gazef glanced to when he heard those words was the katana in Brain's hand, but he realized that wasn't what the other man meant. It wasn't the sword that was broken, but—

"Tell me, are we strong?"

Gazef couldn't answer in the affirmative.

What came to Gazef's mind was the incident at Carne. If the mysterious caster Ainz Ooal Gown hadn't come to his rescue, he and all his men would have died. That had been the extent of his strength, even if he was said to be the strongest in the kingdom. There was no way he could puff out his chest and say he was strong.

How did Brain interpret that silence? He replied, "Weak! We're weak. In the end, we're only human. Our skills with swords are garbage. Humans—we belong to an inferior race."

It was true that humans were feeble.

The gap in physical strength between humans and dragons, the most powerful race, was obvious. Dragons had tough scales, sharp claws, wings that carried them into the sky, and breath that could annihilate anything, whereas humans had nothing comparable.

That was precisely why warriors aspired to slay dragons. There was honor in overcoming that overwhelming gap with cultivated ability, comrades, and gear. It was a feat reserved for those so strong they could be called ultra-warriors.

So had Brain failed to kill a dragon?

Had he aimed too high to reach and thus lost his balance and fallen?

"...I don't know. Doesn't every warrior know that? That humans are weak."

No, he didn't understand why this was suddenly so upsetting to Brain. Everyone knew there were heights that couldn't be scaled.

People sang his praises, calling him the strongest warrior, but Gazef himself wondered if he really deserved the title. For one thing, there was a good chance the theocracy was hiding warriors stronger than him. Also, subhumans like ogres and giants had higher base physical strength than the human Gazef. If they acquired the same level of ability he had or even a little lower, he probably wouldn't be able to win.

The pinnacle was simply beyond sight. Gazef knew full well it still existed. Had Brain not understood something so basic, something that any warrior should know?

"There are heights to aspire to. That's why we train ourselves to win, right?"

Believing you'll get there someday.

But Brain shook his head emphatically. His soaking wet hair flung drops of water everywhere.

"No, I don't mean that level!" he cried in a pained voice.

Gazef saw the man before him superimposed on his memory. Gazef felt the soul of Brain's attacks had been present in that shout, even if the declaration itself was antithetical.

"Stronoff! The true peaks can't be reached even with hard work! Humans can't touch them. That's the true nature of peaks. In the end, we're nothing more than children with sticks. It's a continuation of the knight games we used to play as kids!" He turned to Gazef quietly with an emotionless face. "...Hey, Stronoff. You have confidence in your sword, too, right? But...that thing is garbage. You only take up that junk and feel like you're protecting people!"

"You saw something that beyond our grasp?"

"I did. I learned. There's a peak that humans will never scale. No—"

Brain practically laughed at himself. "What I saw wasn't even so high. I wasn't even capable of seeing the true summits. It was a game. Actually, it's a funny story."

"So if you train to be able to glimpse that peak…"

Brain's face twisted up with rage. "You don't understand anything! No human could ever even approach that monster's ability! You can swing your sword infinite times, but you'll never reach it! …What a joke. What was I even aiming for?"

Gazef couldn't respond.

He'd seen people with wounded psyches like this before, people whose friends had died before their very eyes and had their spirits simply broken. There was no way to save them. It couldn't come from outside. No matter how many people tried to help, if the fallen couldn't gather the resolve to stand up again, it was futile.

"…Unglaus."

"…Stronoff. The power you can obtain with a sword is meaningless! In the face of true dominance, it's trash."

No, there was nothing of his former bravery now.

"…I'm glad I was able to meet you at the end."

Gazef watched with sorrowful eyes as Brain turned to go.

He couldn't summon the energy to call after the receding, pitiful, worn-out figure who had once been his great rival. But Gazef couldn't miss the few brief words that Brain uttered as he left.

"Now…I can die."

"Wait! Wait, Brain Unglaus!" he cried out after him with burning emotion.

He strode forward, grabbed the retreating man by the shoulders, and yanked.

There was none of the former brilliance in that stumbling figure. But though Gazef had pulled him using all his strength, though Brain's stance broke, Brain didn't fall—because his body was well trained, and he possessed a supreme sense of balance.

Gazef felt a little relieved recognizing that his onetime opponent hadn't gone weak. It wasn't too late. He couldn't let him die now.

"...What are you doing?"

"We're going to my house."

"Stop it. Don't try to save me. I want to die... I'm tired of being scared. No more jumping at shadows, thinking someone's creeping up behind me. I don't want to face reality anymore, I don't want to think how happy I was wielding a piece of crap..."

Listening to Brain's practically pleading voice irritated Gazef. "Shut up and follow me."

Although he'd instructed Brain to follow, Gazef seized Brain's arm before walking off. The way Brain stumbled along without any resistance disgusted Gazef in a way he couldn't put into words.

"You're going to get changed, eat, and go straight to bed."

26 Mid-Fire Moon (August) 1:45 PM

Re-Estize Kingdom's royal capital, the city of Re-Estize...

"The old city" was the best way to describe the capital that nine million people called home, not only in the sense that it had history but in other ways as well—the days plodding along, the depressing backwardness, the lack of change.

A mere stroll down its streets was enough to understand.

Many of the houses lining the streets were old and roughly made, completely lacking in dynamism and brilliance. But different people saw this in different ways. Yes, there were probably some people who saw the city as traditional and calm, while others found it boring and eternally stagnant.

It seemed like the capital would continue to be as it always had, without change—even though nothing stays the same forever.

The royal capital had many unpaved roads, so as soon as it rained, the paths became muddy. The sight made it hard to believe this was inside the city. The kingdom wasn't necessarily underdeveloped, though. It was an error to compare it to the empire or theocracy in the first place.

Since the roads weren't very wide (and no one walked straight down the middle in front of the carriages), pedestrians bunched up along the side of the lanes, making for the picture of squalor. The residents were used to it, so they weaved their way through. They approached one another head-on and deftly dodged at the last second.

The road Sebas was walking down, however, differed from most places in the capital. It was a broad street nicely paved with cobblestones.

From a glance to either side, it was easy to see why. The houses lining the street were large and splendid. One could practically smell the affluence.

That was because this lively promenade was the capital's main boulevard.

As Sebas walked in his dignified manner, most of the women in the street turned to watch him, charmed by the refinement of his middle-aged face. Some even stared directly at him with obvious passion, but Sebas paid them no mind, only keeping his posture erect and his head forward as he strode on without a single step out of rhythm.

He wouldn't stop until he reached his destination—at least that was the impression his gait gave—but then he suddenly halted, and after looking both ways for carriage traffic, he turned at a right angle to cut across the street.

He headed toward an old woman. She'd set down a frame pack piled high with baggage and was rubbing her ankle beside it.

"What seems to be the matter?"

Perhaps surprised by the sudden question, the old woman had eyes filled with suspicion when she raised her head. The moment she saw Sebas's good looks and fine clothes, however, her expression softened.

"You seem to be having some trouble. May I help you?"

"N-no, it's nothing I would trouble you with, sir."

When Sebas grinned, the old woman's cheeks reddened. This charming gentleman's wonderful smile broke through her remaining defenses in an instant.

She'd finished business at her stall for the day and was on the way home when she twisted an ankle, which was now giving her a hard time.

This main avenue wasn't dangerous, but that didn't mean everyone present was a good citizen. If she asked the wrong person for help, it was possible they'd steal all her goods and profits.

She knew things like that actually happened, so she was hesitant to seek help indiscriminately.

So this was a simple matter.

"I shall accompany you. Would you show me the way?"

"Are you sure, sir?!"

"Of course. It's only natural to help someone in trouble."

The woman thanked him repeatedly, and he turned his back to her. "Now please, get on."

"I—I could never!" She sounded embarrassed. "My grimy clothes will soil your fine garments!"

But—

Sebas smiled kindly.

What did dirty clothes matter? Such things needn't be taken into account when helping someone in trouble.

Suddenly the faces of his colleagues from the Great Tomb of Nazarick came to mind. Dubious looks, furrowed brows, and even open contempt. But no matter the feelings of Demiurge, who would probably be the first to react in such a fashion, Sebas believed this was the correct thing to do.

It was right to help someone.

She protested several times, but Sebas finally convinced her to climb aboard. Then he hoisted up her pack with one hand.

The old woman—and everyone else who saw him steadily carrying that apparently very heavy luggage—sighed in admiration.

He set off according to his passenger's directions.

Chapter 1   A Boy's Feelings

Chapter 1 | A Boy's Feelings

1

2 *Late Fire Moon* (September) 11:30 PM

The man lit the lantern at his hip. He used a special type of oil, creating a blazing green that bathed the area in an eerie light.

When he stepped outside, he felt a rush of heat. He made a face, but there was nothing he could do about the season. This time of year, every place in the kingdom was sweltering, even after the sun set. The year's hottest days were over, so it was supposed to be getting gradually colder, but there was no sign of that yet.

"Agh, it's hot again tonight."

"Sure is. I heard, though, that if you go up north or near the sea it's a little cooler." The man's partner for the night responded to his griping.

"If it would rain, at least things would cool off a bit." He gazed up as he spoke, but counter to his hopes, the clear sky contained not a single cloud. It was the usual night sky spreading out above them, its stars appearing strangely large.

"Yeah. Rain would be great... Well, shall we get to work?"

It wouldn't be quite right to call these two men typical villagers. First, there was their gear. With longswords at their waists and leather armor, they were far too well equipped to be the community watch group. Plus, the men's builds and faces didn't fit people who worked the fields—they seemed accustomed to violence.

The men walked without saying a word.

Nothing could be heard besides their footfalls in the quiet village enveloped by the night's darkness. It felt eerily like everything had gone extinct, but the men moved on unfazed. Their calm was proof that they'd done this many times.

The village they marched through was completely encompassed by a high wall, and there were six watchtowers visible from their current vantage point alone. The towers were sturdily constructed, even better than those in regions where monsters frequently appeared.

More than a settlement, this was a strategic point.

But still, if a third party saw it, they might assume it was a normal village with stricter security than most. That said, what came next would probably provoke some confusion.

The sight was that strange. Normally walls surrounded residences and storehouses, while fields spread out beyond. Cultivating fields inside the village meant that an extensive wall had to be built around arable land, which took too much time and labor. But in this village, they'd enclosed the green plants waving in the breeze as if they were protecting gold.

The men walking through this weird village felt someone's gaze following them from one of the watchtowers. They had friends armed with bows and arrows there. If something happened, they could wave their lanterns overhead to call for assistance.

Considering the archery skills of their comrades, the two felt it would be best to refrain from requesting support fire, but it was incredibly reassuring to know that everyone would get up if the tower bell rang.

If the patrolling men waved their lanterns due to a misunderstanding, all their sleeping colleagues would be angry, but if there were signs of anything strange, they planned to call for backup right away.

The pair didn't want to die.

Not that they thought anything would happen. They'd been doing the same thing over and over for months, and they would probably go on doing it.

Even though they'd lost interest in what would come next, they walked through the village along the specified route.

Right as they reached the halfway point of their patrol, something slipped over the man's mouth like a snake. No, "snake" wasn't right. It had attached to his mouth and would never come off—it was more like an octopus's tentacle.

Next, his jaw was yanked up, and a searing pain tore across his exposed neck. This all took less than a second.

A sound like something drinking reached him from his neck—and that was the last thing this man heard in his life.

The hand over the man's mouth let go and moved to support him from behind so he wouldn't crumple to the ground. After confirming that the magic weapon, Vampire Blade, had drunk all the blood, another hand extracted it from the man's throat.

The figure propping up the man was dressed all in black. Every part except the eyes was covered with pitch-black cloth. The outfit itself may have been cloth, but atop it, the wearer wore vambraces and greaves to improve defense. There was also a metal plate worn over the chest, which had a distinctly female contour to it.

Another figure, similarly dressed all in black and with a similarly contoured breastplate, stood behind the other man. The first woman looked her way and moved her head in a single, slight nod.

She took note of their stealth kills and scanned the area. It didn't seem like anyone had noticed.

In a corner of her mind, she was relieved.

The lanterns still gave off light, but the women stuck close to them, so the ones in the watchtower probably couldn't tell what had happened. The only thing she'd been worried about was the possibility of detection in the moment they attacked, when they used Darkness Crossing to teleport the short distances between shadows—but that fear was past now.

Still holding her dagger, redder after draining her victim's blood, she supported the corpse so he didn't fall.

To the guards in the watchtower, it must have looked as if the men patrolling had stopped, so if the bodies remained standing still for too long or crumpled to the ground, it would arouse suspicion.

That's why they needed to move immediately onto the next step, but that wasn't her job.

Suddenly, her hands sensed the vibration of something like a pillar running through the man's body. The corpse jerked into motion a second later, proving it was not her imagination.

She wasn't surprised the man was moving despite being dead. It was all according to plan.

She let go and used a skill at the same time. It was one of her ninja skills, Shadow Dive. The ability allowed her to completely melt into the surroundings, anywhere there was shadow, rendering her impossible to discover with normal eyesight.

Leaving behind the two who had vanished into the darkness, the pair of corpses advanced as if their chains had come off—along the original route they were supposed to follow. It was as if they'd just remembered what their jobs were. The only difference was their movements had become slow and heavy. The reason no blood spurted from their necks, even though their wounds hadn't healed, was simply that there wasn't any left.

There was only one reason they would be moving in such a state. They'd been made into zombies and were moving according to their master's orders.

It wasn't the two women who had turned them.

A casual glance would reveal only the two men they expected, and even if an observer could glimpse the women's murky forms, there would still be only four people. But there was a fifth. It was this person who had created the zombies.

The women couldn't see the fifth, either, but a ninjutsu technique they had mastered allowed them to perceive beings hidden by magic or skills, so they could detect a presence directly in front of them.

"Preparation here is complete."

"Perfect," they responded in low voices.

A similarly quiet voice replied, "Yeah, I know. I was watching. I'm moving to the next location. We have to catch the high-ranking guys if we can." This was also a woman's voice, but it was higher pitched and had an air of immaturity, like a child's.

"I'm also going on to the next raid. Where are the other two?"

"Probably off screwing around, since they don't have anything to do."

"I don't think so. They're hiding out near the village, ready to simultaneously attack the front and rear in case of an emergency. All right, I'm going to go to the highest-priority location. You guys should also proceed according to plan."

Their invisible comrade, whom they could sense only by her presence, floated lightly up into the sky. She was using Fly to travel through the air.

The receding presence moved toward the building she had called the "highest-priority location." It was one of the buildings in this village and a critical foothold they needed to capture first.

Normally they would want to prioritize other buildings, but the reason that one was designated as the most urgent was due to the magic spell Message.

Many people avoided conveying information via Message because it was often unreliable and difficult to confirm the authenticity of dispatches. At the same time, some used the spell without worrying about the shortcomings, such as the empire, where magical education was promoted on a national level. There were also several major merchant networks that prioritized gathering information as fast as possible, and the enemies who controlled this village were much the same. So first, it was necessary to capture the communications person in that building.

Now that their comrade had departed, the pair needed to quickly hide out in the vicinity of their objective. It was important to execute everything at the same time and complete the raid before anyone realized it was happening.

With sharp exhalations, the two ninjas set off running.

No normal person would notice them, moving like they were, from shadow to shadow. Even high-level adventurers would have had a hard time discovering intruders equipped with their magic items. In other words, no one in this village could see them.

Her companion running parallel to her dexterously moved her fingers. All she did was bend her digits in various ways, but the meaning had been clear. "Good thing they didn't have a dog."

She answered with her fingers. "Agreed."

It was the sign language of assassins. When one was as proficient as they were, it was possible to convey information just as fast as talking. They'd taught it to their comrades, but unfortunately, they could use it for only simple signs and instructions. These two, however, had speed and vocabulary suitable for daily conversation, so they used it for clandestine small talk like this often.

"No doubt about it. It's so much easier when they don't come gather around the scent of blood."

If the men had had a dog, things wouldn't have gone this smoothly. They'd prepared a way to render an animal powerless, but there was nothing better than not having to deal with more problems.

After her reply, her comrade's fingers moved speedily. "Then I'll head to my target building according to plan."

When she replied with a "Got it," the comrade running next to her gradually veered away.

Left alone, she glanced sidelong at the fields while she sprinted.

What was being cultivated there was neither wheat nor some other grain, nor was it vegetables. The plant was used as raw material in the manufacture of the most rampant illegal drug in the kingdom, Black Flour. There were several fields inside this walled village, but they were all growing the same thing. That proved that this village was a narcotics production base.

Black Flour, also sometimes called Lyla Powder, was a black powdered drug taken by drinking it in solution.

It was mass-produced and cheap, as well as a simple, effective route to intoxicated euphoria, so it was the most well-known narcotic in the kingdom. Moreover, while the drug was addictive, there were supposedly no side effects, so it was in widespread use.

Thinking on the information about the drug they had, she snorted.

There was no such thing as a drug with no side effects. The "I can quit whenever I want" misunderstanding was also ridiculous. She'd performed autopsies on dead Black Flour addicts, and all their brains had shrunk to about four-fifths their original size.

In the first place, Black Flour produced from wild plants was a powerful poison. Where did anyone get off believing a plant that toxic wasn't also addictive?

Street-ready Black Flour could be categorized as a narcotic but only because it was not very potent.

Even so, it was extremely addictive and remained in the body for a long time. Most users wound up taking another dose before the first one had completely left their system. Unless they went to a priest to have the substance forcibly removed via magic, it was virtually impossible for people who reached a certain degree of addiction to completely quit of their own free will.

The most problematic thing about this horrible drug was that the symptoms of withdrawal from it were not pronounced, and even if people had a bad trip, they didn't go on a rampage or hurt anyone around them. Consequently, the kingdom authorities failed to understand the threat and spent all their efforts exposing the evils of other drugs—practically giving people tacit permission to use Black Flour.

She knew the empire even claimed that the kingdom was secretly supporting the industry.

For her part, when she'd been an assassin, she had occasionally used drugs, and her organization had grown them, so she wasn't against them. Narcotics could in fact have wonderful effects when used properly. They were basically medicinal herbs with a dangerous element.

But this time she was out on a job, so her personal opinion didn't enter into it. However—

Requests that don't come through the Adventurers Guild are dangerous. She wasn't really convinced the job was the best idea, either.

She frowned under her face covering. The client was a friend of her team's leader. They were being paid a fair amount, but there were all sorts of issues that could crop up from taking a job without going through the guild—even if they were one of only two adamantite adventurer teams in the kingdom.

Er, wait, there are three now, I think? As she remembered that she had recently heard news of a new adamantite team, she arrived at the building they had code-named "Number Two."

Her role was to gather all the intelligence she could find inside. When that was done, she had to set fire to the fields.

The smoke from the burning narcotic plants would be poisonous, but if she didn't do it, she couldn't complete her mission.

Depending on the direction of the wind, some villagers might be harmed. But there was no time or means to have them evacuate. *They're necessary sacrifices...* She told herself this and hurled her concern for the villagers' safety into oblivion.

Raised as an assassin, she was rarely moved by a loss of life, particularly if it was someone she didn't even know. Then no matter what happened to them, she wouldn't so much as twitch an eyebrow. The only thing she considered was how she hated the look on her leader's face whenever there were innocent victims. But for this operation, they had their leader's approval, so she didn't feel even the slightest inclination to try saving anyone.

More importantly, after this raid was over, she would teleport straight to another village and burn down the fields in exactly the same way. The plan fully occupied her head.

This wasn't the only village where they produced the base for the drug. According to their research, there were ten places in the kingdom where large-scale growing operations were located. And there were probably still others they hadn't discovered. Otherwise it would have been impossible for these groups to yield the estimated amount necessary for the drug to spread all over the kingdom like it had.

We have to pick the weeds where they grow... It might be in vain, but it's all we can do...

If there were written orders from the organization in this village, that would be excellent, but she didn't expect things to go so smoothly. The most they could hope for was that the village's overseer would have some information.

Our leader would be happy if I could unearth at least part of the org, though…

The huge crime syndicate manufacturing the narcotic was called the Eight Fingers. Their name derived from a deity subordinate to the god of earth—the god of theft, who had eight fingers. It was a massive organization that dominated the kingdom's underworld.

The outfit was split into eight divisions: slave trafficking, assassination, smuggling, thievery, drug dealing, security, moneylending, and gambling. It was said that they were behind every underworld crew in the kingdom. And because the group was so large, the full truth about it was shrouded in mystery.

However, there was one thing that proved how far the Eight Fingers had reached into the kingdom—and that was the village before her eyes.

They were growing illegal drugs right out in the open. This fact proved to her that the noble holding power in this land was an accomplice. But even if she exposed the crime, she would be unable to accuse the lord or lady.

If the royal family made an inquiry or the judicial officials became involved, that would be a different story, but they would still encounter difficulties in pinning the crime on a landed aristocrat. This fiefdom's ruler would probably claim, *I had no knowledge this was being used to make a narcotic,* or say, *The villagers did it on their own,* to shift blame.

Charging nobility directly wasn't very effective, and even if efforts were made in an attempt to suppress circulation, the Eight Fingers had seduced several nobles who were now involved in the distribution routes. The situation had become impossible to resolve using guards and other regular means.

That's why they were currently relying on the violent last resort of burning the fields; it was the only option left.

Honestly, she didn't think burning the fields would work to address even the symptom. That was how far the syndicate had undermined the kingdom—it was too powerful, and it had reached its tentacles into the government.

"We're merely buying time… If we can't strike a target where we can turn the tables with one blow then this, too, will all be in vain…"

2

It was raining.

The sound was so intense it grated on the ears.

The kingdom's roads weren't built with drainage in mind, especially when it came to the backstreets. As a result, the alleys transformed into huge lakes.

The rain beating down on the surface of the water sent up little splashes. The wind whipped up the spray and filled the air with its scent. It felt as if the royal capital itself had sunk into a body of water.

In this world colored gray by whirling droplets, there was a boy.

He lived in a shack. No, it could not even be called a shack. The main beams holding it up were about as thin as an adult man's arms. Instead of a solid roof, rags draped over the shelter to cover it, and the walls were no more than the ceiling cloths sloppily hanging down.

In this dwelling, which offered hardly any shelter from the elements outside, the boy of about six years of age lay on a thin cloth spread out on the floor, curled up like a casually tossed piece of garbage.

If one stopped to think about it—the wooden beams, the scraps that formed the ceiling and walls—it seemed like the kind of thing a child could build, even just for fun.

The only real benefit of this home was it kept the rain from falling directly on him. The endless deluge had drastically lowered the temperature and enveloped the boy in a shivery chill. His foggy exhalations provided but momentary evidence for his existence before they faded away as the air stole their warmth.

Prior to his sheltering here, the cold rain had drenched him, and his body heat was deserting him at a terrible pace.

He had no way to stop the shivering.

The single minuscule silver lining of this miserable situation was probably that the permeating chill felt good to his bruised and beaten body.

Still lying on his side, the boy looked out at the world, at the alley no one walked down anymore.

The only sounds he could hear were the rainfall and his own breathing. The scene gave him the impression there was no one else in the world. That was the extent of the calm.

Although he was young, he understood that he would likely die.

Not old enough to fully understand what death entailed, the boy wasn't very afraid. That, and it didn't seem that life was worth holding dear. The only reason he'd managed to hang on so far was a sentiment similar to the desire to avoid pain.

If death would come without pain, only cold—like how he felt at that very moment—then dying didn't seem so bad.

He gradually lost feeling in his wet body, and his consciousness clouded.

It would have been better to move somewhere the wind and rain wouldn't come in before the weather turned, but he'd run into some nasty men and received a beating, so getting back here had been all he could manage.

There was one tiny, happy thing. Did that mean everything else was sad?

The fact that he hadn't eaten in two days was normal, so that wasn't sad. His parents were absent, and no one else would care for him. This had been the case for a long time, so it wasn't something to be upset about. That he was dressed in rags and smelled bad was only natural. Eating rotten food and drinking dirty water to fill his belly was all he'd ever known.

Following this train of thought, was it sad the abandoned house where he had been living had been stolen from him, the hut he'd worked hard to build had been trashed for someone's amusement, and drunk men had beaten him, leaving injuries all over his body?

No.

The heartbreaking truth was that the boy couldn't even understand what was sad or why.

But this was the end.

The sorrow he didn't even understand would end here.

The grave called for the lucky and the unlucky alike.

Yes, death was absolute.

He closed his eyes.

Keeping them open was too much effort for a body that had ceased to feel even the cold.

He could hear his tiny, frail heartbeat in the darkness.

In a world where only that and the rain could be heard, another strange sound appeared. It was like something blocking the rain.

Despite his fading consciousness, he mustered the curiosity peculiar to children and urged his eyelids to move.

In the thin strip of his field of vision, he saw it.

The boy's nearly closed eyes popped wide open.

Something beautiful.

For a moment, he couldn't understand.

Perhaps *like a jewel* or *like a nugget of gold* were the right descriptors, but to someone who'd been abandoned, who'd lived eating half-rotten food, those words didn't come to mind.

No.

He thought one thing.

Like the sun.

That was the most beautiful thing he knew, the most out of reach.

The world dyed gray by the rain. Dark rain clouds reigning in the sky. Was that why? *Is the sun here with me because it went on a trip when no one could see it?*

He wondered to himself.

It reached out its hand and caressed his face. And then—

The boy hadn't been a person.
There had never been anyone who saw him as a person.
But that day, he became one.

•

3 *Late Fire Moon* (September) 4:15 AM

The Re-Estize Kingdom, at the royal capital…
At the innermost part of the city sat Ro-Lente Castle, which occupied an enormous space. The curtain wall around it, almost a mile long, was furnished with twelve giant cylindrical towers that formed the defense network.

The room was in one of those twelve towers.

In the not-so-large, unlit space, there was a single bed. Lying on it was a child whose age fell right at the vague border between "boy" and "young man."

His blond hair was cropped short, and his skin glowed with a healthy tan.

Climb.

Though that was the only name he had claim to, he was a soldier attending the woman often titled "golden," permitted closer to her than any other—a position many looked upon with envy.

He woke up early, rising before the sun.

By the time he noticed his consciousness returning from the deep, dark world of sleep, his mind was clear and his body was primed for the most part. One of the things he had pride in was how he could fall asleep and wake up with ease.

Climb's almond-shaped eyes, with the whites visible below the iris, opened wide and revealed his iron will shining within.

Pushing back the rather heavy blanket covering his body (even in summer, nights surrounded by stone were chilly), he sat up.

He touched his face near his eyes. The fingers came away soaking wet. "...That dream again?" Climb wiped the tears off his face with his sleeves.

Maybe the heavy rain from two days ago had reminded him of his childhood.

They weren't grieving tears.

How many people did one meet in life whom they could respect? Was everyone lucky enough to serve a person for whom they would give their life without hesitation?

That day, Climb had met a woman whom he firmly believed he could die for without a bit of regret.

What he had wiped away were tears of joy. He had cried out of gratitude for the miracle that began with that meeting.

With determination on his face, still appropriately childish for his age, Climb stood up.

In this dark world bereft of even a single light, Climb whispered in a voice hoarse from too much training. "Shine."

In response to Climb's keyword, a white light appeared in a lamp suspended from the ceiling, illuminating the room. It was a magic item imbued with Continual Light.

Although this type of item was commonly available, it was still expensive. The reason he had one wasn't entirely due to his special position. It was unsafe to burn something, even for lighting, in a place like a stone tower where air did not circulate very well. For that reason, despite the significant initial cost, almost all the rooms were equipped with a magic light.

The floor and walls illuminated by the white light were hewn from rock. A thin rug provided as much protection as it could against the cold hardness of the floor. The other things in the room were a coarsely made wooden bed, a wardrobe that seemed large enough to hold armor, a desk with a drawer, and a wooden chair covered by a thin cushion.

Perhaps it seemed shabby to an outsider, but for someone of Climb's rank, it was undeserved luxury.

Soldiers didn't get private quarters, usually bedding down together in large rooms with shared bunks. The only other furnishing they were provided was a wooden lockbox to store personal belongings.

In addition, he also had white full plate armor enshrined in one corner of the room. Rank-and-file soldiers would never be supplied with such well-made gear so lustrous and unblemished it seemed to gleam from within.

This special treatment certainly wasn't anything Climb had earned through his own actions. The gear was a token of affection from his master. It was no wonder people were jealous of him.

Opening the wardrobe, Climb removed some clothes and dressed himself using the mirror found inside.

After putting on a shirt that smelled metallic from frequent use, he donned a shirt of mail over it. Normally he'd put armor above the mail, but he didn't do that now. Instead, he slipped on a vest lined with many pockets and a pair of pants to finish the outfit. In his hand, he carried a bucket with a towel in it.

Lastly, he checked the mirror to make sure nothing was strange and ensure nothing about his outfit was in disarray. Any failure on his part could be used to criticize his master, the Golden Princess Renner, so Climb took the utmost care. His purpose wasn't to cause trouble for her. He was there to give his master everything he had.

He closed his eyes before the mirror and imagined her face.

The Golden Princess Renner Theiere Chardelon Ryle Vaiself…

She possessed such heavenly beauty she could easily be mistaken for a goddess. She radiated with a compassionate spirit befitting her noble blood and superior wisdom that gave birth to her government policies. She was a noble among nobles, a princess among princesses—the supreme woman.

Climb could not allow himself to put so much as a nick in the untarnished gem that sparkled like gold.

If their relationship were a ring, Renner would be a large brilliant-cut diamond, while Climb was nothing but the prongs surrounding her. Since his make was cheap, he lowered the item's overall worth, but he couldn't allow it to fall any further.

Climb was unable to stop the passion from building in his chest every time he thought of her. Even a devout believer in the gods could not surpass Climb's current fervor.

He gazed at himself for a short time, nodded with the satisfaction that his appearance would not bring his master shame, and left the room.

3

3 *Late Fire Moon* (September) 4:35 AM

Climb headed for the large hall that occupied the tower's entire first floor as a training area.

Usually it was filled with the body heat of soldiers, but of course, no one was there this early in the morning. The empty space was so quiet he could practically hear the silence. Because the room was enclosed in stone, Climb's footsteps echoed loudly.

Quasi-permanent magic lights brightly illuminated the hall. Inside were standing suits of armor fastened to posts, as well as straw figures used as archery targets. Along the walls were shelves lined with a variety of dull-bladed weapons.

There was a reason a training area normally found outside had been built indoors. Valencia Palace was housed within the Ro-Lente Castle compound. If soldiers trained in the open, it was possible for visiting messengers to see them. As this was not very dignified, several facilities were built inside the towers.

It was also an option to show off the manly training soldiers as a diplomatic stratagem, but that wasn't the kingdom's style. The prevailing mindset was to present an elegant, gorgeous, and noble picture of the realm.

That said, there were some exercises that required being outside. These were performed stealthily in a corner of the grounds, on an athletic field beyond the walls, or removed from the capital entirely.

Climb entered the hushed room, penetrating the chilly air, and began leisurely stretching in a corner.

After a thorough thirty-minute stretch routine, Climb's face was more than a little flushed. Sweat beaded on his forehead, and his exhaled breaths brimmed with excess heat.

He put a hand to his forehead and wiped off the perspiration before approaching the weapon shelf and choosing a fairly thick, large, dull iron practice sword. The hand around it was hardened from repeatedly forming and popping blisters. He tested out different swords until he found one that fit his grip perfectly.

Next, he placed lumps of metal in his pockets, buttoning them to make sure the contents wouldn't fall out. With several pieces inside, the vest had taken on the same weight as a full suit of armor. In exchange for being sturdy, ordinary full plate armor was heavy, and the limited range of movement was also a disadvantage. If one wanted to practice under conditions similar to actual combat, training in armor was ideal. But taking out a full suit of armor just to practice wasn't something Climb did very often. Besides, he couldn't wear the white mail he'd been given for training. That's why he resorted to this substitute instead.

Climb tightly gripped the iron weapon larger than a great sword. He raised it over his head and lowered it slowly as he exhaled. As its tip was about to touch the floor, he brought it up again, inhaling. Gradually increasing the speed of his practice swings, he concentrated intently, staring into space with a penetrating gaze.

He did over three hundred repetitions.

Climb was bright red, and sweat dripped down his face. The heat building up in his body dramatically raised his breath's temperature.

Climb was a fairly well-built soldier, but the weight of the oversize great sword was still extreme. It was especially difficult slowing the sword so the tip didn't touch the ground—the amount of strength needed for this was not insignificant.

After five hundred repetitions, both his arms began cramping, as though screaming out to him. A waterfall cascaded down his face.

Climb was aware that this was his limit. Still, he didn't seem interested in stopping.

But—

"That's enough, don't you think?" someone else called out to him.

Climb was flustered as he turned to look in the direction of the voice, and he immediately noticed a man.

There was no word more fitting for him than *robust*. He was like steel incarnate. Because his craggy face was frowning, the ensuing mass of wrinkles made him appear older than his actual age. His bulging muscles showed he was no ordinary man.

There probably wasn't a single soldier in the kingdom who didn't know this figure.

"—Captain Stronoff."

Captain of the Royal Select Gazef Stronoff. He was the strongest warrior in the country, and it was said he had no equals in neighboring realms, either.

"Any more than that is too much. No point in killing yourself."

Climb lowered his sword and watched his spasming arms. "You're right. I might have pushed myself a bit too hard."

Climb expressionlessly thanked Gazef as the older man shrugged. "If you really think so, then it'd be great if you wouldn't make me say the same thing all the time. I wonder how many times it's been…"

"I'm sorry."

Gazef shrugged once more at the boy's head bowed in apology.

The pair had exchanged these lines many times, almost like a greeting. Usually this was where it ended, and they would each become absorbed in their own training, but today was different.

"How about it, Climb? Want to try sparring?"

Climb's expressionless mask began to crack for a moment.

Up until now, these two had met in this place before, but they never sparred. It was an unwritten law. There were no benefits to training together. No, there were benefits, but there were too many drawbacks.

At present in the kingdom, the nobles' faction—comprising three of the six great noble families—and the king's faction were in a struggle for power. The country's straits were so dire that some believed the only thing holding everything together was the yearly war with the empire.

There was no way the king's right-hand man, Captain of the Royal Select Gazef Stronoff, could possibly lose. But supposing he did, the nobles' faction opposing them would use it as ammunition to attack the king under the present circumstances.

Likewise, if Climb lost, the nobles would probably take it as a chance to claim he couldn't be trusted to protect the princess. The fact that a common soldier of dubious pedigree had been appointed to guard the peerlessly beautiful and unwed princess rubbed many nobles the wrong way.

And so, their respective positions would not forgive a loss.

It was out of the question to show any weakness, expose a vital point, or allow openings that could be attacked. They both acted with the utmost prudence to avoid causing any trouble for their masters, a priority they shared due to their origins as commoners.

What reason could Gazef have for breaking this rule?

Climb looked around.

It couldn't be simply that there wasn't anyone else there. The walls had eyes in this place. The chances were high that someone was observing from afar or watching in the shadows. But he couldn't think of any other explanations.

Unsure if it was a good reason or a bad one, Climb was confused and shaken, though he didn't let it show on his face.

Before the boy stood the warrior said to be the strongest in the kingdom. Gazef keenly detected the split-second disturbance in Climb's emotions that normal humans would have naturally missed before he gave his response. "I was shown recently how green I still am. I'd like to train with someone who'll pose a bit of a challenge."

"You, green, sir?"

Under what circumstances would Gazef learn he was "still green"? It was then that Climb remembered the unit he commanded had been missing members of late.

Since Climb didn't have any close friends, he'd only heard the rumors bouncing around the mess hall. Apparently, the Royal Select had been caught up in something and lost a few men.

"Yeah. If that charitable caster hadn't helped me, I probably wouldn't be here right now…"

Hearing that, Climb felt his iron mask crumble; he couldn't help it. But who wouldn't be surprised? His curiosity got the better of him, and he asked, "A charitable caster?"

"…His name was Ainz Ooal Gown. I'm not sure, but I think he's on the level of the empire's monstrous casters."

It was not a name Climb had ever heard before.

The young soldier admired heroes and had a secret hobby of collecting sagas—regardless from what race the epic originated. Not only that, but he also collected as many exciting stories as he could from famous adventurers in the region, but he didn't recognize the name Gazef mentioned.

Of course, there was always the possibility it was a pseudonym.

"S-so, nngh!" Climb suppressed his desire to ask details. *I can't blithely ask about an incident that cost him some of his men. One can only be so rude…* "I'll commit that name to memory… So is it really all right for you to train me?"

"I'm not training you. We're sparring. Whether you learn something from it or not is up to you. You're one of the best soldiers this country's got, you know. It'll be meaningful exercise for me, too."

That was high praise, but Climb considered nothing more than polite decorum.

It wasn't as if Climb was remarkably strong. The standard he measured against was simply low. The kingdom's soldiers were only marginally stronger than the average citizens and weak compared to the empire's knights, who were full-time. No member of this kingdom's army was famous enough to be known throughout the region. The men directly under Gazef were strong, certainly, but still not quite as strong as Climb.

Out of the adventurer ranks of bronze, iron, silver, gold, platinum, mythril, orichalcum, and adamantite, Climb was probably gold. It wasn't as if he was weak, but there were always many more who were stronger.

Could someone like him really engage in a sparring match worth the time of someone like Gazef, a warrior who was undoubtedly adamantite rank?

Climb chased all the discouraging thoughts from his mind.

It would be an extremely valuable experience to learn from the strongest man in the kingdom. Even if he ended up disappointing Gazef, Climb would have no regrets.

"Okay, then I'd like to go a round, please."

Gazef grinned and nodded once with enthusiasm.

They walked to the weapon rack together and equipped swords that were exactly the right size for them. Gazef chose a bastard sword, and Climb selected a small shield and a broadsword.

Then Climb took the lumps of metal out from his pockets. It would be rude to face someone stronger while still wearing them. Not to mention that if he didn't fight as hard as he could, he wouldn't grow. His opponent was the strongest warrior in the kingdom. Confronting this considerable challenge would require his all.

Soon Climb finished his preparations, and Gazef asked, "And are your arms okay? They're not numb anymore?"

"No, sir. I'm fine now. They feel a bit warm, but there's no problem with my grip."

Climb waved his arms, and Gazef saw from the way they moved that the boy was telling the truth and nodded. "Okay. Hmm. But in a way, that's kind of too bad. You run into all kinds of situations on the battlefield and can't always fight at your best. If your grip is weak, you need to adjust your style appropriately. Are you working on that?"

"N-no, I'm not. In that case, I'll do more practice swings—"

"Oh no, you don't have to go that far. But you're protecting the princess most of the time. It wouldn't be a waste to practice things like how to fight if you get attacked somewhere you're not allowed to carry a sword and familiarize yourself with different weapons."

"Yes, sir!"

"There are nine basic disciplines of armed combat: swords, shields, spears, axes, daggers, combat gauntlets, bows, bludgeons, and throwing weapons. If you try to learn too many, you'll end up neglecting all of them. I recommend narrowing it down to two or three and practicing those. Okay. Apologies for the boring commentary."

"It wasn't boring, Captain Stronoff! Thank you!"

Gazef smiled awkwardly and waved off Climb's gratitude. "If you're ready, then let's get started. For now, come as you are. Later…well, I can't train you, but I'll give you some tips on fighting in the other disciplines."

"Yes, sir. Looking forward to it."

"Right, but know that it's not my intention for this to be a drill. Come at me like it's a real battle."

Climb slowly moved into a stance with his sword held low, facing Gazef with the left side of his body hidden behind the shield. His eyes were sharp—already treating this as more than practice. He could sense Gazef was also taking it seriously.

They stared each other down, but Climb couldn't move.

He was nimbler after removing the lumps of metal from his pockets, but Climb still didn't feel like he could beat Gazef. In both physical strength and experience, Gazef completely surpassed him.

If he was careless in how he advanced, the captain would effortlessly intercept him. His opponent was superior, and there wasn't anything he could do about that. But if this were a real battle, would Climb simply lose his life because there was nothing to be done?

So then what?

He would have to meet Gazef with something Gazef didn't have.

Climb lost out on strength, experience, and mental fortitude—everything a warrior needed. If there was an exception, it would be in gear.

Gazef had a bastard sword. Climb, however, had a broadsword and a small shield. If they were magical equipment, one blade could be superior to another, but these were made for training. In terms of weapons, he wasn't ahead.

But whereas Gazef had only one, Climb had two—a shield could be used offensively as well. In exchange for dividing his attack power, Climb had an advantage in versatility.

He could deflect a blow with the shield and then swing the sword or parry with the sword and strike with the shield.

Climb observed Gazef's movements carefully, aiming for opportunities to counterattack.

After a few seconds, the older man smiled slightly. "You're not going to charge? Then I'll start—here I come."

Displaying absolute calm, Gazef held his sword aloft. He lowered his hips slightly, suffusing his frame with energy like a tensed spring.

Climb braced himself as well, so he'd be ready to defend whenever the sword was swung.

Then Gazef rushed forward and swung down at Climb's shield.

He's fast! Climb gave up on maneuvering the shield to deflect the oncoming hit. He transferred all his attention and ability into the basic defensive act of withstanding the assault.

In the next moment, a tremendous shock assailed his shield.

Did it break from that one attack? It certainly felt like it, as the blow was so mighty it immobilized Climb's shield-bound hand. The strike was the kind that he had to block with his entire body.

Deflect?! How could I even match his speed like this? If I could at least get it to glance off smoothly… As Climb chided himself for being so naive, another shock assaulted his stomach. "Guh-hagh!"

The young boy's body went flying. He landed hard on his back, and the stone floor knocked the wind out of him. One glance at Gazef was all it took to find out what had happened.

The older warrior retracted his leg after launching that heavy kick. "Don't pay too much attention to the sword just because it's all your opponent is carrying. You might get kicked like this. That time, I aimed for your stomach, but usually they'd go for a less guarded area. They'll try to shatter your knees or…even if you've got your groin padded, a kick from metal greaves can rupture things… You need to keep an eye on your opponent's entire form and watch their every move."

"…Yes, sir." Climb resisted the dull pain in his stomach and stood up.

Gazef had tremendous physical strength. Kicking at full power, he could have easily broken Climb's ribs, mail shirt or no, and rendered him unfit for combat. It was clear he hadn't kicked at full power and had instead aimed his foot to send Climb flying and used no more strength than necessary.

So this is training after all… Thank you. It was sinking in that this was a lesson from the kingdom's strongest warrior, and full of gratitude, Climb reassumed a fighting stance.

How precious was this chance? He had to take care not to let it end too soon.

Climb raised his shield again and inched forward. Gazef silently watched. If things continued like this, it would merely play out the same as last time. As Climb approached, he was forced to rethink his strategy.

Climb sensed overwhelming composure coming from the calmly waiting Gazef. He hadn't managed to draw out even a hint of his opponent's true strength.

Being frustrated about his inability would probably be arrogant.

Climb was already starting to reach his limits. Even though he always got up early to hone himself, his progress was slower than a snail's. Ever since he first picked up a sword, he had not improved fast enough. Even if he could condition his body to swing faster with heavier swords, he would probably still be unable to obtain specialized combat abilities.

Surely it was rude to wish that Gazef, the embodiment of talent, would use his full abilities when Climb was so incapable. He lamented that his own skill wasn't enough to warrant them.

Telling him to approach their bout as if it were a real battle and not practice had probably been Gazef's way of saying that if Climb didn't fight with the intent to kill, he wouldn't even be worth sparring with.

Climb ground his teeth audibly with a *crk* sound.

He hated how weak he was. If only he were stronger, he could be more useful. With more power, he would be the princess's weapon and face head-on those who sullied the kingdom, who caused the people to suffer.

The princess had only one fragile sword, so she had to be careful when she wielded it, which racked Climb with guilt.

But he immediately cleared those thoughts from his mind. What he needed now was to avoid drowning in negativity in this endeavor to enhance his abilities, even slightly, by clashing with everything he had against this man who stood at the heights of human potential.

He had only one thought in his heart.

I want to be useful to the princess...

"Ohh?" Gazef murmured approvingly, his expression shifting slightly.

It was because of the minute change he saw in the boy on the cusp of manhood in front of him. Up until a moment ago, Climb had been excited, like a child meeting a celebrity. But after the kick, that bubbly attitude had vanished and been replaced with the face of a warrior.

Gazef raised his guard a notch.

He thought more of Climb than the boy knew. He held an especially high opinion of that unwavering desire to better himself. His fervent devotion was akin to a religious faith. And then there was his swordsmanship.

No one had taught Climb. He'd gleaned what he could by watching others train. His form was awkward and contained many extraneous movements. But unlike those who had unthinkingly studied exactly what they were taught, Climb considered the significance of each strike and cultivated a style that focused on real combat or, to put it darkly, a killer's style.

Gazef thought it was absolutely wonderful.

In the end, a sword was a tool for murder. Someone trained for sports and display wouldn't be effective in a serious battle. Such a style wouldn't protect or save anyone.

But Climb was different. He would cut down his enemies and safeguard whatever was precious to him.

However—

"Your attitude may have changed, but there's a clear gap between our ability levels! What are you gonna do about that?"

To put it bluntly, Climb had no innate talent. Without that, he couldn't reach the heights of Gazef or Brain Unglaus, no matter how much harder than everyone else he tried, regardless of how cruelly he tortured his flesh.

Climb's attempts to be the strongest were nothing but a dream or a delusion.

So why was Gazef training Climb? Wouldn't it be more beneficial to spend his time on someone with more aptitude?

The answer was simple. He couldn't stand around watching Climb expend pointless effort. If humans had a limit to their potential, then this boy was single-mindedly throwing himself at that wall over and over, and Gazef pitied him for it.

He wanted to show Climb another way.

It was his belief that even if there was a limit to ability, there was no limit to experience.

The other reason was that Gazef regretted his greatest opponent's appalling state. *It's like I'm doing this to make up for that…which isn't fair to Climb, but…still, it's not like he loses anything from going at it with me for a round.*

"Come on, Climb!"

A response with the spirit to break through Gazef's internal monologue came back to him.

"Sir!"

At the same time he replied, Climb dashed forward.

Unlike before, Gazef slowly lifted his sword with a serious face.

Then he brought it down from up high.

If Climb received it with his shield, his approach would be halted completely; if he blocked with his sword, he'd be repelled. It was an attack that rendered defense purposeless. It was a bad idea to defend, but Climb had a broadsword whereas Gazef had a bastard sword—Climb's weapon was shorter.

All he could do was leap. Gazef knew that, so he was waiting to intercept.

It was like entering a tiger's den—but the young soldier hesitated only for a moment.

Climb came within range of Gazef's sword.

Gazef's swing was perfectly timed, and Climb braced against it with his shield. The tremendous shock was even more intense this time. Pain ran up Climb's arm and made him grimace.

"Too bad it ended up playing out the same as before."

Gazef seemed slightly disappointed as he aimed his foot at Climb's stomach, but then—

"Fortress!"

The moment Climb shouted, Gazef's face registered slight surprise.

It wasn't as if the martial art Fortress couldn't be used without a sword or shield. It was quite possible with either a hand or armor. The reason it was commonly activated when defending with a sword or shield was due to how tight the timing needed to be. One false move when using it with armor could end with the warrior suffering the hit unprotected. So according to human psychology, most would want to activate it when blocking with something.

But Climb knew when Gazef's kick would come, which solved the timing problem.

"You meant for that to happen?"

"Yes, sir!"

The power in Gazef's kick vanished as if something soft had absorbed it. His leg extended fully, and unable to drive any strength into it, he gave up and began to bring it back down. While Gazef was in this disadvantaged posture, Climb moved in to take his shot.

"Slash!"

Climb activated the martial art as he brought his sword down from high above.

Create a single move that you can unleash with confidence.

He possessed no inborn talent, but he'd taken to heart the advice a warrior had once given him and desperately polished his overhead attack.

Climb's body was not covered in an ostentatious layer of muscles, nor was he blessed with a physique that easily put on muscle in the first place. It wasn't as if he had the agility to put extra bulk to good use anyhow.

So he had toned his body and achieved a specialized build through what had seemed like infinite repetition.

The result was his downward swing from up high—his singular strike achieving a speed that could be considered extraordinary, which practically summoned a gale in its wake.

That was what fell toward Gazef's head.

The idea that if his attack connected it could be fatal did not occur to Climb. He'd unleashed his move with absolute conviction that a man of Gazef's caliber wouldn't die from something like this.

A sharp *clang* rang out as the bastard sword rose to meet the descending broadsword.

Gazef had anticipated even this far ahead.

Climb used all the energy in his body to try and throw the older warrior off-balance.

But Gazef's body didn't budge.

Even in an unsteady position on one foot, Gazef had no problem stopping a blow bearing the entirety of Climb's might. The man was like a great tree with thick roots deeply seated in the earth.

Climb had used his martial art and all his strength. Even with those two things combined, he couldn't match one-footed Gazef. He was surprised to realize this and then looked to his stomach.

Slicing with the broadsword had meant closing the distance, and thus it was possible for Gazef to kick him again.

He jumped away right as it arrived.

Just a little dull pain. Then the two of them stared each other down a few paces apart.

Gazef's eyes were happy, and his mouth curled in a grin.

His expression was amused, but it contained no ill will. It was only a refreshing smile. It made Climb fidget, how Gazef beamed at him like a father proud of his son's improvement.

"Nice work. I'm gonna take this next one a little bit seriously." Gazef's expression changed.

Fear coursed through Climb's entire body. The kingdom's strongest warrior had finally shown himself.

"I actually have one potion. If you end up with a broken bone or something, we can fix it up, so don't worry."

"…Thank you."

Hearing Gazef basically announce, *I'm gonna break one of your bones, that's all*, made Climb's heart pound. He was accustomed to injuries, but that didn't mean he liked them.

Gazef charged—twice as fast as Climb's previous approach.

The bastard sword traced an extremely low arc aimed at Climb's feet, its tip practically scraping the ground. Flustered by the speed and centrifugal force, Climb protected his feet by gripping his broadsword blade-down, as if to stick it into the floor.

The two crashed together. That's what Climb thought, but suddenly, Gazef's bastard sword rose back up, slicing along the edge of the broadsword.

"Kgh!" Climb turned his entire body and face away from the bastard sword, which missed him by a tiny margin. The draft blew a few of his hairs away.

Climb was terrified by how quickly Gazef had been able to corner him. He followed the bastard sword with only his eyes but saw it suddenly stop sharp and come back around.

Faster than he could think.

His survival instinct seemed to drive him to thrust his shield forward when the bastard sword crashed into it with a shrill *clang*.

And then—

"Gah!"

With a sharp pain, Climb's body sailed sideways. When he fell to the floor, the shock knocked the weapon out of his hands.

The bastard sword had rebounded off the shield to the side, delivering a heavy impact to Climb's wide-open flank.

"Flow. Don't think, *First attack, then defend*—you have to move in a way that connects you to your next stroke. Defending is but another part of the attack." As Climb retrieved his fallen sword and made to get up while holding to his side, Gazef gently spoke to him, saying, "I held back so nothing would break. You're still good, right? …What do you want to do?"

In contrast to Gazef, who didn't seem the least bit out of breath, Climb was panting from the pain and stress.

If he couldn't last for more than a few exchanges like this, he was wasting Gazef's time. But he still wanted to improve, even if only slightly.

He nodded at Gazef and held up his sword.

"Okay, then let's keep going."

"Yes, sir!" With a hoarse shout, Climb raced forward.

After being struck, launched away, and occasionally kicked or punched, Climb collapsed on the floor, out of breath. The cold stones leeched the heat out of him through his mail and clothing, which felt good.

Panting, he didn't even move to wipe the sweat off his face. Rather, he didn't have the energy to.

Enduring the pain welling up in various locations, Climb was overwhelmed by the fatigue coursing through his entire body, and he lightly closed his eyes.

"Good work. I tried to swing so you wouldn't get any breaks or fractures, but how are you feeling?"

"…" Still lying on the floor, Climb moved his arms, examining the painful spots before opening his eyes. "There doesn't seem to be anything wrong. I'm hurting, but it should only be bruises."

The throbbing aches he felt were far from serious. They wouldn't prevent him from guarding the princess.

"Okay… Then you don't need the potion, huh?"

"No. Because if I overuse them, I won't get any of the benefits of strength training."

"Letting your muscles heal naturally makes them stronger, but if you use magic to restore them to their original state, then that doesn't happen. I getcha. Are you off to be bodyguard for the princess now?"

"Yes."

"Then I'll give it to you. Use it if you have any problems."

He placed the potion next to Climb with a *clink*.

"Thank you." Climb sat up and regarded the man his sword had been unable to approach even once.

The unscathed warrior asked in puzzlement, "What?"

"Nah, I was thinking that you're amazing…"

Gazef had barely any sweat on his forehead. He wasn't out of breath. Sighing, Climb acknowledged the gap between the strongest man in the kingdom and himself, a boy splayed out on the floor.

In response, Gazef grinned awkwardly. "…Oh. I see."

"How—?"

"I can't really answer the question of how I got this strong. I just had some inborn talent, that's all. By the way, I learned to fight during my mercenary days. The nobles are always screaming about how vulgar my kicks are, but I learned those back then, too."

There were no tricks to getting stronger. Gazef had declared it so. He denied with ease the small hope Climb had clung to, the belief that he might be able to grow more powerful if he continued his current training.

"In that sense, it's a good style for you, Climb—punching, kicking, a style where you use your arms and legs like that."

"You…think so?"

"Yeah, not being trained as a swordsman or soldier will work in your favor. People tend to focus on bladework once they have a sword in their hands…but I don't think that's very smart. In a real fight, a doctrine that fully utilizes the hands and feet with the sword as simply another offensive option should prove more useful. Well, it's kinda fighting dirty…but it works for adventurers."

Climb dropped his usual expressionless manner and smiled. He never thought the strongest man in the kingdom would hold such a high opinion of his sword skills or his inconsistent, unorthodox movements. Climb knew the nobles scoffed at his style from the shadows, so praise like this was a big deal for him.

"All right, I'm going to head out. I need to be ready for breakfast with the king. Are you okay on time?"

"Yes. The princess will have a visitor today."

"A visitor? One of the nobles?"

Gazef wondered who the princess would be entertaining, and Climb answered, "From the Aindra family."

"Aindra? …Ohh, then which one? Blue, right? I can't imagine it'd be the red one."

"Yes, from the Blue Roses."

Gazef was visibly relieved. "Aha…I see, so her friend is coming…"

Gazef seemed to guess that Renner didn't want Climb at breakfast with her friend, but Climb had actually declined an invitation. Even if he had the kind of relationship with her that allowed it, refusing an offer from one of the royal family would definitely have made Gazef frown, so Climb said nothing and left the details up to the older man's imagination.

As for Aindra herself, she was also acquainted with Climb through Renner and was friendly with him. She wouldn't react badly, like the other nobles, if he came to breakfast. But Renner had few female friends, and he figured she could get more of that rare girl talk without a guy around.

"Thank you for today, Captain Gazef."

"Nah, don't worry about it. I had fun, too."

"…If you don't mind, could you train me again sometime?"

Gazef wasn't sure what to say, but faster than Climb could notice and apologize, the captain responded. "Sure, as long as we can find a time and place where no one else is around."

Climb knew what the conflict had been, so he didn't say anything awkward. He flexed his creaking muscles and stood up. He did, however, express his honest thoughts. "Thank you."

Gazef gave a benevolent wave and got moving. "Okay, let's clean up. There'll be trouble if I don't make it to breakfast on time. Oh, and that swing from overhead is pretty good. You just need to think about how to follow up—in case your opponent dodges or blocks it."

"Yes, sir!"

4

3 *Late Fire Moon* (September) 6:22 AM

After leaving Gazef and wiping himself down with a damp towel, Climb went to a place very different from the large practice hall.

This room was as spacious as the training area he'd come from. Many people sat on benches, chatting. An appetizing scent suffused the warm atmosphere.

It was the mess hall.

Cutting across the room, weaving through the noise, Climb joined the line behind a few others.

Following the people in front of him, Climb took dishes from the arranged stacks. On his tray, he placed a wooden plate and a wooden stew bowl. Then a wooden cup.

Everyone received their food in order.

A large steamed potato, brown bread, a white stew with a decent helping of fixings, pickled cabbage, a sausage—from Climb's perspective it was a luxurious meal.

The array of all those things on his tray gave off inviting smells. Suddenly feeling hungry, Climb looked out across the mess hall.

The soldiers ate with no small commotion, making idle chat with their neighbors about what they would do on their next day off, the food, their families, mundane stories about their work, and so on.

Climb spotted an empty seat and made his way through the busy room.

He straddled the bench and sat down. There were soldiers on either side of him, having nice chats with their friends. As Climb sat down, the ones nearest him spared him just a glance before looking away in apparent disinterest.

It was like there was a lull that surrounded only Climb.

From the outside, it seemed odd.

Lively conversations went on all around Climb, but not a single person called out to him. Certainly not many people would randomly talk to a stranger. But considering they were soldiers serving at the same place, entrusting their lives to one another when on duty, this treatment was a bit strange.

It was like he didn't exist.

Climb didn't make an effort to talk to anyone, either—he knew where he stood.

The guardians of Ro-Lente Castle were not ordinary military.

The kingdom's "soldiers" included levies outfitted by landed nobility, soldiers who were like a private army whose wages were paid by city officials, and the guards who mainly patrolled the city. They all shared one thing—their commoner backgrounds.

But there were various problems with entrusting peasants of unknown origin with the castle's protection and bringing them so close to the royal family and all the kingdom's sensitive intelligence. Accordingly, the soldiers who guarded Ro-Lente Castle needed a recommendation from a noble. If a soldier caused any issues, the vouching noble would be held responsible, so the candidates were necessarily of clearly established identity with no evidence of problems with their thoughts or behavior.

But something had developed as a result of this system.

Factions.

The nobles who supplied castle guard nominees all belonged to one or another of them. Naturally, the soldiers aligned themselves with the affiliations of their patrons. Those who would defy their noble would never be elected in the first place, so it wasn't an exaggeration to say there were virtually no soldiers who eschewed factionalism.

At first glance, this setup appeared to be wholly detrimental, but if there was an advantage to speak of, it was that because conflict between factions could potentially spark a war, the soldiers were expected to apply themselves diligently. Even if they still couldn't match up to the empire's knights, the soldiers who guarded the castle were fairly skilled.

Of course, Climb was a few notches above them, and that was another reason the nobles resented him—he was stronger than the soldiers they backed.

It was possible to conceive of a sponsoring noble who didn't belong to a faction. But in the current power struggle between the king's faction and the nobles', there was only a single noble who was skilled enough to strategically flit back and forth like a bat between them.

And among the soldiers, there was only one who had not joined up with either faction besides the troops endorsed by that exceptional noble.

That was Climb.

Climb's position was a very difficult one.

Normally someone of Climb's background wouldn't be able to serve as Renner's personal attendant. The role of protecting a member of the royal family would normally never be an option for a lowborn citizen. It was generally accepted that the only ones fit to protect the royal family were of noble rank.

But there was the exception of Gazef Stronoff, the strongest soldier in the kingdom, and his elite men. That, and more importantly, there weren't many who could openly oppose Princess Renner if she strongly desired something. Maybe a relative could speak frankly with her, but if the king approved, no one could dissent.

The reason Climb had a private room was due to this difficult position.

If he were an ordinary soldier, he would have shared a big common room instead.

Although Renner's authoritative pronouncement was part of the reason he had his own room, the other part was to isolate him. They didn't know where to place him because he didn't belong to a faction. He was a problem.

Considering Climb's own circumstances and his position, he would naturally belong to the king's faction. But the king's faction was comprised mainly of nobles who swore loyalty to the king. Climb was a nobody whose existence the nobles would undoubtedly frown upon.

So the group wouldn't know how to treat him if they took him in, and he would naturally cooperate with them if they left him alone. Whereas for the nobles, it would be quite a prize to win Climb over, but it would also be dangerous.

Still, each faction contained countless nobles. It wasn't as if their thoughts and opinions were monolithic. In the end, a faction was no more than a gathering of similarly minded people who desired the advantage of banding together. So of course, there were some in the king's faction who detested Climb—the beautiful Golden Princess's closest aide despite his uncertain peasant background—and some in the opposing nobles' faction who wanted to befriend him.

In any case, no one thus far had been so imprudent as to cause schisms in their faction over one guy.

The result was that although everyone wanted to avoid his going to the other side, they didn't want to go so far as to have him on theirs.

That's why no one talked to him, why he dined alone.

He ate his meal without chatting with anyone and looked to neither side. He finished his breakfast in less than ten minutes.

"Okay, guess I should get going." Satisfied, he talked to himself under his breath—a growing habit from being alone so much—as he stood up, and a soldier who happened to be passing by bumped into him.

The man's elbow jabbed a spot he'd hurt training with Gazef that morning, and although his face remained expressionless, he stopped short from the pain.

The soldier who'd bumped into him kept walking without saying a thing. Naturally, none of the surrounding soldiers spoke up, either. Some of the ones who had witnessed what happened furrowed their brows a tiny bit, but still, no one moved to say something.

Climb exhaled slowly and walked off with his empty dishes.

This degree of harassment was all too common. He was just glad it hadn't happened when there was hot stew in his bowl.

Someone would stick a leg out and trip him. Someone would bump into him, pretending it was an accident. These things happened all the time.

Still—

What about it?

Climb walked on, unconcerned. They couldn't do anything more than that, either, especially in a place like the mess hall where there were so many people watching.

Climb kept his chest out. He kept his eyes facing forward and his head high.

If he did anything shameful, it would cause trouble for his master, Renner. The reputation of the woman he devoted his whole self to was on the line.

Chapter 2   The Blue Roses

Chapter 2 | The Blue Roses

1

Perfectly outfitted in his white full plate armor with his sword strapped to his hip, Climb stepped into Valencia Palace.

The palace was made up of three main structures, and he entered the largest one, where the royal family resided. Unlike the mess hall he had just come from, the palace was designed to allow in so much light that the interior itself brightly shone.

He walked down a long corridor so clean that it seemed unlikely one would find even a speck of dust, never mind garbage. His gear made hardly a sound because it had been forged from a mix of mythril and orichalcum, as well as enchanted.

Along the broad and spotless hallway stood the elite soldiers who guarded the palace, clad in full armor, standing rigidly—the kingdom's knights.

In the empire, *knight* meant an ordinary person who was transformed into a professional soldier, but in the kingdom, the word referred to those who had life peerage. Third or fourth sons of nobles, men who wouldn't inherit their houses, often aimed to join the knighthood. That said, the royal household paid consummate wages, so only those skilled enough were chosen. Not even a noble could get by on connections alone.

The most straightforward way to describe the kingdom's knights was perhaps "the king's bodyguards."

Incidentally, Gazef's title of warrior captain was something the king fabricated because a great many objected to knighting a commoner. Correspondingly, the elite soldiers he hand-selected to serve under him became known as the Royal Select.

Climb bobbed his head toward the knights. They, at least, usually returned his greetings. There were a few who did so unwillingly, but some actually meant it, too. These men were nobles, but at the same time, they were loyal to the king and had the hearts of warriors. Naturally, they had plenty of respect for an outstanding soldier who would never lapse in his devotion to the king.

At the same time, there were others Climb passed in the corridors who directed outright hostility at him—the maids. Most made unpleasant expressions whenever they saw him.

Unlike the average servant, most maids who worked in the palace were the daughters of noble households, hoping to raise their prestige through service. In a way, these maids were higher in status than Climb. Quite a few were from elite noble families, particularly the maids who closely attended the royal family. Their discontent at having to pay obeisance to a lowborn man was clear in their angry faces.

True, Climb's social standing was lower than theirs, so they probably wanted to express their displeasure when Renner wasn't around. Climb understood that, and he didn't protest.

But those feelings made for a blank expression in response, which the maids mistook to mean he was ignoring them. This further increased their dislike for him, resulting in a vicious cycle to which Climb was completely oblivious. In fact, if he were better able to realize these sorts of things, he would've been better at handling all sorts of situations.

The young soldier was a bit dense, but walking through the palace like this did place a little mental strain on him.

Naturally, there were other members of the royal family around besides Renner and Ramposa III.

Ack!! Seeing one draw near, Climb shifted to the side of the hallway, stood at attention, and raised a hand to his chest in a salute.

There were two people. The one bringing up the rear was tall and lean with blond hair slicked back. His name was Marquis Raeven, one of the six great nobles.

The problem was the plump man walking in front of him. His name was Zanac Valléon Igana Ryle Vaiself. He was second in line for the throne, the younger of the two princes.

His feet stopped, and his flabby face twisted into a sarcastic grin. "Oh, if it isn't Climb! Going to pop in on the monster?"

There was only one person Prince Zanac called a monster. Though Climb knew it was disrespectful to speak out, he couldn't just stand there and do nothing. "Your Highness. With all due respect, Princess Renner is in no way a monster. As kindhearted and beautiful as she is, one could say the princess is the kingdom's treasure."

If a woman who proposed policies like eliminating slavery to help the populace wasn't a treasure, then who was? Due to the nobles' interference, not many of her plans had seen the light of day, but Climb was certain. He knew how much Renner thought about the people.

Zanac, who did nothing, had no right to utter even a single word about the kindhearted woman who shed tears before Climb every time her proposals were mocked and rejected.

He was taken by the urge to shout the prince down, to pummel the rotund man with his fists.

Zanac's words were not something a person should say about their blood relatives—half siblings though they may have been. But it would be unforgivable for Climb to reveal his inner rage.

Renner had warned him, "My brother is trying to provoke you into saying something defamatory. He wants an excuse to separate you from me. Climb, don't ever show him any weakness."

Climb remembered the day he had sworn to her sorrowful countenance— to his master denied by her own family—that he would never betray her.

"It's not like I was calling Renner a monster or anything. You must just think she is, in your heart…is what I would say, but I won't spout anything as clichéd as that. But a 'treasure,' huh? Do you think she actually expects her proposals to pass? I have the feeling she brings them up knowing all the while that they're futile…"

That can't be true. Impossible. This is just the envy of a man who can only make groundless accusations. "I do not believe that to be the case."

"Heh-heh-heh-heh-heh. So you really can't see that she's a monster, huh? Got any eyes in that head of yours? Or is she just that clever? …It wouldn't hurt to doubt her a little bit, right?"

"Doubt her? Princess Renner is the kingdom's treasure. My conviction on that point will never waver." *Everything she does is right.* Climb could declare that precisely because he watched her closer than anyone.

"I see, I see. How amusing. Then will you tell the monster something for me? …Our elder brother thinks her a tool in his schemes, but if she cooperates with me, I can revoke her succession rights and set her up with a domain on the frontier."

Climb was assailed by an unpleasant feeling. "…You jest. I can't believe you would speak of such a thing here. I'll pretend I didn't hear it."

"Heh-heh-heh-heh-heh. That's too bad. Shall we, then, Marquis Raeven?"

The man who had been silently observing the two bowed his head slightly.

Climb wasn't sure about where the nobleman stood. Marquis Raeven always seemed to keep his distance, but when under his gaze, Climb got a different feeling from him than the other nobles. Renner had never told Climb how to behave around him, either.

"Oh. The marquis agrees that she's ghastly. No, it would be better to say that we've formed an alliance because our opinions align on that matter."

"Prince—"

"Let me tell him, Marquis Raeven. So, Climb. If I thought you were too far gone I wouldn't say this, but…I have to warn you, since you might be getting duped by that beast… She's a monster!"

"I beg your pardon, but allow me to inquire. What is it that makes you think Princess Renner is a monster? Is there anyone who thinks more of the people, of the country, than her?"

"It's because almost everything she attempts ultimately ends in failure. Too many of her plans go nowhere. At first I thought she was just bad at laying the groundwork, but then I spoke to Marquis Raeven one day, and suddenly it dawned on me: *What if it's all according to plan?* When thinking about it that way, everything started to make sense. If that's true, then that would mean that a woman who doesn't even have a decent contact with the nobles, who is basically shut up in the palace, is still somehow manipulating them all… If that's not a monster, then what is?"

"It's just a misunderstanding. Princess Renner isn't that kind of person," Climb declared.

Those tears couldn't be fake. Princess Renner was a compassionate, kindhearted person. Climb, whom she'd plucked off the streets, knew that better than anyone.

But his words didn't reach the prince. Zanac flashed a wry smile and walked away with Marquis Raeven following behind.

In the now-empty hallway, Climb whispered, "Princess Renner is the kindest person in the whole kingdom. I may be a nobody, but I guarantee it. If…" Climb swallowed the words that came next. But he continued his monologue in his head. *If Princess Renner ruled the kingdom, it would be a wonderful country that always considered its people.*

Of course, considering the succession, it was an impossible wish. Still, Climb couldn't abandon the thought.

3 *Late Fire Moon* (September) 8:11 AM

Eventually, Climb arrived at the room in the palace he visited the most.

He scanned the area a couple of times before turning the knob. Not knocking flew in the face of common sense, but that was the princess's wish. She wouldn't allow him to knock no matter how much he protested.

So Climb gave in. He would be in too much of a spot if the princess started crying. He did manage to get her to allow for special circumstances.

For example, certainly when the king was watching, he couldn't enter without knocking.

It was true, though, that pushing the door open without knocking caused him a lot of anxiety. It was no wonder he got stressed when the thought running through his head was *There's no way this is okay*.

He was about to push it wide open when he heard a heated exchange through the crack, so he stopped his hand.

There were two voices, both women's.

Climb was still outside, but the owner of one of the voices didn't notice him because of how absorbed she was in the conversation. He didn't want to ruin the moment, so he stood immobile and listened in on the voices inside. He did feel guilty for eavesdropping, but he would have felt worse if he disrupted such passionate discussion.

"—what I'm telling you. People generally focus on the immediate benefits that are right in front of them."

"I dunno…"

"Your plan is to rotate different crops. And…I don't really think that'll make them grow better, but…when would we see a result?"

"By my rough calculations, it would take about six years."

"So during those six years, what are the estimated financial losses due to changing crops?"

"It depends on the crop, but…if we say a usual yield is one, then point eight. So a point two loss. But after six years we should end up with a steady gain of point three. And if we can get the livestock grazing in a cultivated pasture, that should increase even further…"

"If they were only hearing that last bit, anyone would go for it, but will they accept a point two loss for six years? I wonder."

"…What if the government lent that point two with no collateral and no interest and only asked them to pay it back once they could? I don't think there would be a problem… And if the yield doesn't go up, then they won't have to pay it back, or something like that. If the yield does go up, they'd be able to pay it off in four years…"

"Seems like a hard sell."

"Why?"

"I've been telling you! People focus on the immediate benefits they can see—most people want stability. Even hearing they'll have one point three times more in six years, it's only natural to hesitate."

"I...don't really get it. The test fields are doing fine..."

"The tests might be going well, but that doesn't make the results absolute."

"...That's true—the results aren't certain because the test can't account for every possible scenario. Considering variations in soil quality and climate, and we'd have to do a pretty large-scale test..."

"So it's not very persuasive. I don't know if that point three increase is the minimum or the average, but it won't be very convincing in the face of all those qualifiers. You have to be able to promise enough long-term benefits *after* promising immediate benefits."

"So if we offered them the point two without asking them to pay it back?"

"That'll make the opposing nobles happy, since the king will lose some of his power."

"But if after six years we can really get that boost in agriculture, the kingdom's power should increase..."

"That means the nobles against us would get stronger, too. And the king's power would lessen. The nobles supporting him will never allow that."

"In that case, we could appeal to the merchants..."

"You mean the wealthy ones? They have their own considerations. If they cooperate too much with the king's faction, they could potentially lose business with the other faction."

"This is hard, Lakyus..."

"Your plans fall through all the time because you're no good at laying the groundwork and making the necessary preparations... I mean, I understand that it's harder because there are two large opposing factions... How about implementing your plan only on lands directly within the king's demesne?"

"My brothers would never let me."

"Ah, those idi— Honorable men who left all the wisdom inside your mother for you."

"...........Well, it's not as though we share a mom."

"Then it's from the king? Really, it's so sad if the royal family can't even agree."

The room quieted down, and Climb realized there was a lull in the conversation.

"Oh, you can come in anytime. It's okay, right, Renner?"

"Huh?"

Climb's heart nearly leaped out of his chest. He was shocked she had noticed him, but it also made sense. He slowly opened the door. "Excuse me."

The familiar decor appeared before his eyes.

This room was luxurious without being gaudy, and at a table near the window sat two blond-haired ladies. They were both beautiful, and their pretty dresses suited them.

One was obviously Renner—it was her room.

Across from her sat another woman. Both her green eyes and pink lips had a healthy glow. She wasn't as beautiful as Renner, but she overflowed with a different sort of charm. If Renner had the glitter of a jewel, then this woman was filled with the spark of life.

Her name was Lakyus Alvein Dale Aindra.

One would never guess from the pale-pink dress she wore at the moment, but she led one of the kingdom's only two adamantite-rank adventurer teams, as well as being Renner's best friend.

Her overwhelming natural ability must have been what allowed her to perform so many feats and achieve adamantite rank at the young age of nineteen. Sometimes, deep inside, Climb felt jealous in spite of himself.

"Good morning, Princess Renner, Lady Aindra."

"Morning, Climb."

"G'morning."

Having greeted them properly, Climb moved to stand in his usual spot behind and to the right of the princess, but she stopped him. "Climb, not there, over here." She was gesturing to the chair on her right.

Climb was confused. There were five chairs around the circular table. That was the usual number. But there were three cups of tea: one in front of Renner, one in front of Lakyus, and one at the place next to Lakyus—not where Renner was indicating he should sit. He scanned the room but didn't see a third person.

Feeling strange, Climb gazed at the chair.

His master was asking him to commit the disrespectful act of sharing a table with royalty despite being a commoner, had ordered him to come in without knocking (as a favor for her), and more. Most of his master's orders weighed heavily on him.

"But…" Climb looked to the other woman for a lifeline.

His plea to be spared from sitting with them met a simple rejection. "I'm fine with it."

"B-but…Lady Aindra…"

"I told you before, you can call me Lakyus." Then to Renner, she said, "Climb's special."

"…Grah." At Lakyus's syrupy tone, as if the sentence was punctuated by an affectionate heart, Renner forcibly smiled as she voiced her displeasure. If it was possible to call upturned lips with completely serious eyes a smile.

"Lady Aindra, no more jokes, please."

"Okay, okay, Mr. Straitlaced. Maybe you should learn a thing or two from me about how to relax."

"Huh? You were joking?" Renner asked in surprise.

Lakyus froze in response as if on purpose, then let out an exaggerated sigh. "Of course. Well, Climb is definitely special, but it's because he's *yours*."

Climb awkwardly averted his gaze from Renner as she blushed and held her face in her hands when his eyes suddenly popped open.

Melted into the shadow remaining in the corner of the room was someone sitting against the wall, holding their knees. A woman wearing all black, formfitting clothing, she didn't match the atmosphere of the room at all.

"What the—?!" Taken by surprise, Climb reached for the sword at his hip, lowering his center of gravity, and moved to protect Renner.

Lakyus sighed. "See, you surprised Climb because you're dressed that way."

There was no caution or panic in her composed voice. The tension left Climb's shoulders as he realized what that meant.

"Got it, boss." The woman sitting in the darkness leaped to her feet.

"Ah yeah, you haven't met her, huh, Climb? She's one of my team members—"

"Her name's Tina." Renner finished Lakyus's thought.

Climb's understanding was that the adamantite-rank team the Blue Roses comprised five women: the leader, a faith caster, Lakyus; a warrior, Gagaran; an arcane caster, Evileye; and the two who had mastered thief skills, Tia and Tina.

The former three he had met before but not the other two.

She's… I see. She's just like the rumors said. With her slim body swathed head to toe in clinging black fabric, she certainly looked the part.

"…Please excuse me. How do you do? My name is Climb." He bowed low to Tina.

"Huh? It's no big deal."

After waving off Climb's apology, she approached the table almost soundlessly with sleek movements akin to a wild animal. Then she pulled out the chair next to Lakyus and sat down. Apparently, the cup was hers.

There were three cups on the table, so the number alone suggested she wasn't here, but Climb intently scanned the area anyway for the other woman he hadn't met.

Lakyus realized what he was doing immediately. "Tia didn't come. Gagaran and Evileye also said they hate formalities… It's not even that fancy! I dressed up just in case, but it wasn't like I was going to force them to," she said. In reality, formal dress was the correct attire for meeting the princess. Climb, however, didn't have any intention of pointing that out to a woman who was Renner's friend and a noble besides.

"I see. But I'm very happy to finally meet the famous Lady Tina. I hope you'll remember me kindly should we meet in the future."

"How about sitting down and *then* chatting, Climb?" Renner said, serving tea into a fresh cup. Steam rose from the tea pouring out of the magic item, Warm Bottle, as if it were freshly steeped.

The Warm Bottle would maintain any drink's temperature and quality for about an hour and was one of Renner's favorite items. She used it especially often when welcoming guests who were important to her. In fact, she rarely used it otherwise.

With no avenues of escape left to him, Climb accepted his fate, sat down, and took a sip of tea. "It's delicious, Princess Renner."

Renner beamed, but in truth, Climb had no idea whether it was delicious or not. He just figured that since she had prepared the tea, it must be.

Suddenly, he heard a level voice whose emotions were difficult to discern. "She should be out collecting intelligence today—on the orders of someone who gave her work even though we were supposed to all come to the palace together. It's all our demon leader's fault." It went without saying the voice belonged to Tina.

Averting his eyes from Lakyus and the terrible smile that appeared on her face in response to the words *demon leader*, Climb said, "Is that so…? I'd like to meet her sometime."

"Climb, Tina and Tia are twins, and their hair is about the same length."

"So seeing one of them is enough."

It wasn't about what was enough or not, but Climb indicated his understanding for the time being.

He started feeling flustered under Tina's unreserved gaze. He thought he would just endure it, but then he wondered if she had noticed something he'd carelessly missed, so he made up his mind to ask. "What is it?"

"You've gotten too big."

"…Huh?" That made no sense. Climb had several question marks over his head when Lakyus interrupted to apologize.

"Never mind, it's just her thing. Don't worry about it, Climb. Really, don't worry about it. Really."

"I see—"

"What are you talking about, Lakyus?" Climb had forced himself to accept the explanation, but unable to do so herself, Renner interrupted.

Lakyus made a whiny face at her. "Ugh, whenever it comes to Climb…"

"Oh, I just—"

"Shut up. The reason I didn't bring Tia is because she's always trying to put weird ideas into Renner's head. So can you just understand that and be quiet?"

"Aye-aye, demon boss."

"But… Lakyus. What is it?"

At Renner's follow-up, Lakyus's face twitched violently with an expression of agony.

Right when Climb thought he should maybe chime in, she suddenly turned to him. "Uh…Climb, looks like you love wearing that armor."

"Yes, it's fantastic armor. Thank you."

The word *forced* was far from enough to describe the change of topic, but hoping to prevent the princess's guest from losing face, he replied and ran his hand over the white armor he'd received from Renner. It had been constructed from quite a bit of mythril and a little orichalcum; was enchanted with various spells; and was surprisingly light, sturdy, and mobile.

The Blue Roses were the ones who had offered to supply the mythril for his equipment, free of charge. No amount of bowing could possibly be enough to express his gratitude.

He was about to lower his head when Lakyus stopped him. "No worries. We just gave Renner the leftovers from when we made our own mythril armor."

Even mere scraps of mythril could fetch an extremely high price. An orichalcum-ranked adventurer might have had the means to forge a full set of mythril plates, and a mythril rank could have possibly owned a mythril weapon. But the only ones who could hand over the material like it was nothing were probably powerful adamantite-ranked adventurers.

"Besides, it was Renner who asked. We couldn't say no."

"You wouldn't take my money. I even saved up my allowance for it…"

"…Isn't it weird for a princess to have an allowance?"

"The money from my estate is separate. I wanted to make Climb's armor with my allowance…"

"Yeah. You wanted to give him armor you made with your own money."

"If you knew, then why did you give the metal to me for free? You jerk."

"Do I really deserve to be called a jerk for that…?"

Pouting Renner and smirking Lakyus started quarreling without really fighting.

Watching the two, Climb's stoic expression nearly broke, but he held it together.

The fact that he was able to see this—this peaceful, warm scene—was thanks to his master, who had taken him in. But he couldn't ever open up and reveal his feelings. Showing his gratitude was proper, but he had stronger feelings deep inside, those he couldn't show.

They were…love.

Climb shoved them down and suppressed them. Instead, he said the words he'd repeated many times. "Thank you, Princess Renner."

The way he held his body clearly demarcated a line between their respective positions—clarifying their relationship as master and servant. Renner reacted to this with a smile that contained the faintest hint of sadness, which Climb only noticed precisely because he watched her more than anyone every single day.

"You're welcome. Now, we seem to have gotten a bit off track. Let's return to our earlier discussion."

"About the Eight Fingers, right? You got that we snuck into three villages growing the drugs and burned the fields, right?"

At that name, Climb mentally frowned behind his blank visage.

The Eight Fingers was a criminal organization operating in the kingdom's underworld. His beloved and respected master was figuring out what to do about them.

If they torched the drugs supplying the livelihoods of those villagers, the question of what would become of them didn't have any good answers, but they were necessary sacrifices in eradicating the narcotics eating away at the kingdom.

Someone with absolute power would have had a number of ways to solve the problem, but despite being the princess, Renner had virtually no support. Consequently, she had to make realistic choices as to who she could save and who she needed to ignore.

If she petitioned her father, the king, she might have been able to attack with military and authoritative might wherever she wished. But since the Eight Fingers had clear ties to various nobles, intelligence would most certainly leak, allowing the criminals to anticipate her moves and destroy all the evidence of their crimes.

That's why Renner had chosen to rely on her friend Lakyus and her team directly.

Climb knew that such a request was a risky move. Normally, adventurers fielded jobs via the guild; accepting jobs directly was not permitted. What they were doing was against the rules.

Granted, the guild couldn't very well penalize or banish a team at the highest rank. Still, breaking the rules could hurt their reputation internally and put them at a disadvantage in the future. The reason they undertook the mission regardless must have been because the Blue Roses loved their country and saw Renner as a friend.

She was putting herself and her team on the line, making Climb even more grateful to her.

Lakyus felt it was about time to bring up a certain topic, so she opened the bag Tina had brought and withdrew a piece of parchment.

It was something the Blue Roses hadn't been able to decipher. Lakyus thought Renner, who had the best brains of anyone she knew, might be able to figure it out.

"We found these when we were lighting the narcotic fields. They seem like some kind of instructions, so we brought them back with us, but…can you make anything of them?"

On the unfurled parchment were symbols from no writing system for any country they had ever seen. Renner answered nonchalantly after just a glance, "It's a substitution cipher."

A substitution cipher was a type of code where symbols or other characters were substituted for single or multiple character units of normal writing. If A is Δ and B is $\square$, then $\Delta\Delta\square\square\Delta$ is *AABBA*.

"That's what I thought, too. So I looked everywhere for the key, but unfortunately I couldn't find it. It's possible they have it memorized, so it made sense to charm the man we captured into being our ally and get it out of him that way. He seemed like someone in charge. But as you know, charm magic is less effective when the same person casts it on the same target multiple times. I wanted to make sure the first round was a good one, so I thought we should check with you first."

"I see... Why was this at the scene anyway? Is it a trap...? Or was there some other reason? Then they wouldn't use something very hard to crack. Right. I think this is pretty easy to decipher."

Lakyus's eyes widened. She exchanged a glance with Tina beside her in spite of herself.

She couldn't believe it. On the other hand, well, it was Renner.

"Uh, so, in the language of the kingdom, the first letters will represent either the masculine article, the feminine article, or the neuter article, so... One second..." As the princess mumbled, she got up, still holding the parchment, and grabbed a pen and paper.

Then the letters started to flow onto the paper.

"This is a pretty simple cipher, since each symbol stands for a single character. And we're lucky they were using the language of the kingdom. If the key were a book from the empire or something, it'd be pretty much impossible. With this...well, if you can figure out one letter, it's just about filling in the rest from there. Anyone can decipher this with a little effort."

"Noooo, it's easy to say that, but it's impossible unless you know tens of thousands of words, right?" said Lakyus.

"These are instructions written in code! You wouldn't expect any overly complex phrasing, and the possibility of there being difficult vocabulary is extremely slim. It should be written in plain language even a child could understand, so that narrows it down quite a bit."

A figurative sweat drop dangled in Lakyus's mind.

Her friend talked like it was simple, but it wasn't such an easy thing. *She can do it, but…she really is incredibly smart.*

Every time they met and talked, she was surprised anew. Lakyus didn't know anyone who fit the word *genius* as well as Renner.

Lakyus secretly had the creeps, but Renner was relatively nonchalant when she said, "I got it! It wasn't instructions, though," and handed over the paper. It was a list of various places in the kingdom. There were seven in all.

"I wonder if it means there are drugs stored here or that they're important strategic locations," Lakyus suggested.

"I doubt they would write down such important information and leave it lying around a mere production facility… They must be decoys."

"Decoys? You mean it's a trap?"

"Hrm, I don't think so. Uh, the Eight Fingers is one organization, but people say it's split into eight organizations that kind of work together, right?"

Lakyus nodded.

"So they're intentionally giving away information about the other seven organizations, er, divisions, I guess, to divert attention from themselves."

"They prepared intelligence on the other seven divisions…? I expected the organization was far from a monolith, but I didn't expect them to be this…" To adventurers, betraying one's comrades was disgusting. "I knew we'd have to move fast, but yeah, I guess if we don't, we'll have issues."

Renner nodded and Lakyus asked another question.

"So then, what about that brothel? Apparently, it's a pretty nasty one where you can do anything." Just saying that made her insides boil with rage. *Those filthy pieces of trash! Garbage who can't think of anything except their own desires should drop dead!* She snarled in her mind, recalling the information she had on the brothel, not as a noble's daughter but as an experienced woman adventurer. She didn't even need to guess what "anything" meant. She knew that multiple people, men and women, had been killed for pleasure.

Back in the days when there was slave trafficking, a few of those types of brothels existed in the underworld. But right before her eyes, by the work of her friend, slavery became illegal, and those facilities began disappearing. This place could very well be the last brothel in the royal capital or even the kingdom.

That was precisely why it couldn't be expunged so easily. They would surely meet strong opposition. It was the last filthy paradise for people with unspeakably sleazy tastes.

"Hey, Renner. Since there's no way to use your authority to carry out a search, why not have us force our way in and blow the lid off the place? There won't be any trouble as long as we find evidence, right? If the slave-trafficking division is really running the brothel, it'll be a huge blow to the Eight Fingers if we take it down, and depending on what evidence we find, it could also be a heavy strike against the nobles who do business with them."

"Maybe, Lakyus. But won't that cause troubles for your family, the house of Alvein? So it's tricky. It's tricky if we mobilize the Blue Roses…but it'd be impossible for Climb to go in and take them out on his own…"

"I'm sorry I'm not strong enough."

When Climb bowed his head, Renner cupped his hand in hers and smiled kindly. "Sorry, Climb. I didn't mean it like that. It's the only underworld brothel in the capital. No one could take it out alone… I trust you the most, Climb. I know how hard you work for me. But don't do anything reckless, okay? And I'm not asking as a favor—that's an order! If anything ever happened to you…"

Even Lakyus, watching from beside Renner, felt the peerless beauty's teary eyes pierce her heart. How was Climb's heart doing?

He frantically tried to keep a straight face but couldn't quite manage it. On the contrary, his blushing cheeks said it all.

If a bard were to title this scene, it would be *The Princess and the Knight*—it was moving, but a touch of fear unsettled Lakyus. She didn't think it was possible, but if Renner was doing all this on purpose, then she knew every trick in the book—it was unbelievable.

What am I thinking? That's not the kind of thing you should think about a close friend. Everything she's done speaks to the fact that she's not a bad person like that. If I can't believe in the Golden Princess who's done so much to help people, then who can I believe in?

Lakyus shook her head and spoke, in part to clear away those horrible thoughts. "By the way, Tina and Tia's research turned up the names of a few nobles with connections to the slave-trafficking division chief, Coccodor. The only thing is...it's too soon to move on the info, since we haven't confirmed whether it's true or not yet."

When she listed the names of several nobles, there was one that prompted a simultaneous reaction from both Renner and Climb.

"His daughter is one of my maids."

"I can't imagine he had her placed here to spy on you...but there's no guarantee she's only here to cultivate prestige."

"Yes. I should be careful how I'm handling information. You remember that, too, Climb."

"Okay, let's decide what to do about those places we learned from the coded message. And Renner. Can I borrow Climb? I want him to go tell Gagaran and the others it seems like we'll be making a move really soon."

2

3 Late Fire Moon (September) 9:49 AM

Climb walked down one of the capital's broad streets. There was nothing about his appearance that made him stand out, so he melted completely into the crowd.

His white full plate armor certainly would have attracted attention, so he'd taken it off. If he used a special alchemical item, he could change its color, but he didn't feel like going to that much trouble just to wear it. There was no need to equip full armor just for a walk around the city anyway.

So he was dressed lightly, with mail hidden under his shirt. The only thing that set him apart from an ordinary civilian was the longsword at his hip. That was about the same level of gear as the patrolling soldiers—guards—mercenaries, and other people on the street wore. Even if some people gave him a relatively wide berth, he wasn't armored heavily enough that the crowd parted or anything.

Any ponderously outfitted people were adventurers. This style was less for necessity and more to stand out.

For an adventurer, dressing to attract attention was not strange. It was advertising. Some even dressed in a particularly eccentric way to create a strong impression, spread rumors, and make a name for themselves. In other words, style was like an adventurer's trademark.

But for adventurers at the level of the Blue Roses, whom Climb was currently going to meet, there was no need for fashion statements. At their rank, a stroll down the street was enough to get people talking.

Eventually, on one side of the street, an adventurer inn came into view. On its grounds were the inn proper, a stable, and a yard large enough to practice with a sword. The fantastic exterior made it easy to imagine the beautiful interior, and the windows of the guest rooms were fitted with clear glass.

That top-class hotel was a gathering spot for adventurers confident in their skills and able to pay the fairly high rate.

Ignoring the guards on either side, Climb opened the door.

For how large it was, there were few adventurers in the spacious bar and dining hall that took up the entire first floor. There just weren't very many elite adventurers to begin with.

After a slight murmur traveled through the group, their curious eyes gathered on Climb. He paid no mind and scanned the room.

The occupants were all extremely powerful. Any one of them could have easily defeated him. Every time he came to a place like this, he was reminded how insignificant he was.

Climb endured the depressing thought and held his gaze on one particular point in the bar.

He was focused on two people sitting at a round table all the way in the back.

One was small and cloaked in a black robe.

The figure's face was hidden. It wasn't because of the quality of the light but because the person was wearing a strange mask, with a crimson jewel set in the forehead, that covered their entire face. There were eye slits, but even the color of the irises behind them was out of sight.

Then there was the other person.

The one in robes was small, but this character was overwhelmingly large—to the point it brought to mind the word *megalith*. The entire body was thick in a way. But it was not wrapped in body fat.

The figure's arms had the girth of logs. The neck supporting a square head seemed about the size of a woman's thighs put together. A broad jaw clenched with effort, and eyes resembling those of a predatory beast kept tabs on the area. The short blond hair prioritized only function. The chest conspicuously bulging under the clothing brought to mind the image of pectoral muscles trained to extremes—frankly, it was no longer the chest of a woman.

The adamantite adventurer team comprised entirely of women—the Blue Roses.

This curious pair contained two of its members—the arcane caster Evileye and the warrior Gagaran.

Climb continued his approach, and the one he had been aiming for called out in a husky voice, "Hey, virgin!"

The gazes that had left Climb gathered on him once again, but no one jeered. On the contrary, the adventurers lost interest immediately and averted their eyes with something resembling pity.

The reason for this detached treatment was that everyone knew getting involved with a guest of Gagaran's was not brave but reckless, even for an orichalcum- or mythril-ranked adventurer.

Shamed, Climb kept walking nonetheless.

Gagaran wouldn't change his nickname no matter how many times he told her, so giving up and just pretending he didn't care was the most effective thing he could do.

"It's been a while, La— Er, Gagaran. And Lady Evileye." When he arrived in front of them, he bobbed his head.

"Yeah, long time no see! Did you come to get laid?" she asked with a wild, animalistic grin on her face, gesturing with her chin for him to sit down, but Climb remained expressionless and shook his head.

This could be called Gagaran's usual greeting, but she wasn't kidding. If Climb responded affirmatively, even as a joke, she would probably drag him up to a private room on the second floor. He would have no way to resist her overwhelming muscles.

She endlessly professed her fondness for relishing "fresh cherries"—that was the kind of person she was.

In contrast, Evileye faced straight ahead, unmoving. Climb couldn't tell where her eyes were focused under the mask.

"No, Lady Aindra asked me to come."

"Hmm? Our leader?"

"Yes, I have a message for you. She says it seems like you'll be moving very soon. Details will come when you get back, but she wants you to be combat ready at any time."

"Whoa. Well, sorry you had to come all the way here just for that." Gagaran laughed heartily, and Climb remembered he had something else he needed to tell her.

"Today I was blessed with the opportunity to receive training from Captain Stronoff, and he praised that move you taught me, the overhead strike."

Gagaran had taught him that move in this inn's backyard. She broke into a smile as if Gazef's praise had been for her. "Oh, that? Hmm, nicely done. But you know…"

"I know. I won't be satisfied with this. I'll train even harder."

"Well, that too. Assume that move won't work out, and come up with the next thing and chain it."

Curiously, or perhaps because it was just common sense among top-class warriors, Gagaran's advice bore a strong resemblance to Gazef's. Climb was surprised at the coincidence, but Gagaran must have read his reaction as something else. "Of course, the downward slice I showed you has no point if you don't use it with the intent to make it a one-hit kill."

She laughed. "Really, the correct answer is to have countless moves and choose the appropriate ones as you go, but you can't do that." She remarked in a roundabout way that he lacked innate talent. "So make a chain of three moves so that even if your opponent blocks them, they can't transition into a counterattack."

Climb nodded.

"Well, there will be times that it won't work, like when your opponent's a monster with lots of arms, but you'll be fine against a human. If they learn your pattern, you're doomed, but for first-time opponents, it'll be pretty effective. Make a chain so you can push, push, push."

"Got it." Climb nodded emphatically.

That morning, the only time he'd been able to penetrate Gazef's space as far as he had was when he had used that move. Except for that, the captain had seen through him instantly and left Climb defending against counterattacks.

But did Climb lose confidence because of it? No.

Did he despair? No.

Just the opposite.

An ordinary person had come that close to the strongest warrior in the kingdom—no, in the entire region. He knew it was because his opponent had been holding back, but for Climb, going down his pitch-black path devoid of light, that was plenty encouraging.

Your hard work isn't all for nothing.

Remembering that, he realized what Gagaran was trying to say.

He wasn't sure he would be able to devise a chain attack, but still, the passion to do it bubbled up inside him. He wanted to get strong so that next time he sparred with the captain of the Royal Select, he would be worth just a little more of his superior's effort.

"...Oh yeah. You were asking Evileye for something, too, right? Magic training, was it?"

"Yes." Climb glanced at Evileye. When he'd asked her, she'd scoffed at him from under her mask, and the conversation had ended. Since nothing had changed, if he brought it up again, he would probably get the same response.

But—

"Kid." Her voice was hard to hear. Even ignoring the effect of the mask, the tone of her voice was very mysterious. Despite the mask, as long as it wasn't too thick, it should have been possible to tell what sort of voice she had to some extent. But Evileye's didn't betray her age, emotions, or anything like that. The sole, barely discernible trait was that it belonged to a woman. She sounded both old and young. Her voice was detached and flat.

It was probably because the mask she wore was a magic item, but why did she need to go to such lengths to hide her voice?

"You don't have the aptitude. Pour your efforts into something else." She made the dismissive declaration as though that was all she had to say to him.

But Climb knew that perfectly well.

He had no magic aptitude—no, not only magic.

No matter how many times he swung his sword, no matter how many times his blisters bled, popped, and healed over, he hadn't been able to reach the realm he aspired to. Someone born with talent could scale that wall easily, but for Climb, it was an unapproachable precipice.

But that didn't mean he could neglect his efforts to overcome it. Without aptitude, all he could do was work hard and trust that he would be able to advance even one step forward.

"You don't seem convinced." Apparently noticing Climb's emotions beneath his expressionless facade, Evileye continued. "Gifted people show it from the beginning. Some people say that ability is like a flower before it has bloomed and that everyone has the potential, but…hmm. If you ask me, that's nothing but wishful thinking. Something inferior people say to console themselves. But that's what the leader of the Thirteen Heroes was like, too."

The leader of the Thirteen Heroes… The legends said that he was originally an ordinary person. He'd been weaker than everyone, but as he continued fighting with his sword, getting injured along the way, he became a hero stronger than anyone had ever seen. He had potential that endlessly grew.

"He already had it, it just hadn't bloomed yet. But you're different. You work hard and stay the same… That's right. Natural aptitude is unmistakable. There are those who have it and those who don't. So…I won't say to give up, but just know where you stand."

Evileye's harsh words invoked a moment of silence. And it was Evileye who broke it again.

"Gazef Stronoff…he's a good example. That's a man with potential. Climb, do you really think you can close the gap in your abilities with hard work?"

His words wouldn't come out. He had been reminded today during his training bout with Gazef that it was a distance he couldn't cross.

"Well, it's probably unfair of me to compare you to him. I don't know anyone equal to him with a sword besides the Thirteen Heroes, perhaps. Gagaran here is pretty skilled, but she can't beat Gazef."

"Don't be ridiculous! That guy's already got one foot in the realm of heroes."

"Hmm. People say you're a heroine yourself…although there's a question mark with regards to your gender."

Evileye faltered for just a moment, but Gagaran smiled and said, "Hey now, Evileye. Isn't the definition of a hero a monster with extraordinary power who's transcended human limits?"

"I don't deny it."

"In that case, I can't set foot in the heroic realm. I'm a human."

"…Still, you have a gift. You're different from a human like Climb with none. Climb, you're not meant to spend your time chasing after the stars."

Climb knew full well he was lacking, but this constant confrontation with the fact drove it home. Still, that didn't mean he intended to change his way of life.

I exist for the princess. To do her will.

Evileye must have sensed something martyr-like about him. She clicked her tongue from under her mask. "…You probably won't quit just because I said all that."

"You're right."

"What a fool you are. Truly a fool." She shook her head and exclaimed how she couldn't understand. "Those with dreams that can't be attained destroy themselves, you know. I said it before, but you need to know your place."

"I understand."

"But you don't feel like listening? You are a man who's beyond foolish. The type who dies an early death… Is there anyone who would cry if you were killed?"

"What's this, Evileye? You're harassing him so much because you're worried about him?"

At Gagaran's words, Evileye bitterly slumped her shoulders. She turned to face Gagaran, reached out with a gloved hand to grab her collar, and shouted, "Shaddup for a second, meathead!"

"But it's true, isn't it?"

Gagaran was unfazed, even held by her collar, and her remark left Evileye speechless.

The robed woman sank into her chair and, to change the subject, directed her frustration at Climb. "First, learn about magic. If you increase your knowledge, you'll be able to understand the intentions of an opponent who uses magic. That way you can take more appropriate measures against them."

"Aren't there too many types of magic for him to study them all?"

"No. There are relatively few core spells that casters rely on. He can start with those." Evileye added dismissively that if he couldn't do that much, he should just give up. "Besides, as long as he learns up to tier three, he should have no problem."

"Hey, Evileyyyye. They say there are spells that go up to tier ten, but no one can use them, right? So how do we know about them?"

"Hmm…" With the air of a teacher instructing her students, Evileye did something beneath her robe. Suddenly, Climb felt all the sounds around them grow distant, as if their table had been placed inside a bubble. "Don't panic. I just used a trifling item."

He wasn't sure how wary of surrounding ears she had to be to use the item, but Climb sat up straighter when he realized the answer to Gagaran's question was important enough to take precautions.

"In one of the myths, there are beings known as the Eight Kings of Avarice. It's said that they stole the powers of the gods and ruled this world with their enormous strength."

Climb knew the story of the Eight Kings of Avarice. It was far from popular as a fairy tale, but people who possessed a certain degree of knowledge knew the story.

To summarize, five hundred years ago, the Eight Kings of Avarice appeared. Described as taller than the sky and dragon-like, they obliterated a country in the blink of an eye and conquered the world with their overwhelming power. They were unaccountably greedy, however, and fought because they coveted one another's possessions. At the end of the story, they all died.

It was only natural that a tale like that would be unpopular, but where opinions split was whether it was a fairy tale or something else. Personally, Climb thought it was rather embellished. But among adventurers, there were some here and there who believed it depicted actual beings—those more powerful than any that existed in the present day.

As grounds for this belief, they pointed to a city said to exist far away to the south in the desert. Supposedly it had been built by the Eight Kings of Avarice to serve as their capital when they ruled the continent.

While Climb stewed in his own thoughts, Evileye continued. "It's believed the Eight Kings of Avarice possessed countless powerful items, and among them was a grimoire known as the *Nameless Spellbook*. That's your answer."

"Huh? You mean it was all written down in that book?"

"Indeed. Supposedly all the spells are listed in that unimaginably powerful magic item left behind by the legendary kings. Rumor has it that, perhaps through the workings of some magic, every new spell created is listed automatically."

Though Climb knew the story of the Eight Kings of Avarice, he had never heard about this book before. Vaguely realizing what a rare piece of knowledge this was, he focused again on listening.

"That's how we can be certain tier-ten spells exist. Of course, few know even this much—that the *Nameless Spellbook* is real."

Climb gulped. "H-have you ever tried to find it? The *Nameless Spellbook*?" He asked precisely because these two stood at the pinnacle of adventurers.

Evileye snorted as if to say, *Don't be absurd!* "Hmph. According to someone who's laid eyes on the thing, it's protected by such a strong magic charm that no one but its rightful owner can touch it. It reportedly has power equal to an entire world, but that just means it's equally dangerous. I know my place, so I have no intention of coveting that sort of item and dying a foolish death like the Eight Kings of Avarice."

"You say that even knowing the leader of your team is famous for owning a weapon that belonged to one of the Thirteen Heroes?"

"It's supposedly on a whole other level, that book. Well, it's secondhand info from someone who saw it, so I don't really know the details. Aren't we off topic? Anyhow, that's the answer, Gagaran. Got it?"

After that, Evileye seemed to hesitate a bit, a rare occurrence, and turned to Climb. "Climb, don't do anything foolish like giving up your humanity just because you want power."

"Giving up my humanity…? You mean like demons in the stories?"

"That or becoming undead or a magic being."

"A normal human can't do those things."

"Yeah… Most people who turn undead end up warping their minds. They're passionate about their ideals, so they pursue that route to realize their desires, but…the physical changes strain their mind too much, and they transform into something horrific."

No emotion was visible behind the mask, but Evileye's voice was clearly tinged with pity. Watching her adopt an apparent faraway gaze, Gagaran spoke in a terrifically cheery voice. "Plus, if the princess woke up and Climb was an ogre, she'd go into shock!"

Evileye must have understood the feelings driving Gagaran's remark. Her voice returned to its previous inscrutable state. "...Well, that's one thing you could do. Using transformation magic, you could change temporarily. In all seriousness, that is an option! For increasing physical ability, I mean."

"I think I'll pass."

"It's effective in the sense of purely physical enhancement. Humans don't have a terrible amount of ability to start with, you know? Given the same talent, starting from better basic attributes would naturally give you an advantage."

That was obvious. At the same skill level, the one with better physical ability would have the edge.

"Actually, most of the Thirteen Heroes hailed from other races, not humanity. By the way, we say the Thirteen Heroes, but really, there were more. Only a mere thirteen made it into the legends... The fight against the evil spirits united beings across racial boundaries, but people focused on humans, probably not willing to spread sagas featuring the exploits of other species," Evileye remarked sarcastically. Then her demeanor changed entirely, and her narration turned nostalgic. "The warrior wielding the whirlwind ax was chief warrior of the air giants, and there was a royal family of elves that shared the characteristics of the ancestral elves, as well as the original owner of our leader's sword, Killineiram, the Black Knight, who possessed the Four Great Swords of Darkness and was part demon."

"The Four Great Swords of Darkness...?" asked Climb.

One of the Thirteen Heroes, the Black Knight, was said to possess four swords: Evil Sword, Humiris; Demonic Sword, Killineiram; Canker Sword, Coroquedavarre; and Death Sword, Sufiz. One of them was currently in the possession of none other than the leader of the Blue Roses, Lakyus.

"The most powerful Sword of Darkness, created by condensing infinite shadows, Demonic Sword, Killineiram... Sooo, is it true that if you unleash its power completely it would radiate enough dark energy to swallow a country whole?" asked Gagaran.

"What in the world?" Evileye seemed confused.

"I heard it from our leader. She said it when she was on her own the other day. She was holding her right hand and saying something about how only a woman who serves the gods like her could control its full power, et cetera, et cetera."

"I never heard anything about that..." Evileye cocked her head, puzzled. "But if the owner of the sword said so, it might be true."

"Then is it true that there's a dark Lakyus born from the mind of that darkness?"

"What?"

"Nah, I mean, she was mumbling that to herself a different time. She didn't seem to realize I was there, so I listened in to see what was up, and she was saying this crazy stuff like, 'If you get careless, I, the black root of all darkness, will rule your flesh and unleash the power of the Demonic Sword.'"

"I...can't say that it's entirely impossible. Some cursed items take over their owners' minds... It would be a massive pain in the neck if Lakyus was possessed, though."

"It seems like she wants to keep it a secret, but I bet if we ask her straight, she'll blush and tell us not to worry about it."

"Hmm. As a priest who's supposed to break curses, she's probably embarrassed that we'd worry about her being cursed instead. Does that mean she's determined not to make us worry and bottling it all up?"

"I haven't seen anything like that happen since then, but... Do you remember? She started wearing those meaningless armor rings right after she got that sword, right?"

"I thought they were just a fashion statement, but are you saying they might be magic sealing items or catalysts?"

Climb couldn't maintain his stoic mask any longer and furrowed his brow.

From what he'd heard just now, it sounded like Lakyus might be falling under the control of an evil item. Thinking about where he'd just come from, his uneasiness grew. "Is Princess Renner in danger?"

He seemed ready to fly out the door, but Evileye held him back. "Don't panic. It's not like anything's going to happen this second. Even if she were about to lose herself to a dark power, it's not like it would happen before she realized what was going on. The fact that she hasn't told us about it probably means she thinks she can control it. I mean, she's mentally strong, right? But…I had no idea that sword had such power!"

"Should we tell Azus just in case?" asked Gagaran.

"Having to borrow the strength of a rival is somewhat unfavorable, but…she's his niece, so yes, we should probably tell him."

"Okay, I guess we should do that right away? We have to figure out where he is first."

"Yes. We should be ready to support Lakyus at any moment."

"Plus, the only ones who can stop an adamantite rank are other adamantite ranks."

"Hmm? Oh! Speaking of which, Gagaran. There's supposedly a third adamantite-rank adventurer team now in E-Rantel."

"What? Really? First I've heard of it… Did you hear about them this morning at the Adventurers Guild?"

"No…uh, oh—sorry, I forgot to tell you: Apparently, they're black."

"Black? There's red and blue, so I thought for sure the next would be brown or green!"

"Black is one of the colors used in the Six Gods faith, so it's not really surprising. Perhaps next will be white."

"I'm not really a fan of the Slane Theocracy. There was that one time we wound up really getting into it with those secret unit guys, you know?"

Climb felt like he was hearing something terribly dangerous, but they ignored him and kept going.

"You don't like them, Gagaran? …They're trying to kill me, but I agree with their policies. Or rather, the task they've set for themselves, the vow they made to protect humanity, isn't wrong from the human race's point of view."

"Huh? So it's okay to kill subhumans and elves who didn't even do anything wrong, then?" Vivid disgust appeared on Gagaran's face, and flames of intense anger burned in her eyes.

Evileye shrugged off the heat directed her way. "In this area, you have several human countries: the kingdom, the sacred kingdom, and the empire. But Gagaran, did you know that the farther you get from here, the fewer human-majority countries you find? Subhumans and other races superior to humans are building nations. There are even some places where humans are slaves! One of the biggest reasons there aren't countries like that around here is because the Slane Theocracy has for years beat back any subhumans on the rise."

Gagaran quieted down and began to sulk. "Well, yeah, subhumans are physically superior to humans. If they were to gather in one place and develop their civilization, there wouldn't be much humans could do at that point..."

"If you're a human, you should appreciate what the theocracy is doing. Certainly, some of what they do is heartless, but there is no one serving humans more than them. Of course...whether I'd be able to say the same thing from the perspective of the unwanted minorities is another question. Also, there's a very good chance the Slane Theocracy were the ones who created the model for adventurers' guilds."

"Seriously?"

"Who can say? The truth is unclear, but there's a good chance. The guild system appeared after the fight with the evil spirits when humans were weak. The theocracy authorities were saving their strength, so they probably created the adventurer framework as assistance that they could offer without creating international conflict."

The silence particular to a lull in conversation descended on the table. Unable to bear it, Climb spoke up. "Sorry to interrupt, Lady Evileye. About the new adamantite-rank team, what are the members' names?"

"Hmm? Ah yes. I believe one was named Momon. He's the leader and known as the Dark Hero. Apparently, they don't have a team name. But I guess people call them Jet-Black."

"Whoa. Huh. And the other members?" asked Gagaran.

"It's a two-person team. He works with an arcane caster named Nabe, known as the Beautiful Princess."

"Huh? Just two people? What's up with that? Are they just ultra-confident idiots…? Well, no, they're adamantite rank. So they have some tricks up their sleeves, then. And? What'd they do?"

Climb listened in, too. This was a team that reached adamantite rank. They must have done things no ordinary person could imagine. He knew even before hearing them that the stories would be thrilling, and his heart buzzed in anticipation.

"I heard they did it all in the span of two months, but…first they handled an incident in E-Rantel with several thousand undead. Then they wiped out a coalition of goblin tribes coming up from the south, gathered ultrarare herbs in the Tove Woodlands, subdued a gigantic basilisk, and destroyed a division of undead that streamed in from the Katze Plain. I also heard they took out an immensely powerful vampire."

"A gigantic basilisk…?" Climb gasped.

Basilisks were huge monsters similar to lizards or snakes, over thirty feet long, with a petrifying gaze and bodily fluids so poisonous they caused instant death. Their skin was so thick it was comparable to mythril—in short, they were the worst enemy. If this party could defeat a monster capable of devastating an entire city, it was no wonder they had reached adamantite rank.

There was just one problem. That was…

"That's…pretty amazing! But did they really do it with just two people? A gigantic basilisk has to be impossible to manage with just a warrior and a caster. That can't be true."

Yes, that was the catch. It would be virtually impossible to do it with two people. Especially with only a warrior and a caster—how did they heal? They couldn't possibly have a way to defend against a basilisk's every special attack—the petrifying gaze, poisonous fluids, and so on.

"Oh, sorry! I guess I can't say they are just two. They also tamed the Wise King of the Forest so it serves them."

"...The Wise King of the Forest? What kind of monster is that?" asked Gagaran.

Climb remembered hearing the name in some folktales, similar to the sagas of adventurers. But he felt it would be rather impertinent to chime in at this juncture.

"I don't know the details, but folklore has it that the Wise King of the Forest is a magical beast who has reigned in the Tove Woodlands since eons ago. Its might is supposedly unrivaled. Someone I know went to the Tove Woodlands a long time ago...mm-hmm, some two hundred years ago, and didn't see it, but..." She said two hundred years with a shrug of her shoulders.

If she were an elf or something, that age would be entirely possible, but from her attitude Climb concluded she must have been joking.

"Whoa. So how much of all that is true? It has to be mostly exaggeration, right?"

That's how it usually played out. When people told stories, they exaggerated unconsciously. Corpses found in pieces made it difficult to accurately count, and on occasion, adventurers themselves made outlandish claims, so stories simply became wilder and more grandiose.

In response, however, Evileye wagged a finger disapprovingly and said, "Tsk-tsk-tsk. No, apparently all this is true. The first rumors circulating after the E-Rantel incident claimed that he defeated an undead giant by throwing a sword and then broke through an undead mob thousands strong. That info is from surviving guards who witnessed it, and they all said the same things, so it doesn't seem to be exaggerated. The fact that they beat the two ringleaders behind the mob was confirmed with corpses. And that was *after* they defeated two skeletal dragons."

Climb asked the speechless Gagaran, "Would that be hard even for you?"

"If the several thousand undead were zombies and skeletons, then it wouldn't be a problem. I could break through. I could probably also manage two skeletal dragons somehow, but the two ringleaders who caused that big of an incident? I dunno. I can't say for sure if I don't know their abilities."

"The unofficial consensus is that they were from Zurrernorn."

"Are you serious, Evileye? Ahh, if we're talking about *their* disciples, that'd be the end for me. It would be rough after all that other stuff. And if I made the slightest wrong move—got poisoned or paralyzed—I'd be done. How do they heal? Do they rely on potions? Or maybe the warrior Momon can use faith magic like our leader. Or maybe the Beautiful Princess can?"

"Can't deny the possibility." Evileye nodded.

"But a giant basilisk would be…impossible. For a warrior, someone who mainly fights at close quarters, that's a serious challenge. I have Gaze Bane, but I'd still be in trouble without support."

"There's your answer, Climb. Apparently, it'd be impossible for Gaga-ran on her own. So it would depend on what the woman, Nabe, can do. If we fought together, we could do it…probably?"

"Yeah, if she were on your level, they'd be more than strong enough. If you made it a mostly ranged battle, you could probably beat a gigantic basi-lisk on your own without even going all out, no?"

"Mm, no, that would be impossible. I would need to apply my full power."

"If you were with me, the only opponents it would make sense for me to handle out of those two incidents would be the skeletal dragons…so I'd basically be relying on your strength. With an orichalcum-rank caster… there'd just be no way."

Climb felt puzzled. *Is Evileye really that powerful of a caster?* Usually teams were composed of members around the same strength. Plus, Evileye and Gagaran had been adventuring together all this time. Would such a significant gap really open up under those circumstances?

"That's not true. I know how strong you are, Gagaran. You can defi-nitely match these newcomers," Climb assured her.

"Hoo-whee! Thanks for the praise. All right, wanna sleep together?"

"No, I respectfully decline."

"And that's why you're a virgin! It's like not eating when a meal's put in front of you. You don't get a prize for keeping your virginity forever, you know. What are you going to do when it's time to sleep with your real woman? Do you want her to complain about how bad you are? Is that what you're into? Are you a masochist?" Having made all those assertions without waiting for Climb's response, Gagaran heaved a conspicuous sigh. "Well, I won't force you. I'm good for it anytime, so if you want to, just say the word… But hey, how embarrassing is 'Beautiful Princess' as a nickname? She can't possibly live up to it, right?"

"Apparently, Nabe is quite beautiful. At least, according to what I heard"—Climb sensed Evileye's gaze for just a moment and understood right afterward that she had indeed glanced his way—"she's as beautiful as the Golden Princess."

Gagaran turned mischievous eyes on Climb. Anticipating what she was going to say, Climb made the first move. "Appearances are a matter of personal taste, and for me, there's no one more beautiful than Princess Renner."

"I *see*." The tone was distinctly disappointed.

"Hmm. We've been chitchatting too much. Sorry to make you go along with this nonsense. We'll follow Lakyus's orders and begin preparations now."

Gagaran and Evileye stood up. Climb followed their lead.

"Sorry, Climb! There's a lot of things I'd like to *do* with you, but it seems we don't have time for that anymore."

"Please do not worry about it, Gagaran. And Lady Evileye, thank you for the informative discussion."

Gagaran looked at Climb and gave a tired laugh. "Well, that's fine. Okay. So you're probably going back now, right? Take care of our leader. Counting on you, virgin! …Oh, and make sure you equip your items. That sword on your hip isn't your usual weapon, right?"

"No, this is a backup."

"You never know what will happen. Whatever you do with your armor, you should always carry your sword! That's the proper attitude for an adventurer, especially as a warrior. And do you have the items I gave you?"

"The bells? Yes, I have those right here." He patted a pochette on his belt.

"Okay, good. Remember this: All we warriors can do is swing our weapons, but sometimes that's not enough. What fills in that gap for us is magic items. Acquire lots of them, and don't let them go. And make sure you always have at least three healing potions. That's saved me before."

He had three potions but was currently carrying only two. Climb indicated his acknowledgment.

"You're surprisingly caring..."

"Don't make fun of me, Evileye... Sorry to have held you up. What I mean to say is, don't slack on preparation and precaution."

"Understood." Climb bowed deeply to Gagaran.

3

3 *Late Fire Moon* (September) 6:00 AM

There were nine men and women seated at the round table.

Despite the fact that the chiefs from all eight divisions of the Eight Fingers had gathered, they hardly spared a glance for one another. Instead, they examined the papers in their hands or exchanged words with their subordinates behind them.

The atmosphere made it seem like eight completely separate groups were holding a meeting. It wasn't quite a powder keg situation, but everyone was obviously cautious, as though they were surrounded by threats. Still, this was the natural state of affairs for them. Although they shared loosely symbiotic relationships within the same organization, they often fought over conflicting interests, and true cooperation rarely materialized.

For instance, the drug-dealing division oversaw every aspect of their business, from production to distribution. They would never work with the smuggling division in the drug trade. Even if the divisions were never openly hostile, it was utterly ordinary for them to obstruct and frustrate one another behind the scenes.

Detrimental behavior like that was the result of once separate underworld syndicates coming together.

These people weren't on good terms with one another, but they participated in the regularly held Eight Fingers division chief meeting in the capital for a good reason. Those not in attendance were often purged on suspicion of potential treachery. That made it so even those who rarely visited the capital came all the way over for the meeting.

Even those who normally stayed holed up in safe places came, in a sense, out in public. It was no wonder many feared assassination and brought along escorts—a pair of elites, the maximum number of attendants allowed from each division.

Only one came alone…

"Okay, everyone's assembled. Let the regular meeting begin." At the sound of a voice, chairs creaked as people settled in.

The speaker was the man who would run the meeting, the leader of the Eight Fingers. His age appeared to be around fifty, and he wore a water god sigil. With his gentle face, he didn't seem at all like the type to be deeply involved in the criminal sphere.

"We have a number of issues, but the first we need to deal with is—Hilma."

"Aye." The one who answered was a pearly-white woman. Her skin was so pale she seemed ill, and she was dressed completely in white. A snake tattoo climbed to her shoulder from her hand, which held a pipe emitting noxious purple smoke. Her lipstick was the same shade of purple as her eye shadow. Clad but lightly, her figure exuded the decadence of a high-class prostitute. She yawned conspicuously. "Could we have done this any earlier?"

"…We're discussing the raids on your narcotics cultivation facilities."

"Yeah, someone attacked some villages with production equipment. It cost a fortune. It may result in reduced supply for distribution."

"Do you have any information about the raiders?"

"Nope. They did a perfect job of it…although that's why I have an idea who it might have been."

"Which color?"

Everyone there knew exactly what he meant.

"I don't know! We just found out about it. How could I figure that out so fast?"

"I see. Well, everyone, that's the situation. If you have any information, raise your hand."

There was no response. They either had no information or they did and didn't want to share it.

"Then next—"

"—Hey!" There came a low sound, a tremendously powerful man's voice.

All eyes gathered on him. It was a bald man whose face was half-obscured behind a beast tattoo. Everything about him was big. The bulges of his muscular physique were clearly visible even through his clothes. The cold gleam in his eyes gave off the impression of a warrior.

Every other chief had brought escorts, but there was no one behind this man. Of course there wasn't. What good was it to bring someone along who wouldn't be any help?

He glared at Hilma, chief of the drug-dealing division. No, he probably didn't mean to glare at her, but it was hard to see a look from his razor-thin eyes as anything else.

The escorts behind the woman caught their breath for just a moment— a natural response because they understood the gap between their abilities and his.

That man was a monster capable of massacring everyone in the room.

"Why not hire us? Your small fries don't have what it takes to guard the facilities, right?"

Zero was in charge of the security division, which provided everything from doormen to armed escorts for nobles. He was even more famous for having the highest combat ability in all the Eight Fingers. But his proposal—

"No need."

—was flatly rejected.

"We don't need you. And we can't have outsiders knowing where our critical bases are."

That was the end of that. Zero's eyes closed, as if he'd lost interest. It was like he'd turned into a rock.

"In that case, I'll take you up on the offer." The one who had spoken was a slender man. His lithe build was the exact opposite of Zero's. "Zero, I'd like to hire a man."

"What, Coccodor? Can you pay?"

If Hilma's drug dealing was fairly lucrative, Coccodor's slave trafficking was on the decline. Since the Golden Princess had made slavery illegal, he'd had to shelter his business further underground.

"I'm good for it, Zero. And I'd like one of the best of the best, preferably Six Arms–class."

"Ohh?" Zero seemed interested for the first time in the meeting, and his eyes opened back up.

He wasn't the only one who was surprised. Almost everyone there felt the same.

The Six Arms was a collective term for the six members of the security division with the highest combat ability; it came from the fact that the god of theft's sibling had six arms.

Of course, at the top was Zero, but the other five were no less powerful. There was one said to be able to cut space, another who manipulated illusions, and even one who was an immensely powerful undead—an elder lich.

If Gazef Stronoff and adamantite-rank adventurers were the strongest of those in the light of day, the Six Arms were the strongest of the underworld. Employing one of them meant only one thing.

"You're in that much trouble? Okay, then. Take heart. My man will guarantee the safety of your assets."

"So sorry to trouble you. An issue came up with a woman we were planning to dispose of. It might be going overboard to enlist so much power, but if our shop gets taken out, I'll have problems. So yeah, I'll consult you later about the contract and fee."

"That's fine."

"Is immediately after the meeting all right with you? There's something I'd like you to do right away."

"Got it. I brought a man with me, so I can lend him to you."

"…Okay, I'm moving us onto the next topic. Is there anyone here who knows the new adamantite adventurer Dark Momon? Has anyone invited him to join us?"

Intermission

Cha-ling, cha-ling came the sound of precious metals clinking together.

Upon confirming there was nothing left inside the leather pouch he'd upended, Ainz lined up the gleaming coins on his desk.

He made stacks of ten each, gold ones and silver, and counted them.

After tallying the mountain over several times, he picked up the bag and peered inside again.

There's really nothing in here. After confirming it, he flung the bag away and held his head in his hands.

"There's not enough... I don't have anywhere near enough money..."

The human face he'd created using an illusion warped darkly. Of course, the pile of coins before him was a fortune, a sum an ordinary person from this world wouldn't be able to earn even over dozens of years. But as the ruler of the Great Tomb of Nazarick, as well as the only one earning foreign currency, he felt extremely uneasy about the amount.

Since Ainz's emotions were forcibly calmed if they fluctuated beyond a certain range, his shocked mind would be immediately stabilized if he were in the extremely bad situation of having, say, a single silver coin. When he had some gold coins, however, that didn't happen due to the slight reassurance in a corner of his mind, so he experienced a steady irritation.

Ainz shook his head and began allotting the coins in front of him to different uses. "First, these are additional funds for Sebas."

He removed a huge chunk from the mountain, and his face twitched.

"Then this is the money Cocytus requested to support the restoration of the lizardman village and cover equipment costs."

The mountain moved again, and all that was left were a few gold coins.

"...The stuff we'll be sending to the lizardman village are necessities, so if I buy at the Adventurers Guild, I can use my adamantite connections. I should be able to get everything a little cheaper...for maybe this much?"

A few coins returned from Cocytus's funds.

Ainz counted the remaining money and muttered, "...Getting some merchant to sponsor me would be the ideal...to earn some kind of regular income besides adventuring."

Including Ainz's, there were only three adamantite-rank parties in the kingdom. Because of that, merchants occasionally requested him by name. In general, the kind of work they wanted was simple compared to how much he got paid, and he wanted to take those jobs by all means, but he had been hesitant up until now.

He wanted to avoid giving the impression that the adventurer he was playing, Momon, was greedy for cash or would take on any job as long as he was paid.

His plan was to make Momon into the kind of adventurer everyone would praise and then transfer all that glory to Ainz Ooal Gown when the time came. For that reason, he had to pay attention to his reputation.

"But I have no moneyyy. I really don't need a room like this."

Ainz scanned his splendid surroundings.

He was renting the nicest room in the best hotel in E-Rantel, so the cost was nothing to sneeze at. Ainz didn't even need to sleep, so there was no point in his taking a room this splendid. He would have wanted to use this money for other things.

That went for food as well. Even if he was offered luxurious meals, Ainz couldn't eat, so they were meaningless. It would have been smarter to refuse and save the money.

But Ainz knew full well he couldn't do that.

Ainz—no, Momon—was the sole adamantite adventurer in this city. There was no way someone like that could stay in a flophouse.

Food, clothing, and shelter were points of easy comparison. An adamantite adventurer had to maintain the lifestyle of an adamantite adventurer.

It was all about looks and honor.

That's why Ainz couldn't downgrade his inn, even though he knew it was a waste of money not to.

"If I'm worth anything to them, I could probably get the guild to arrange lodgings for me... Ahh, if I just asked them, I bet they would..." But he didn't want to owe anyone. Up until now, he'd done things like taking on last-minute requests in order to incur debt. Once he'd saved up enough favors, he intended to collect on them, even if it took a near threat. If he asked a favor for such a mundane thing as this, his plan would get messed up.

"Agh, I don't have any money. What should I do? I guess I have to take a job... But it doesn't seem like there are any high-paying requests lately. And taking on too many is asking for ill will from the other adventurers."

If he was going to make Ainz Ooal Gown into an enduring legend, he wanted it to be in a good way, not a bad way. Ainz gave an imitation sigh and counted up the rest of the gold coins to burn into his mind how much spending money he had.

"Speaking of money, what should I do about the guardians' salary?" Ainz hmmed as he leaned back in his chair and lifted his gaze to the ceiling.

The guardians all insisted that they didn't need a salary, that there was nothing that made them happier than serving a Supreme Being, and that receiving some kind of consideration for it would be absurd.

But Ainz wondered if it was really all right to take advantage of them like that. *There should be a fair price for their work.*

When the guardians declared that being able to devote themselves completely to the Supreme Beings was consideration enough, Ainz had a hard time accepting it.

Maybe it was just him, who used to be a human working as a company employee for pay, but he couldn't simply discard the idea that work deserved compensation.

He was worried about throwing these children who knew nothing of salaries into it, but he still felt a system was worth adopting as an experiment.

"The problem is what to pay them with." His eyes moved from the ceiling to the small amount of gold coins on the table.

"If I gave some of the guardians the going rate for managers, it'd be fifteen million yen... Shalltear, Cocytus, Aura, Mare, Demiurge, and then Albedo should be even higher? In other words, times six. Yeah, there's no way. I can't make that much."

Ainz held his head in his hands, but suddenly his eyes popped open.

"Oh! I can just substitute something else! I can make a currency that can only be used inside Nazarick—like toy money—and say that one is worth a hundred thousand or something!"

After he'd finished shouting, Ainz frowned again.

How will I have them use the money?

Everything inside the Great Tomb of Nazarick was free, so even if he created a currency, there was nothing for them to spend it on.

"Maybe they could buy items from this world with it?" Ainz compared the items of this world with those of Nazarick and wondered if anyone would even want them. "But making free facilities suddenly cost money would be totally backward... What should I do?"

After thinking for a little while, he had a brilliant idea.

"That's it! All I have to do is make the guardians think about it. I just have to ask them what they want badly enough that they would pay for it!" Delighted, he murmured, "Genius, it's a genius idea," until his expression suddenly soured. "Man..."

I really talk to myself a lot these days, thought Ainz.

He'd been aware of his growing tendency to talk to himself back in the game when no one was coming around anymore, but he wondered why it hadn't gone away now that the NPCs all moved according to their own wills.

Was it already a habit? Or...?

"Maybe it's because I'm still alone..." He smiled a desolate smile.

It probably wasn't fair to the NPCs, who had minds now, to say he was alone, but that was how he felt—perhaps because he was killing Satoru Suzuki in order to play the leader of the Supreme Beings, Ainz Ooal Gown.

As he sighed and focused once more on the array of coins on the desk, there came a knock at the door.

After a moment, the door opened. When he saw his guest was who he thought it was, Narberal Gamma, Ainz made a certain face.

The expression was snobbish with one side of his lips curled up.

Because the low-level illusion forming Ainz's face expressed his emotions honestly, there was a chance it could display something unbecoming of the ruler of Nazarick. For that reason, in order to create the picture of a dignified ruler in front of others, especially Narberal, he took great pains to stick to this single expression, which he had practiced in front of a mirror.

"What's the matter, Nabe?" He used his normal Ainz voice.

"Ma— Sir Momon."

"...Ah, you still call me master sometimes, huh? I guess we just have to admit it's a habit of yours. But when I point it out, you stop for a while, so I guess that's where we stand. Ahh, you don't have to bow your head. I'm not mad, and as for the extra respect, well, it's fine. The heads of the guilds seem to be laboring under some misunderstanding, too. Anyhow, what's wrong?"

"The iron ore you ordered the merchant to collect is ready."

I didn't order him! It was a normal business transaction! Ainz thought, but the dignified expression he'd put on earlier remained firmly in place.

"I see. And where is this iron ore from? From all eight spots?"

"My apologies, but I didn't ask."

"...Fine. I have plenty of gold. Even if we don't know where it's coming from, I have enough gold to buy it all."

Ainz confidently packed all the coins on the desk into the bag, tossed it at her feet, and watched her respectfully pick it up.

"Understood. But may I ask you something?"

"The reason I'm buying iron from all different locations?"

Narberal nodded, and Ainz explained. "It's to throw it in the exchange box. Basically, I want to find out if there is a difference in price depending on where it's collected."

The exchange box didn't take shape into account. For example, an elaborate stone carving dropped into the box would get the same assessed value as a rock of the same weight with no craftsmanship involved. So what about composition—difference in quality? That was why he was collecting iron from various locations.

"As you know, we assessed some wheat recently." *It took so much to get just one gold coin,* Ainz grumbled in his head.

That meant they could make money if they produced a lot of it, so he'd come up with a plan to create wheat fields outside Nazarick. He figured if they used undead and golems, they should be able to create vast fields.

Granted, there was a pile of problems that needed to be tackled before they could get there.

"I understand. Then I will go and make the purchase right away."

"Okay. But do be careful. We can't say for sure that we're not being targeted. In that case…you know what to do, right?"

"I'll take a shadow demon to guard me, prioritize safety over intelligence gathering, and if the situation takes a turn for the worse, retreat at full speed. In that event, I will teleport to the fake

Nazarick Aura has been building and let the enemy collect false information."

"Good. Focus on safety. Don't take an unpopulated route where it would be easy to attack you. And even if people try to pick a fight or call out to you, don't injure them too badly. That time a guy came crying to me for help, saying all he did was hit on you was, frankly, shocking. You can't be whipping out your intent to kill like that. Smashing the hand of a pickpocket might not be so bad, but don't do it too often. And definitely do not call humans worms or other names. Basically, have some restraint when it comes to hurting or killing humans. We're Momon and Nabe, lauded as 'Raven Black,' adventurers of the highest rank."

Narberal expressed her understanding, and Ainz nodded, thinking that was about all he had for warnings.

"Yeah, that's it. Okay, then. Go, Nabe."

With the leather pouch in hand, Narberal bowed once and left the room. Watching her go, Ainz sighed deeply despite his lack of lungs.

"…Expenses always go up right when you have no money. Honestly, this sucks."

Chapter 3 The Finders and the Found

Chapter 3 | The Finders and the Found

1

26 *Mid-Fire Moon* (August) 3:27 PM

After taking the old woman to her house, Sebas proceeded toward his original destination.

He arrived at a place with a long wall.

Beyond the wall were three five-story towers. With no buildings higher than that nearby, they seemed especially tall.

Those towers were surrounded by several long, thin two-story buildings.

This was the headquarters of the kingdom's wizards' guild. They needed spacious grounds because they were developing new spells and training arcane casters. The reason they had so much land despite receiving barely any support from the government was probably because they were the sole producers of magical items.

Eventually the sturdy-looking gate came into view. The latticed door was open wide, and multiple armed guards occupied the two-story towers on either side.

The guards didn't stop him—just glanced at him—and Sebas went through the gate. Beyond, there was a broad, gently sloping staircase and a door leading to an impressive, old white-walled building. Of course, the door was open to welcome visitors.

Inside was a small entrance hall and then a lobby. From the double-height ceiling hung several chandeliers burning with magic light.

On the right was the lobby lounge, which had several sofas and a few casters engaged in conversation. On the left side was the board. Figures clad in robes appropriate for arcane casters and other people who seemed like adventurers were studiously observing the pieces of parchment posted there.

In the back, a few young men and women were seated behind a counter. They each wore a robe with the emblem displayed at the building entrance embroidered on their chests.

To either side of the counter stood what resembled life-size mannequins, slender figures with no eyes or noses—wood golems. Apparently, they were guards. The lack of human guards, except for the ones outside, was likely a display of the wizards' guild confidence.

Sebas's measured footfalls clicked across the floor as he approached the counter.

A young man at the counter noticed him and communicated a modest salutation with his eyes. Sebas gave a slight bow in return. He visited often, so they knew each other.

The young man smiled in a barely perceptible way when Sebas arrived in front of him, and he greeted him as always. "Welcome to the wizards' guild, Sir Sebas. What can I do for you?"

"I would like to buy a magic scroll. May I see the usual list?"

"Yes, sir."

The young man quickly put a rather large book on the counter. He'd probably secretly gotten it ready the moment he caught sight of Sebas.

The book was a splendid item with high-quality thin white paper inside and a leather cover. Considering the letters of the title were sewn in with gold thread, this item itself had to be worth quite a bit.

Sebas pulled the book nearer and opened it.

Unfortunately, the writing was not in letters he could read. Or rather, no one from *Yggdrasil* would be able to read them. Even if they could understand spoken language through some strange law of this universe, writing was different.

But Sebas had received an item from his master to resolve just such a problem.

Sebas reached into his pocket, took out a case, and opened it. Inside was a pair of eyeglasses. The slim frames were made of a metal similar to silver. Upon closer inspection, one could make out tiny characters, like crests, etched into them. The lenses were blue frost crystal, cut and polished thin.

When he put on the glasses, he was magically able to read the letters.

While carefully yet quickly turning the pages, Sebas's hand suddenly stopped. He looked up from the book and addressed the woman sitting next to the young man behind the counter. "Did you need something?"

"Oh no…" The woman blushed and lowered her eyes. "I was just thinking…you have nice posture."

"Thank you." He smiled faintly, and the woman's face turned even redder.

Sebas was a white-haired gentleman people fell for just from looking at him. Not only did his attractive features draw attention, but his air of elegance did as well. When he walked down the street, nine out of ten women, regardless of age, turned to watch him. If the woman at reception lost herself staring at him, there was nothing to be done, and it happened often enough, anyway.

Now that he understood the situation, Sebas turned back to the book. He stopped again on a specific page and asked the young man, "Could you give me a detailed description of what this spell, Floating Board, does?"

"Yes, sir." He began the explanation without missing a beat. "Floating Board is a tier-one spell that creates a translucent hovering board. The size of the board and maximum weight limit depend on the caster's magical energy, but when it's cast with a scroll, the board is about three feet squared and the weight limit is one hundred and ten pounds. The board can go up to five yards away from the caster, and the caster can have it follow them. It only follows, however; it's not possible to push it forward, and if the caster should turn around, it will slowly circle around to remain at the rear. It's a spell that is generally used for carrying things, often seen on public works construction sites."

"I see." Sebas nodded. "Then I would like to buy one of these."

"Yes, sir."

The young man showed no surprise at Sebas buying a spell that was not terribly popular—the reason being that Sebas almost always bought unpopular spells. The guild was grateful for it, since it helped get rid of their excess inventory.

"Will that be one scroll, sir?"

"Yes, please."

The young man nodded slightly at the man sitting next to him.

The man, who had been listening to the conversation, stood immediately, opened a door in the rear wall that led to the back, and went in. Scrolls were very expensive. It wouldn't do to just have big stacks of them there at the counter, even if the place was guarded.

About five minutes later, the man returned. In his hand was one rolled-up piece of parchment.

"Here you are, sir."

Sebas examined the scroll on the counter. The rolled-up parchment seemed very sturdy and looked different from run-of-the-mill writing material. The spell's name was written on it in black ink, and Sebas made sure it matched the spell he had requested. Then he finally took off the glasses.

"Yes, that's the one. I'll take this, please."

"Thank you." The young man politely bowed his head. "This scroll is a tier-one spell, so that will be one gold and ten silvers."

A potion of the same level made only with magic cost two gold, so the scroll was relatively cheap. That stemmed from the fact that a person usually couldn't activate scrolls unless they could already use the same family of spells. It made perfect sense that potions, which anyone could use, would be more expensive.

Of course, even if the spell was cheap, it was still quite a sum for an ordinary person—it was a month and a half's salary. But for Sebas—no, for the master Sebas served—it was not so much.

Sebas took a leather pouch from his breast pocket. He loosened the opening, removed eleven coins, and gave them to the young man.

"With exact change." The young man didn't do anything like checking to make sure the coins were proper currency in front of Sebas. He was a frequent enough customer to have built that kind of trust.

•

"That old man is so cool!"

"Totally!"

As Sebas left the wizards' guild, the receptionists, especially the women, chatted together excitedly.

They acted more like girls who had met the prince they pined for rather than women of poise and intelligence. One of the men behind the counter had a slightly jealous frown on his face, but he didn't say anything because he himself could see how elegant Sebas was.

"He must have experience serving a pretty important noble. I wouldn't be surprised if he was the third son of a noble himself!"

Nobles who didn't inherit their houses often became butlers or maids, and the higher a noble's rank, the more likely they were to specifically hire this type of person. Sebas's bearing was so impeccable, it made sense to think he must have been of noble blood.

"He carries himself so beautifully."

Everyone seated behind the counter nodded.

"If he invited me to tea, I'd definitely go!"

"Yeah, me too! Definitely!"

The girls squealed.

The men talked among themselves with sidelong glances at the girls, who were still going on about how he probably knew tremendously sophisticated places and how he would do absolutely everything an escort should do.

"He seems to be incredibly knowledgeable. Do you think he's a caster?"

"I wonder. Maybe."

All the spells he chose had been developed only recently. From that, they could infer that he had some degree of magical knowledge. If he were coming to buy something on orders from a superior, he shouldn't have needed to look at the book; he could have just asked for the scroll by name.

The fact that he didn't do so—but consulted the reference himself—meant that Sebas was the one choosing what to buy.

It was only natural to think that he was no mere old man but had to be someone with specialized magic education—a caster.

"And those glasses… They looked really expensive."

"I wonder if they're magic."

"Nah, they just seem like high-quality glasses—made by dwarves or something."

"Yeah, it's amazing he has such fancy glasses."

"I wanna meet that pretty lady he brought with him that one time again," one man murmured, but he was met with disagreement.

"Really? She seemed kinda all appearances and nothing else, you know?"

"Yeah, I felt bad for Sebas. Seems like she really works him hard."

"She was pretty, but her personality is definitely awful. Even the way she looked at us was the worst. I really pity him having to serve someone like that."

The men fell silent as the women began criticizing the lady. Sebas's master was a peerless beauty, the type who could steal hearts in the blink of an eye. The women there were each beautiful enough to be chosen to represent the wizards' guild, but the difference between them and her was night and day. The guys wanted to tell them, *Don't be jealous*, but it was obvious what would happen if they did that.

None of them was that stupid, so…

"Okay, that's enough chatter." The young man spotted an adventurer walking toward the counter, and the group immediately changed their focus and expressions.

•

26 Mid-Fire Moon (August) 4:06 PM

Exiting the wizards' guild, Sebas casually checked the sky.

Things had taken longer than planned because he'd escorted that old woman home, and the blue was gradually turning a deep red.

When he took his watch out of his breast pocket, it was already the time he'd planned to be home, but he still hadn't finished his errand. *It's fine if I leave it for tomorrow, so should I put it off? Or should I get home later than planned but finish everything today?*

He hesitated only a moment.

The incident with the old woman had been his own doing, so he needed to fulfill his duties.

"Shadow demon…"

A presence squirmed in Sebas's shadow.

"Please tell Solution I'll be back late. That is all."

There was no answer, but the presence stirred and then receded, moving from shadow to shadow.

"Now, then," murmured Sebas as he set off walking.

He didn't have any particular destination; he was attempting to get a complete picture of the capital's geography. He hadn't been specifically ordered to do so, but he'd decided to voluntarily as part of his intelligence gathering.

"Okay, I guess today I'll go that way," he murmured, stroked his beard, and twirled the scroll he carried in one hand. He was acting like a kid in a good mood.

He walked farther and farther away from the safe area at the center of the capital.

After he turned and continued down several roads, the alleys started getting a bit dirty and sending a faint but unpleasant smell. It was the stench of raw garbage and filth. It seemed like it would permeate clothing, but Sebas strode silently on.

He stopped abruptly and looked around. Perhaps because he was on a total backstreet, the alley was so narrow there was only enough room for two people to pass by each other.

Since the sun was low behind the tall, deserted buildings on either side of the small alley, no light came in, and it would have been difficult for a human to walk there. But Sebas didn't have any problem. He walked with noiseless steps, melting into the darkness.

He had turned several corners and proceeded to even more deserted areas, when suddenly his unhesitating steps stopped.

He'd arrived here by walking aimlessly as his whims dictated, but he'd ventured quite a ways from the house that was his base. He had a general instinctive sense of where he was, and he drew a line from there to his base in his mind.

With Sebas's physical strength, it wasn't such a long distance, but that was if he walked in a straight line. If he followed the streets, it would take quite a while. Considering night was falling, it was probably a good idea to head back.

He wasn't worried about Solution, who was living with him.

Even if an incredibly powerful enemy appeared, there was a monster in her shadow, just as there was one in Sebas's. It could definitely buy her enough time to run away. Still…

"Guess I'll go home."

It was true that he wanted to stroll a bit more, but he doubted it was very good to allot too much time to something that was practically a hobby. But even if he was going to withdraw, he wanted to at least see what was up ahead, so he continued down the small alley.

As Sebas proceeded silently through the darkness, a heavy-looking iron door about fifteen yards ahead of him began slowly opening with a grating sound, without warning, and light spilled from inside. Sebas stopped and watched in silence to see what would happen.

Once the door was all the way open, a person's face poked out. The backlighting allowed Sebas to see only the silhouette, but it appeared to be a man's. He scanned the road but apparently didn't discover Sebas because he returned inside without incident.

The man tossed a rather large cloth bag outside with a *thud*. Sebas could see its soft contents bend and change shape by the light escaping through the door.

Although the door was still open, the man who had thrown the bag like it was trash seemed to have gone back inside for the moment and didn't do anything else.

Sebas furrowed his brow for a moment and wondered whether he should stay his course or proceed in a different direction. This seemed like a bad situation.

After some brief indecision, he decided to continue down the narrow alley now that it was quiet again.

"…Unf!"

The opening of the big bag ripped.

Sebas's steps echoed along the alley, finally closing the distance between him and the bag.

As he was about to pass it, he stopped.

He felt a faint sensation as if his slacks had caught on something. He looked down and saw what he expected—a bony hand reaching out to grab the cuff of his pants. And the half-naked woman coming out of the bag.

The mouth of the sack was wide open now, and the woman's upper body was free.

Her blue eyes had lost their spark and gone dull. Her disheveled shoulder-length hair was coarse due to malnutrition. Her face had been beaten until it swelled up like a ball. Her skin, dry as a dead tree, was covered with countless pink spots the size of fingernails.

There was not so much as a thimbleful of life left in her emaciated body.

She was already a corpse. No, she wasn't dead, of course. The fact that she'd snatched Sebas's cuff spoke volumes to that. But can an organism that is only capable of breathing be said to be alive?

"…Could you let go, please?"

There was no response to Sebas's request. It was clear at a glance that she wasn't ignoring him. Her eyes reflected nothing, cast into space through the barely open slits below her swollen eyelids.

If Sebas moved his leg, he could easily shake off those fingers weaker than dead branches. But instead, he asked, "…Are you in trouble? If so—"

"Hey, old man, where'd you come from?" a threatening voice interrupted.

The man had reappeared in the doorway. He had a big chest and thick arms, and hostility clearly showed on his scarred face as he turned his penetrating gaze on Sebas. In his hand, he held a lantern—it glowed red.

"Hey, hey, hey, old man. Whaddaya lookin' at?" The man loudly clicked his tongue and gestured with his chin. "Get lost. If you leave now, you can get home safe."

When he saw Sebas wasn't moving, he took a step forward. Behind him, the door closed heavily. As a threat, the man placed the lantern near his feet with exaggerated purpose. "Hey, old man! You goin' deaf? Can't you hear me?" He rotated his shoulders and stretched his neck. He slowly brought his right hand up and curled it into a fist. It was clear he wasn't the type who hesitated to use violence.

"Hmm..." Sebas smiled. He could be described as an elderly gentleman with a profound smile that put people at ease and made them feel cared for. So why did the man back up a step as if a predatory beast had suddenly arrived?

"Ahh, hey, hey, wh—" Under the crushing pressure of Sebas's smile, words that weren't words trickled from the man's mouth. Without even realizing that his breath had grown ragged, he backed up farther.

Sebas tucked the scroll in his hand, with the wizards' guild seal on it, into his belt. Then he took one measured step toward the man to close the distance between them and reached out. The man couldn't even react. With a sound that was barely a sound, the hand clutching Sebas's slacks fell onto the street.

With that as the signal, Sebas grabbed the man's collar with his outstretched arm and lifted him up with no trouble.

Had there been any witnesses to this scene, they would have thought it was a joke.

Judging the two on appearances alone, Sebas would have had no chance against this man. Youthfulness, breadth of chest, girth of arms, height, weight, and aura of violence—he was beat in any category.

But the elderly gentleman was lifting up this robust, heavyweight-class guy with one hand.

—No, perhaps someone witnessing this scene would have keenly felt the gap between these two men. It's said that the intuitions of humans—their animal instincts—are dull, but they still probably would have been able to detect this unmistakable gap.

*   *   *

The difference between Sebas and this man was the difference between…

…absolute strength and absolute weakness.

The man, who had been lifted completely off the ground, kicked both legs and squirmed. Then he tried to take hold of Sebas's arms, and the fear born of sudden realization shone in his eyes.

It had finally dawned on him—that the old man before him was something completely different from what he appeared, that any futile struggling would only further anger the monster.

"This woman, what is she?" The quiet voice sounded in the petrified man's ears.

The voice flowed with the quiet of a clear stream. It was terrifying precisely because it clashed with the context, how he was effortlessly holding a man aloft with one hand.

"A-an employee of ours," the frantic man replied in a voice cracking with fear.

"I asked you 'what' she is. Your answer is 'an employee'?"

The man wondered if he had said something wrong. But in this situation, that answer should have been the most accurate. The man's bulging eyes flitted around like he was a petrified little animal.

"No, I have friends who treat humans as things. I thought perhaps you might treat them that way as well. In that case, you wouldn't be doing anything wrong. But you told me she's an employee. That means you're taking these actions despite recognizing her as a person. Then allow me to ask another question. What will happen to her now?"

The man thought for a moment. But—

There came a noise like a creak.

Sebas's grip strengthened, and the man suddenly found it more difficult to breathe.

"Gugh!" He let out a strange scream.

Sebas's meaning was clear: *I'm not giving you any time to think—just talk.*

"Sh-she's sick so we're taking her to the shrine."

"I'm not very fond of lies."

"Kgh-eegh!" The man let out another bizarre shriek, his face reddening with every increasing application of force from Sebas's hand.

Even if Sebas made the massive concession of assuming this person had put the woman in the bag to transport her, the fact that she'd been tossed into the road gave no indication of the care of one taking her to a shrine for treatment. It had been more akin to throwing out the trash.

"Sto— Gah!" Now struggling to breathe, the pinned man began fearing for his life and flailed about wildly without thinking.

Sebas intercepted the fists coming at his face without trouble. The man's kicks connected with his body and dirtied his clothes, but the older man didn't budge.

Of course he didn't.

Something so insignificant as a human's feet wouldn't affect a giant lump of steel. Sebas continued speaking, unfazed as if the kicks from the thick legs didn't cause him any pain.

"I recommend telling the truth."

"Gagh…"

Sebas squinted up at the man whose face had gone crimson from lack of air. Aiming for the moment right before the man passed out, he let go.

The man crashed down on the road with a loud *thud.*

"Gehgyaaagh!" The man expelled the last remnants of air in his lungs as a scream.

Sebas stared down at him as he gasped for oxygen and then reached his hand toward his neck again.

"Whoa, w-wait a minute!" Enduring the pain and thoroughly impressed with fear, the man rolled away from Sebas's outstretched hand.

"I— Yes, I was going to take her to the shrine!"

That's a lie, isn't it? You're tougher than you look.

Sebas had thought the man would break immediately under the terror of suffering and death, but although he was scared, he didn't seem ready to talk so easily. That meant the danger he would face after leaking information was equal to the threat Sebas posed.

Sebas considered changing his vector of attack. This was, in a way, enemy territory. The fact that the man wasn't requesting backup from inside meant that he didn't expect anyone would come quickly. Still, if Sebas stayed here too long, it would surely make things more complicated.

His master hadn't ordered him to cause trouble. The order he'd received was to blend in and quietly gather intelligence.

"If you were going to take her to the shrine, then I don't suppose there is any issue if I bring her there myself? I will take custody of her now."

The man's shocked eyes darted around. Then he desperately strung some words together. "…There's no proof you'll actually do it."

"Then why don't we go together?"

"I have an errand to run now, so I can't. That's why I'm taking her later." Sensing something from Sebas's expression, he quickly continued. "She's legally ours. If you lay a hand on her, you'll be violating this country's laws! Just try and take her—that's abduction!"

Sebas froze and furrowed his brow for the first time.

This argument had struck a critical location.

His master had said that attracting attention to some degree was unavoidable, but that was necessary while playing the butler of a rich man's daughter.

If he broke the law, the authorities would be involved, and there was a chance someone would see through his disguise. In other words, it could directly cause a huge fuss—and he would attract the kind of notice his master didn't desire.

Sebas had a hard time believing this coarse man was educated, but his words overflowed with confidence. Someone must have put these ideas about laws into his head. If that was true, there was a good chance this defense would hold.

Now, with no witnesses present, it was a simple matter. He could physically force his captive to talk. He could leave a corpse here by simply snapping the man's neck.

But that was his last resort, to be used only in the event that this situation threatened to affect his master's plans. He couldn't do that for this woman he didn't even know.

So does that mean the correct thing to do would be to abandon her?

The man's vulgar laugh irritated Sebas as he vacillated.

"Should such a splendid butler take on a big problem like this and keep it a secret from his maaaster?"

Sebas frowned openly at the grinning man for the first time.

The man must have gleaned a hint of weakness from his reaction. "I dunno what noble you serve, but…if this blows up, won't it cause trouble for him? Huh? And what if he has a good relationship with us? He'll get pissed, won't he?"

"You think my master can't handle a little thing like this? Rules exist to be broken by the powerful, you know."

The man flinched a bit as if he had an idea how that worked, but he regained his confidence a moment later. "…So you wanna try it, then? Huh?"

"Hmm…" It didn't seem Sebas's bluff was going to make the man stand down. *Does he truly have such a powerful backer?* Sebas judged this line of attack to be ineffective and switched angles. "…I see. Yes, this does seem like it could be troublesome, legally speaking. But there is also a provision in the law that allows forcible rescue when someone calls for aid. I'm simply helping her in line with this clause. To begin with, she's unconscious, so she needs to visit the shrine for treatment, yes?"

"Mn…bu…that's…" The man mumbled, at a loss.

His ignorance was exposed.

Sebas was relieved at the man's inability to act and slow-working brain. He'd told a huge lie, something that sounded plausible, since his opponent had brought up legalities.

If the man were to counter with another argument, even a lie, Sebas didn't have enough knowledge of the laws of this country to fight back. In the end, he had only a smattering of legal knowledge, and not studying it more thoroughly was what had landed him in this situation.

On the other hand, someone with only a fragmentary understanding of the law would hesitate when it was brandished in a fight. Plus, this man had to be an underling. He probably didn't have the authority to make any decisions on his own.

Sebas turned away from the man and held up the woman's head. "Do you want me to help you?" he asked. Then he brought his ear to the woman's dry, chapped lips.

What he heard was faint breathing, respiration that could be mistaken for the last gasp of a deflating balloon.

There was no reply. Sebas shook his head slightly and asked again, "Do you want me to help you?"

Helping her was completely different from helping the old lady. He wanted to assist others whenever he could, but if he got involved with this woman, there was a good chance it would lead to a fair amount of trouble. And when he considered whether the Supreme One would forgive him or whether this went against his will, a cold wind blew through his heart.

Still no reply.

The man quietly laughed that vulgar laugh again.

As someone who understood what hell she had been in, he knew there would be no reply. If she had been able to speak freely, they probably wouldn't have tried disposing of her like this.

True luck would not occur twice in a row—because things that happened so frequently couldn't be called luck.

No, if grabbing Sebas's slacks had been that woman's luck, she wasn't going to receive a windfall again.

Her fortune had been the fact that Sebas happened to come down this alley at the right moment. Everything that occurred after, she achieved with her will to live.

It was **definitely** not luck.

A slight movement...

Yes, her lips made a truly feeble movement. It was not an automatic one, like for breathing. It clearly contained her intent.

"—"

Upon hearing what she said, Sebas nodded emphatically. "…I'm not interested in saving every single person who asks me for help like a plant expecting to bathe in the rain from the heavens. However, when someone is struggling to survive…" Sebas's hand moved to cover the woman's eyes. "Let go of your fear and rest. You are under my protection now."

Clinging to his warm, kind touch, she closed her vacant eyes.

The man couldn't believe it, so naturally, he tried to say what was on his mind. "It's a li—" *You didn't hear her voice*, he was about to snap but froze.

"A lie, you say?" At some point, Sebas had stood up, and now the gleam in his eyes pierced the man.

Those brutal eyes.

The man's breath caught—it felt like his heart would be crushed under such a gaze, one that seemed to weigh on him with physical pressure.

"Are you saying that I lied the way you did?"

"Ah, nn, uh…" The man gulped loudly, swallowing the spit that had pooled in his mouth. His eyes moved to Sebas's arms and stuck there like glue. Perhaps after getting ahead of himself, he remembered his fear.

"Well, I'm going to take her and go now."

"W-wait—I mean, please wait!" The man raised his voice and Sebas glanced at him.

"You still have something to say? Are you trying to buy time?"

"N-no. If you take her away, there's going to be trouble. For you and for your master! You've heard of the Eight Fingers, I'm sure!"

Sebas remembered hearing the name during his intelligence gathering. It was a criminal organization that dominated the kingdom's underground world.

"So I'm tellin' ya, just pretend you didn't see anything. If you take her away, I'll have failed at my job, and they'll punish me!"

Realizing he couldn't win with strength, the man tried for pity, but Sebas turned a chilly gaze on him and answered in an icier voice. "I'm taking her and going."

"Give me a break! They're gonna kill me!"

Should I kill him now? Sebas thought. The man's moaning continued as he calculated out the pros and cons.

It was possible the man was buying time because he was waiting for help, but Sebas judged from his attitude that that wasn't the case. But he couldn't figure out why.

"Why haven't you called for assistance?"

Stunned, the man rapidly explained.

Essentially, if Sebas were to escape while he was calling for help, it would be as good as reporting to his compatriots that he'd made a critical error. And he didn't think he'd be able to win by force even if he called them. That was why he was trying to persuade Sebas to change his mind.

He was so pathetic that Sebas suddenly felt the strength drain out of him, and his urge to kill went away. Still, it didn't mean he was going to hand over the woman. So...

"...Why don't you run away?"

"That's not an option. I don't have that kind of money."

"I doubt it costs as much as your life itself, but...anyhow, I'll pay for it."

At those words, the man's face brightened.

Sebas knew it was safer to kill him, but if he could get him to make a desperate escape, it would buy time. Then he had to heal the woman and take her someplace safe.

Besides, if Sebas killed him here, there was a good chance they'd launch a search for the missing woman. Since it was unclear how she'd gotten in this situation, it wasn't possible to conclude that his actions wouldn't endanger people who knew her.

Mulling it over, Sebas wondered why he was doing something so risky.

He truly couldn't fathom where the ripple in his heart that caused him to try to save her had come from. Anyone else from Nazarick would have ignored her to avoid trouble. They would have stayed hands-off and kept walking.

When someone's in trouble, it's only natural to help them.

*   *   *

Sebas put aside the workings of his heart even he could not explain, since he didn't need to be thinking about them right now, and answered the man. "Take this, hire an adventurer or something, and run with all your might." He took out a leather pouch.

The man's eyes were doubtful. Perhaps he didn't feel the amount in the small bag would be enough.

The next moment, his eyes were riveted on the coins falling onto the street. They sparkled like bright silver—platinum trade currency. Ten coins worth ten gold pieces each lay on the ground.

"Run as fast as you can. You understand, right? And I have a few questions. Do you have time to answer?"

"Yeah, it's fine. I came out to dispose—er, to take that woman to the shrine, so they'll assume I'm a little late coming back."

"Understood. Then let's go." With that, he jerked his chin to say *follow me*, picked up the woman, and set off walking.

2

26 Mid-Fire Moon (August) 6:58 PM

Sebas's lodgings were in one of the royal capital's better neighborhoods, a house in what could be called a luxury residential district.

It was cozy compared to the mansions lining the streets nearby, but it had probably been built with the assumption that two servant families would also live there. It was way too big for only Sebas and Solution.

Naturally, there was a reason they rented such a mansion. As long as they were disguised as a great merchant family hailing from faraway lands, they couldn't very well live in a shabby residence. To do it, though, with no connections or reputation at the construction guild, they'd had to pay an absurd sum up front, many times the going market rate.

When they arrived and went through the door, there was someone to meet them. It was a combat maid in a white dress, Solution Epsilon, who worked directly under Sebas. The other residents included shadow demons and gargoyles, but since they were there as guards, they didn't come to the door.

"Welcome ba—" Solution lost her words and froze mid-bow. She directed a frostier gaze than normal at the woman Sebas held against his chest.

"...Master Sebas, what in the world is that?"

"I found her."

For a moment, Solution gave no response to that short answer, but the air grew heavy. "...I see. It doesn't look like a souvenir for me, so what are you planning on doing with it?"

"Hmm. Well, for starters, could you heal her wounds for me?"

"Wounds?" Solution took a look at the woman, shook her head once she understood, and then fixed her eyes on Sebas. "Couldn't you have left her at a shrine?"

"...Yes. I probably should have thought of that..." Unshaken, Sebas regarded Solution with cold eyes, and for a brief moment, their gazes met. Solution was the first to look away.

"Shall I dispose of her?"

"No, I've brought her this far. We should think of a good use for her."

"...Understood."

Solution didn't have a very rich range of expression to begin with, but her face was blank and even Sebas couldn't comprehend the spark of emotion in her eyes. Still, it was very clear that she was not welcome to this idea.

"First, could you please assess her physical health?"

"Understood. Then allow me—"

"Wait..." Perhaps to Solution, the woman didn't warrant any more care than the absolute minimum, but Sebas didn't think she needed to be examined in the entryway. "We have an open room, so could I ask you to do it there?"

Solution bowed her head silently.

They didn't speak to each other while they carried the woman from the entryway to the guest room. Neither Solution nor Sebas was the type to make idle chatter, but there was another reason—something was off.

Solution opened the guest room door for Sebas, since his hands were full. The room was dark because its heavy curtains were drawn, but it wasn't stuffy at all. It had been opened several times, so the air was fresh, and it was cleaned regularly.

In the room illuminated by only a sliver of moonlight through the gap in the curtains, Sebas gently laid the woman down on top of the bed's clean sheets.

He had performed minimal first aid by pouring chi into her, but given the way she didn't move a muscle, the woman made him think of a corpse.

"Okay, then."

Solution carelessly ripped off the cloth wrapped around the woman and revealed her battered body. It was a pitiful, awful sight, but Solution's unchanging expression was bland and uninterested.

"…Solution, I'll let you take it from here." With that, Sebas left the room.

Solution, who had begun palpating the woman, didn't attempt to stop him.

Once he was in the hallway, he whispered in a voice that wouldn't reach Solution: "This is foolish." The words immediately vanished into the hallway, and naturally, there was no one to respond.

Sebas fingered his beard unconsciously. *Why did I save that woman?* He couldn't hit upon a precise reason. *"The lion spares the suppliant," I guess?*

No, that wasn't it. *Why did I save her?*

Sebas was the butler who performed steward duties at the Great Tomb of Nazarick and had completely devoted himself to the Forty-One Supreme Beings. He should have been serving and surrendering everything to the one who had taken on the name Ainz Ooal Gown, the guild master.

There was nothing fraudulent about his loyalty, and as an utterly faithful servant, he wouldn't hesitate to throw away his life for his master.

Still, if he had to choose only one Supreme Being to swear his allegiance, he knew who he would attend—Touch Me.

Touch Me was the strongest member of Ainz Ooal Gown and Sebas's creator. Second to none, he'd attained the class of world champion.

Their guild grew stronger by killing players, among other things. Who would believe that the original purpose of the group he first formed—the guild's predecessor, the First Nine—was to aid the weak? But it was true.

He'd saved Momon when he was getting PK'd constantly and was about to quit the game out of frustration. Next, he reached out to BubblingTeapot, who couldn't find anyone to quest with due to her unfortunate appearance.

Touch Me's lingering intentions wound around Sebas like an invisible chain.

"I guess this is a curse..." That language was probably blasphemous. If any of the other inhabitants of the Great Tomb of Nazarick—those created by the Forty-One Supreme Beings—heard him, it was possible they would attack him for his disrespect.

"It isn't right to pity those who do not belong to Ainz Ooal Gown," he whispered gravely.

That was completely natural.

Everyone believed that disregarding outsiders was correct, excepting certain members of Nazarick who had been designed by their creators to be different, such as the head maid, Pestonia S. Puppydog.

For example, he'd received a report from Solution that Lupusregina, one of the Pleiades, was getting along well with a girl in Carne, but Sebas knew that if the situation demanded it, she would cut that girl down with zero hesitation.

It wasn't because she was cold-blooded.

If a Supreme One ordered them to die, they had to die, and if they were ordered to kill someone, even a friend, they had to kill them immediately. That was true loyalty. Conversely, anyone who couldn't understand that received pity from their fellows.

Making judgments based on foolish emotions was wrong.

So what about me? Is the action I took correct? Sebas was chewing his lip over his worries when Solution came out of the room. Her face was expressionless as usual.

"How did it go?"

"...She has syphilis and two other STDs. Multiple fractured ribs and fingers. Severed tendons in the right arm and left leg. Both top and bottom front teeth are missing. Her organs don't seem to be functioning very well. She also has an anal fissure. She may be addicted to some kind of drug. Since she has innumerable bruises and lacerations, I'll take the liberty of omitting the details, but...is there any other explanation you require?"

"No, that's fine. There's only one important thing: Will she get better?"

"Easily."

Sebas had expected this immediate response.

Using healing abilities, even someone with their limbs cut off could recover, so if Sebas used his chi kung, he could completely heal her physical damage. Actually, if all of Nazarick weren't in a state of emergency and he hadn't been worried about intelligence leaks, he could have healed that old woman's twisted ankle earlier on the road.

Despite the ability to restore strength, chi kung couldn't properly dispel poison or cure diseases. Sebas hadn't acquired those skills. That was why he needed Solution's help for this.

"Okay, please heal her."

"If you want someone who can use healing magic, it might be better to summon Mistress Pestonia."

"That won't be necessary. Solution, you have the appropriate magic scrolls, don't you?" After she nodded, he continued, "Then please use those."

"…Master Sebas. These scrolls were given to us by the Supreme Beings. I hardly think they should be used on the likes of humans."

She was right. He probably needed to devise a different solution. First, they would heal her wounds to prevent her from dying and fix her poisoned and diseased status at some later point. The question was whether they had that much time. If she was nearing death due to her overall condition instead of merely her wounds, it would be pointless to restore her strength unless he did it permanently.

Sebas hesitated and then, in a steely voice that masked his inner feelings, told her, "Do it."

He thought he saw something reddish black flicker in the back of Solution's narrowing eyes, but the change was hidden as she bowed her head.

"…Understood. I should restore her body back to its uninjured state? Back to before any of those things were done to her?" When Sebas nodded, she bowed politely. "I'll do it right away."

"Then when you're done treating her, can I have you heat up some water and bathe her? I'm going to go buy some food."

There was no one else in the mansion who could make or required meals. If they didn't have a spare magic item that would render eating unnecessary, they would have to arrange food for the woman.

"…Master Sebas. It's a simple matter to treat her body…but I can't treat her mental distress." Pausing there, she looked straight at him. "To care for her mental needs, I think summoning Lord Ainz would be best. Shall I call him?"

"…This isn't important enough to have Lord Ainz come personally. We can leave her mind as is."

Solution made a deep bow, silently opened the door, and went inside. Watching her go, Sebas slowly leaned back against the wall.

What should I do about her?

The best would probably be to help the woman recover to some extent and then, while the ruffian was still on the run and leading his friends on a chase, release her in a location of her choosing. Somewhere away from the royal capital, at least, would be best. Throwing her out into the city would be dangerous and cruel. That wouldn't be aiding her at all.

But is that really the right thing to do as the butler of the Great Tomb of Nazarick, Sebas Tian?

He exhaled deeply. How much easier would everything be if he could expel the other things built up inside him like that? But nothing changed. His thoughts were in turmoil, a white noise invading his consciousness.

"This is foolishness. Why would I...for a human...?"

He quit seeking an answer that wouldn't come and decided to start with something easy. It was only to buy time, but it was the best plan he could come up with for now.

•

Solution lengthened her slender digits into tubelike shapes a fraction of an inch wide. By nature, Solution was an amorphous slime, so she could alter her appearance quite radically. Changing the contour of her fingertips was a piece of cake.

With a glance at the door, she keenly observed the lack of Sebas's presence outside and quietly approached the woman lying on the bed.

"I have permission from Master Sebas, so I'll promptly solve all this trouble. I'm sure you're fine with that as well. You probably don't even know what's going on."

Solution took the hand she hadn't transformed and reached inside her body to take out the scrolls she'd been keeping there.

These scrolls weren't the only things she was secretly carrying. She contained not only consumable magic items but also, of course, weapons and armor. She had enough room to swallow up several humans, so there was nothing surprising about that.

Solution gazed at the unconscious woman.

She wasn't the least bit interested in the woman's features. Solution had a single thought: *She doesn't look very tasty.* That was all.

With this husk of a body, the woman probably wouldn't even struggle if she was melting in Solution's acid. Where was the fun in that?

"If I could have her as a toy after I finished healing her, I would understand Master Sebas's behavior, but…"

She knew her boss's personality. He would never approve of that. Unless they were attacked on the road or something similar, he would never allow her to prey on humans.

"If he's acting on the Supreme One's instructions and was ordered to save her, I suppose I have to accept it, but…is she really worth expending the Supreme One's precious assets? This human?" Solution shook her head to clear her mind. "…Should I just eat her before Master Sebas returns?"

Solution broke a seal and unrolled a scroll. The magic it contained was Heal, an elite tier-six recovery spell that restored a great deal of vitality and cured almost all negative status effects, including sickness.

Usually only those with the class that would allow them to cast the spell normally could use the corresponding scrolls. So to use faith caster spell scrolls, one would need to attain a priest-type class. More specifically, the spell had to be on the list of available spells that the class could learn. However, some thief-type classes provided the ability to sidestep this requirement and "trick" scrolls.

As an assassin, Solution had a number of thief-type classes that allowed her to use the Heal scroll.

"First, I'll make sure she's comatose. Then…" Solution prepared a compound combining a strong sleep-inducing anesthetic with a muscle relaxant and moved over to where the woman lay.

•

26 Mid-Fire Moon (August) 7:37 PM

Sebas came home with food at almost the exact moment Solution exited the room. Solution held a steaming bucket in each hand, both containing towels. The hot water had turned black, and the towels were dirty, showing what an unkempt state the woman had been in.

"Thank you, Solution. It looks like the treatment…went all right?"

"Yes. We finished with no problems. She didn't seem to have any other clothes, so I dressed her in something that was lying around. I hope that's all right with you?"

"Of course. That's fine."

"Very well... The anesthesia should have already worn off... If there's nothing else you need me to do, I shall retire."

"Good work."

Solution bowed and walked past Sebas.

After watching her go, Sebas knocked on the door.

There was no answer, but he could sense someone moving around inside and quietly pushed open the door.

Sitting up on the bed was a girl who looked extremely dazed, perhaps because she had recently woken up.

He practically mistook her for someone else.

Her dirty, disheveled blond hair was now clean and glossy. Her hollow cheeks had filled out with unbelievable speed in such a short time. Her dry, chapped lips now also glowed a healthy pink.

To appraise her overall looks, the word *charming* fit her better than *beautiful*.

It was possible to get some idea of her age. She was probably in her late teens, but her hellish life weighed heavier than her years on her face.

Solution had dressed her in a white negligee, but it was a plain one with as little of the usual frills and lace as possible.

"I think you're fully healed, but how do you feel?"

There was no answer. Her vacant eyes didn't contain the will to look up at Sebas. But he continued speaking without worrying about that. No, he hadn't been expecting much at first. He knew her empty expression indicated she wasn't mentally present.

"Are you hungry? I brought you some food."

He'd bought an entire meal from a restaurant, including the dishes.

The porridge in the bowl had been made with a light-colored broth. The sesame oil added for flavor gave it an appetizing scent.

Reacting to the smell, the girl's face twitched slightly.

"Then here you go."

So she's not completely locked away in her own world, thought Sebas as he held the bowl with a wooden spoon in it out to her.

The woman didn't move, but Sebas didn't press her, either.

After long enough to annoy any third party present, she slowly moved her arm. She was frightened of pain, so it was a stiff motion. Although her physical wounds had been completely healed, vivid memories of suffering still remained.

She grasped the wooden spoon and scooped shallowly into the porridge. Then she brought it to her mouth and put it in.

The porridge, made with ten parts water, was runny to the point where it wasn't even necessary to chew. Sebas had requested that the fourteen ingredients be cut up extremely small.

Her throat rose and fell, and the porridge traveled to her stomach.

Her eyes shifted a bit. It was a truly slight movement, but it was the change from an elaborate doll to a human. Her other hand, shaking, took the bowl from Sebas.

Sebas kept his hands against hers and moved the bowl to where he thought she wanted to put it.

She plunged the wooden spoon into the bowl and wolfed down the porridge without stopping.

Her eating was incredibly rushed. If the food hadn't been cooled to an appropriate temperature, she would have certainly passed out from the burns. She paid no attention to the liquid dribbling out of her mouth onto the front of her negligee. "Drinking" was the best description for how she attacked her meal.

After finishing at a speed incomparable with her previous movements, she sighed, still holding the bowl.

Now that she had become a person, her eyelids grew heavy and began to close.

The effects of her full stomach, fresh and comfortable clothing, and her own clean body combined to relax her mind, and a wave of sleepiness overcame her.

But the moment her eyelids lowered into straight lines, they popped back open and she cringed in fear.

Was she scared to close her eyes? Or fearful her current situation was an illusion that would disappear? Or was there some other reason? Watching from beside her, Sebas didn't know.

It was possible she didn't know herself.

So Sebas spoke to her gently to calm her down. "Your body must want rest. It would probably be good for you to take it easy and get some sleep. You're not in danger here—I guarantee it. When you open your eyes, you'll still be in this bed."

For the first time, her eyes moved to Sebas's face.

Her blue eyes didn't contain much light or energy; however, they were no longer those of a corpse but of a living thing.

She opened her mouth slightly—and closed it. Then she opened it again—and closed it once more. She repeated this several times. Sebas kindly watched. He certainly didn't hurry her up. He just gazed at her silently.

"Th…" Eventually her lips parted and a tiny voice squeaked out. The next words came bit by bit. "Th…than…k…you…"

The first words out of her mouth were not to confirm her situation but to express her gratitude. Feeling like he had grasped a hint of her personality, Sebas did not wear his usual fake smile but a genuine one.

"Don't worry about it. Since I found you, I'll do everything in my power to guarantee your safety."

The girl's eyes widened just a bit. Then her mouth trembled.

Her blue eyes became wet and then overflowed with tears. She opened her mouth wide and started genuinely sobbing.

Soon the curses began to mix in with the weeping.

She cursed her fate, detested the ones who had served her that fate, and resented the fact that help hadn't come sooner. The latter of these was also aimed at Sebas. *If only you had saved me sooner*—that type of blame.

Upon receiving Sebas's kindness—at being treated like a person—whatever was inside her enduring everything for all this time had broken. Or perhaps it's more correct to say that because she regained a human heart, she could no longer bear the memories of all the things she'd been through.

She clawed at her head, audibly ripping out her hair. Countless golden threads curled around her slender fingers. The porridge bowl and the spoon fell onto the bed.

Sebas watched her fit in silence.

Her bitter comments at Sebas were inaccurate and nothing more than spreading blame. Some people might have taken this badly and gotten angry, but Sebas's visage bore no trace of ire, and his lined face was, on the contrary, compassionate.

Sebas leaned over and held her.

It was a hug like that of a father for his daughter, with no ulterior motives, containing nothing but love.

For a moment she stiffened, but sensing the way he held her was different from the men who had devoured her up until now, her frozen body relaxed slightly.

"You're okay now." Chanting those words over and over like a spell, he gently patted her back. It was like he was comforting a crying child.

She sobbed for a moment—then, as if Sebas's words had sunk in, she buried her face in his chest and cried some more. But these tears were a little different from before.

•

Time passed, and when Sebas's chest was completely soaked, the young woman finally stopped crying. She slowly moved away from him and lowered her head to hide her red face.

"Ah…s…rry."

"Please don't worry about it. It's an honor for a man to lend his chest to a woman."

Sebas took a fresh, clean handkerchief out of his breast pocket and offered it to her. "Please use this."

"Bu…t…I can't…some…thing this…beautiful…"

Sebas placed a hand on the timidly hesitating girl's chin and brought her face up. While she was still frozen, wondering what had happened, he gently wiped her eyes and brushed the tear streaks from her cheeks.

Oh yeah, Solution was saying she recently had a long Message conversation with Shalltear… Apparently, she was bragging she had her tears wiped…? Under what circumstances did our master attend to her crying? Puzzled as he was, since he couldn't even imagine Shalltear weeping, his hands didn't stop. Before long, he had finished wiping the young woman's face.

"Ah…"

"Okay, here you go." He pressed the slightly damp handkerchief into her hand. "An unused handkerchief is a pitiful thing, especially one that never gets a chance to brush away tears." He smiled at her and moved away. "Now then, have a good rest. We'll talk about what happens next when you wake up."

Magic was a versatile thing. Solution's treatment had helped the woman's body make a full recovery, and her mental exhaustion was also completely gone. She would probably even be able to function normally right away. But mere hours earlier, she had been in hell. He feared a lengthy discussion would cause her mental wounds to reopen.

Actually, she was not yet psychologically stable. Her earlier outburst was evidence enough. Magic could soothe a mind for a limited time, but it couldn't treat the root issues. It might have been able to heal her physical injuries, but it couldn't heal her gaping invisible wounds.

As far as Sebas knew, the only ones who could fully heal her mental wounds were his master and—maybe—Pestonia.

Sebas tried to get her to rest, but she spoke, bewildered. "Wh…next?"

He wasn't sure if it would be okay to continue the conversation, but she seemed to be in a talking mood, so he went on with a close eye to her condition.

"You probably don't feel safe staying in the royal capital. Is there anyone you can rely on?"

She looked down.

"I see…" Of course, he swallowed the comment *So there isn't anyone…*

Okay, that's a problem, thought Sebas. But surely there was no need for them to take immediate action. It was nothing more than a hopeful observation, but he wanted to believe they didn't need to rush, at least until she regained her strength.

"Okay, then. May I have your name?"

"Oh…I'm…Tsu…Tsuare."

"Tsuare? Oh, that's right, I haven't told you my name yet, either. My name is Sebas Tian. Please call me Sebas. I am the owner of this mansion, and I serve Lady Solution."

That was the story.

Solution was constantly wearing not her maid uniform but a white dress, in case a sudden visitor should call. But while Tsuare was around, Sebas would have to advise Solution to act more like the mistress of the house to keep up appearances.

"La…Solu…tion."

"Yes, Lady Solution Epsilon. Although I don't think you'll see her very often."

"…?"

"She's rather ill-tempered." Sebas closed his mouth as if he'd said all there was to say about her. Then after a short silence, he spoke again. "Okay, please rest well for today. We'll discuss your future tomorrow."

"O…kay."

After making sure she had lain down, Sebas retrieved the empty porridge bowl and exited the room.

As expected, right when he opened the door, Solution was standing there. She had probably been eavesdropping, but he didn't reprove her. Solution showed no sign of expecting a scolding, either—hence her standing there in plain sight with no attempt to conceal her presence. With her assassin classes, if she had wanted to hide, she should have been able to do so more skillfully.

"What is it?"

"…Master Sebas. What have you decided to do with her?"

Sebas was conscious of the door behind him. It was a sturdy barrier, but it wasn't completely soundproof. If they talked here, she would be able to partially hear them.

Sebas set off walking, and Solution silently followed him.

They stopped when he felt sure the sound wouldn't reach Tsuare's ears.

"You mean Tsuare, right…? I'm thinking we'll decide what to do tomorrow."

"You know her name…?" She made no further comment on the subject but, pulling herself together, said, "I apologize for being presumptuous, but I believe there is a good chance that human will be a hindrance. We should dispose of her as soon as possible."

What does she mean by "dispose"?

Hearing her brutal choice of words, Sebas couldn't help but suppose that this was the most correct way for those who belong to Nazarick to think about those outsiders. The way Sebas treated Tsuare was truly unusual.

"You're right. We need to immediately deal with anything that prevents us from following Lord Ainz's orders."

Solution looked mildly puzzled. Her expression said, *If you understand that, why are you…?*

"She might be of use to us. I picked her up, so I shouldn't discard her so easily, but try to think of a way to use her to our advantage."

"…Master Sebas. I don't know where or for what purpose you picked her up, but those types of injuries indicate a certain kind of environment. The people who did those things to her probably won't be pleased she's alive."

"That's no problem."

"…You mean you already disposed of them?"

"No. But if a problem does arise, I'll deal with it in one way or another. So I'd like you to just keep an eye on her. Okay, Solution?"

"…Understood."

Solution swallowed the slight irritation welling up in her as she watched Sebas leave.

Even if she was extremely dissatisfied by his answers, he was her direct superior, so she couldn't say anything. And if no issues came up, giving her tacit approval was probably fine.

Still…

"Using Nazarick's assets on the likes of humans is…"

The riches of Nazarick all belonged to Ainz Ooal Gown and the other Supreme Beings. Would they be forgiven for using them without permission?

No matter how much she mulled it over, she couldn't reach a satisfactory answer.

•

3 *Late Fire Moon* (September) 9:48 AM

Sebas opened the door to the house. Today he'd gone again to the Adventurers Guild first thing in the morning and recorded notes on the postings before the adventurers started taking the jobs.

He wrote down and sent to Nazarick all the information he gathered in the capital, even tidbits no bigger than local rumors. Analyzing the data was extremely difficult so he left that up to the clever ones at the Tomb.

He went through the door and entered the building. A few days ago, Solution would have met him there. But—

"Wel…come…ba…ck."

—now that role belonged to the quietly mumbling woman dressed in a maid uniform with a floor-length skirt.

The day after he'd found Tsuare, they'd discussed things and decided she would work inside the mansion.

He would have been fine letting her stay as a guest, but Tsuare wouldn't accept that.

She didn't want to be treated like a guest on top of having been saved. She didn't imagine it would be a proper thank-you, but she at least wanted to do some work.

Sebas figured that anxiety probably lay behind that desire.

In other words, aware of her unstable position as a seed of trouble for this household, she decided to make what efforts she could to keep from being abandoned.

Of course, Sebas had been telling her he wouldn't forsake her. If he was going to toss out a person with absolutely no place to go, he wouldn't have bothered picking her up in the first place. But it was true that his powers of persuasion weren't enough to soothe the wounds in her mind.

"I'm home, Tsuare. Is your work proceeding smoothly?"

She bobbed her head. Unlike when he'd met her, her hair was now tidily trimmed, and a white headpiece placed on top dipped with the movement.

"There…no problems."

"No? That's good."

Her mood was decidedly dark, and her expression almost never changed, but by living a human life, it seemed like her voice had gotten louder—perhaps because the things tormenting her had lessened a little.

Her remaining uneasiness is because of… Sebas started walking, and Tsuare accompanied him at his side.

Usually, for a maid, walking alongside the butler—her superior—would be improper. But Tsuare had never trained as a maid, so she didn't know the etiquette, and Sebas had no mind to drum the rules into her head.

"What's for dinner today?"

"Stew…wi…pota…oes."

"I see. That's something to look forward to; your cooking is delicious."

Receiving a smile along with the compliment, Tsuare blushed, and she looked down and squeezed her maid's apron with both hands.

"Th-that's no…true."

"No, no, it is. I can't cook at all, so it really helps me out. Do you have all the ingredients you need? If you're running low on anything or there's anything you want me to go buy, please tell me."

"Okay. I…check…later…ask…ou."

Inside the mansion and in front of Sebas, Tsuare could function normally, but she still rejected the outside world. Since they couldn't have her do anything outside, procuring ingredients was Sebas's job.

Tsuare's culinary creations were nothing extravagant. They were humble home cooking.

Because of that, none of the ingredients were expensive, and Sebas could find everything she needed at the market. By familiarizing himself with various foods at the market, Sebas was able to gather information about this world's diet, so he considered it killing two birds with one stone.

Suddenly he had an idea.

"…Shall we go shopping together later?"

A shocked expression appeared on Tsuare's face. Frightened, she shook her head, instantly paled, and broke out in a nervous sweat.

"No, th…you."

Sebas didn't let his thoughts show. *So she still can't…*

Since she had started working, she'd never made an attempt to do anything that involved leaving the house.

She could keep her fear under control because she saw this building's walls as absolute protection. In other words, she could function because she'd drawn a line between the outside world—the world that hurt her—and this dissimilar place.

But she would never be able to go outside like that. And Sebas couldn't shelter her forever.

Given her mental state, Sebas knew that it would be cruel to order her out after only a few days. It would be safer to take some time and acclimate her slowly, but that was assuming they had time.

Sebas had no intention of settling down or spending the rest of his life here. He was just a foreigner who had snuck in on an intelligence-gathering mission. If the order to pull out came from his master…

To prepare for that time, he felt he should give her as many opportunities as possible. Sebas stopped walking and faced Tsuare head-on. Blushing, she looked down, but he took her cheeks between his hands and brought her head up.

"Tsuare, I understand your fear. But please trust me. I'll protect you. I'll thwart whatever danger approaches and keep you perfectly safe."

"…"

"Tsuare. Try to take this step. If you're scared, you can close your eyes."

"…"

He squeezed her hand as she hesitated. Then he said something he felt was unfair. "You don't believe me, Tsuare?"

A veil of silence fell over the hallway, and time passed slowly. With slightly damp eyes, Tsuare parted her lips, to which the color had returned. Her pearly front teeth peeked out.

"N...o fair...Mas...Sebas. If...say that...then I can't...not..."

"Don't worry. I may not look it, but I'm strong enough... Hmm, yes. There are only forty-one people stronger than me... Well, perhaps a few more."

"Is...that...a lot?" Tsuare smiled, figuring that he'd said such a random number as a joke to put her at ease.

Sebas simply smiled and didn't offer any response.

He set off walking again. He knew Tsuare, next to him, was glancing at his profile now and then, but he didn't say anything.

He knew that she had some complicated feelings for him that were not quite a faint crush. He supposed that was something like a conditioned response after being rescued from hell, a dependency on a reliable figure.

Also, Sebas was old, so it was even possible that she was confounding familial affection for the love between a man and a woman.

Even if she really was in love with him, Sebas had no intention of returning her feelings. Not when he was hiding so much and their positions were so imbalanced.

"Okay, I have a few things to talk to the young lady about, and then I'll come and fetch you."

"Lady...Solut...ion?" Her face grew a little dark.

Sebas knew why, but he didn't say anything.

Solution had never interacted with Tsuare, and when they did happen to meet, she would just cast a glance at her and withdraw without a word. That level of disregard would make anyone uneasy, and given Tsuare's position, she must have been quite frightened.

"It's all right. She's like that with everybody. She's not singling you out... Between you and me, she has a pretty difficult personality..." His joking tone and smile lightened Tsuare's mood a little. "Whenever she sees a cute girl, she sulks."

"Bu...I'm...not... She's...so..." Flustered, she waved off his compliment.

Tsuare certainly had a nice face, but she couldn't compete with Solution. Still, beauty was always at least somewhat in the eye of the beholder.

"I prefer you to Solution."

"Wh… How?"

He watched her, his heart warm, as she blushed and looked down, but then furrowed his brow at a sudden change in her expression.

"But…I'm…dirty…"

Her face darkened dramatically, and Sebas sighed in his mind. Then he spoke, facing straight ahead. "Jewels are like that. Clean ones with no scratches are worth more and called beautiful."

Hearing that, Tsuare's face grew even gloomier.

"But humans aren't jewels."

He sensed her head raise suddenly.

"You said you're dirty, but what makes humans clean? For jewels, there are standards of appraisal. But what are the standards to decide a human's purity or beauty? The average? The ordinary? Then does that mean the opinions of the nonconforming minority don't matter?" Sebas took a breath and continued. "Just like aesthetics vary from person to person, if we say human beauty lies beyond appearance, then I believe it resides not in someone's past but within them. It's not as if I know your entire history, but judging from what I've seen of you these past few days together, you're not the least bit dirty in my opinion."

Sebas closed his mouth, and suddenly the only sound in the world was their footsteps echoing in the hall. Then Tsuare spoke, as if she'd made up her mind.

"If you…think…so…then…hold m—"

Sebas embraced her before she could finish. "You're clean and beautiful," he said tenderly, and she didn't make a sound as the tears spilled from her eyes. He patted her back a few times to soothe her and then slowly withdrew his hands.

"Tsuare, I'm sorry, but the young lady is calling."

"I—I understand…"

Sebas parted with Tsuare, who curtsied a bit sadly with red eyes, and knocked on the door. He didn't hear an answer but opened it. As he slowly closed it, he smiled back at her as she watched him intently.

Partly because they were renting the house, but there was barely any furniture despite the many rooms. In this room, however, there was enough furniture not to embarrass them if a guest visited. But the more one examined them, the easier it was to tell that none of the pieces had a history. The room was a facade.

"I've returned, Lady Solution."

"...Thank you, Sebas."

The fake lady of the house, Solution, retaining her bored expression, was seated on a sofa in the middle of the room. In truth, the expression was just an act. Since Tsuare, an outsider, was in the building, she was wearing the foolish-looking mask of a conceited rich girl.

Solution's eyes moved away from Sebas to the door. "...She's gone now."

"It appears so."

They observed each other's expressions, and Solution spoke first.

"When are you throwing her out?"

In response to the question she asked every time they met, Sebas gave his usual answer. "When the time comes."

Normally the conversation would end there. Solution would heave a conspicuous sigh, and it would be over. But today she didn't seem to want to end it there. "...May I ask that you clarify when this 'time' is that you're planning for? There's no guarantee that sheltering that human won't make trouble for us. Doesn't that count as going against Lord Ainz's will?"

"There aren't any problems right now. I don't believe fearing and panicking over the type of problems a mere human could cause is a reaction befitting a servant of Lord Ainz."

Silence fell between them and Sebas exhaled lightly.

This is extremely awkward.

There was no emotion in Solution's expression, but he could tell she was irritated with him. This mansion was their temporary base, but Solution thought of it as a branch of the Great Tomb of Nazarick, and the fact that they had a human there without their lord's consent was intolerable to her.

She hadn't harmed Tsuare yet because Sebas was firmly restraining her, but eventually he wouldn't be able to hold her back.

I don't have much time. Sebas felt it keenly.

"…Master Sebas, if she interferes with Lord Ainz's orders—"

"—I'll dispose of her," Sebas declared, not letting her say any more.

Solution said nothing, gazed at Sebas with unreadable emotions, and bowed her head. "Then I have nothing else to say. Master Sebas, please don't forget what you have just told me."

"I certainly won't, Solution."

"Still…" The intense emotion in her whispered voice was powerful enough to stop Sebas in his tracks. "…Still, Master Sebas, don't you think we should report to Lord Ainz? About Tsuare?"

Sebas was silent for several seconds and then responded. "It shouldn't be a problem. I would feel bad taking up his time to discuss a human."

"…I'm fairly certain you're contacting Entoma via Message at a scheduled time every day. Couldn't you report it then in just a few words? …Are you hiding it on purpose?"

"No, of course not. I would never do something like—"

"Then…you're not acting out of self-interest, right?"

A nervous thrill ran through the atmosphere.

Sebas sensed Solution bracing herself slightly and realized how dangerous his position was.

Everyone in Nazarick was required to devote themselves entirely to Ainz Ooal Gown, to the Supreme Beings. From the guardians on down, it was probably safe to say everyone thought that way. Even the assistant butler constantly scheming to take over the Great Tomb of Nazarick, Éclair, had loyalty and respect for the Forty-One Supreme Beings.

Of course, Sebas also belonged to Nazarick.

Still, he didn't think that was any reason to desert someone in a miserable situation based only on what-ifs. He understood, though, that most members of Nazarick would not share that view.

No, he had thought he understood. Solution's actions a moment ago showed him just how naive his understanding had been.

Solution was serious. She was ready to take on the butler—Sebas, who had some of the highest combat ability of any of the members of Nazarick's administration—depending on his answer. He had no idea she would be willing to go that far to eliminate the problem.

He smiled.

When she saw that, some doubt appeared in her eyes.

"…Of course not. I have no self-interest in not reporting to Ainz."

"Then could you tell me why you're keeping her?"

"I have a very high opinion of her cooking skills."

"C…cooking?" It was like a question mark had appeared over her head.

"Yes. And don't you imagine people might think we're strange, living in this huge mansion, just the two of us?"

"…Maybe."

Solution could sincerely agree there. With such a large house and apparent wealth, the lack of servants would seem strange.

"I think it's only right that we maintain a minimum number of people. Wouldn't it be trouble if someone should visit and we couldn't serve even a single dish?"

"…So you're using the human as part of our disguise?"

"That's right."

"But is that one really so useful…?"

"Tsuare feels indebted to me, so even if she senses something is off, she wouldn't say anything to an outsider. Am I wrong?"

Solution thought for a little while and then said, "No, that makes sense."

"So that's why. We shouldn't need Lord Ainz's permission for something related to our disguise. On the contrary, I think he'd get angry and tell us to think for ourselves," Sebas explained to the silent Solution. "Are you convinced?"

"…Yes."

"Then for now, let's leave it at—" He cut off abruptly at the sound of a hard object colliding with another.

It was very quiet—someone without Sebas's ears probably would have missed it. Someone was undoubtedly causing the arrhythmic noise.

Sebas opened the door and focused his attention down the hallway.

When they realized it was coming from the knocker on the front door, they both froze. No one had knocked on this house's door since they'd arrived in the capital. When they did business, they always went out and never invited anyone to call on them at their residence. It was an extreme measure to not rouse any suspicion for living in such a big house alone.

But today, they had a visitor. That alone was enough to signal trouble.

Sebas left Solution behind, went into the entryway, and lifted the cover of the peephole. Through the hole, he saw a stout man flanked by kingdom soldiers.

The visitor was clean and wore well-tailored clothes with a heavy-looking crest glinting copper on his chest. He had a ruddy, fleshy face with an oily sheen, perhaps due to his diet.

There was also a man who bore a very different appearance.

His skin was so pale it was as if sunlight had never graced it. His sharp gaze combined with his sunken cheeks to suggest a bird of prey—the type that scavenged meat from corpses. His black clothes fit loosely. There was no doubt he was concealing a weapon.

The malice and bloody stench rolling off him triggered Sebas's sixth sense.

It was such a disparate group that he couldn't figure out who they might be or what their purpose was.

"...Who is it?"

"Patrol Chief Staffan Heivish." The fat man in front stated his name in an unexpectedly high-pitched voice.

The patrol chief was an official whose job was to keep the peace in the capital. The position could also be understood as the boss of the patrolling guards, and his work covered a broad span of activities. That was why Sebas wasn't sure why he had come.

Staffan continued, ignoring Sebas. "As you know, we have a law in the kingdom that prohibits slave trafficking... It was Princess Renner who spearheaded the initiative to plan and adopt it. In any case, we caught wind that someone in this mansion might be violating that law, so we're here to ascertain the truth of the matter." Then he asked if they might come inside.

A drop of uncomfortable sweat rolled down Sebas's back, and he hesitated.

He could think of plenty of excuses to refuse, but he worried that turning Staffan away might lead to bigger problems later.

He had no proof Staffan was really an official. He wore the crest of a kingdom official, but that wasn't enough to prove his authenticity. There was a very slight chance—although it'd be a major crime—that it was counterfeit.

Still, what was the issue with letting a few humans into the mansion? If they became violent, Sebas would be able to handle that, no problem. Actually, it would be better for Sebas if the man was faking.

How did Staffan interpret the silence of Sebas's contemplation? He spoke again. "First, I'm sorry to trouble you, but could we meet with the master of the house? Of course, if he's out that can't be helped, but we came to investigate, so we won't be very happy if we go back empty-handed." Staffan's smile contained no trace of apology. Behind it lay a subtle intent to abuse his authority, almost like blackmail.

"Before that, may I ask who the man behind you is?"

"Hmm? His name is Succuronte. He's a representative of the establishment that brought this matter to our attention."

"I'm Succuronte. How do you do?"

Seeing Succuronte's faint smile, Sebas had a hunch he'd been defeated.

The expression was the sneer of a brutal hunter toward his trapped prey. He must have laid all the groundwork before coming here. In that case, there was a good chance Staffan was an actual official. And they'd probably already decided how they would respond if he refused. In that case, maybe it was better to see what they were up to.

"…Understood. I will go inform the lady. Please wait here for a moment."

"Yes, we'll wait, we'll wait."

"But I hope you'll make it quick. We haven't got all day."

Succuronte snorted derisively and Staffan shrugged.

"Understood. Then if you'll excuse me." Sebas closed the peephole cover and turned back to Solution's room. But before that, he would need to tell Tsuare to hide in the back.

Staffan and Succuronte left the soldiers outside the door and entered the room they'd been led to. When they laid eyes on Solution, they were amazed.

They clearly hadn't expected to meet such a beautiful woman. Staffan's expression gradually slackened, and his eyes flitted between her face and her chest. There was something like lust in his eyes as he swallowed a few times. Succuronte's expression, on the other hand, tensed.

Which one should I be wary of? The answer to that question was self-evident. Sebas offered them a seat on the sofa across from Solution.

Solution, Staffan, and Succuronte introduced themselves.

"Now then, what seems to be the trouble?"

Staffan cleared his throat rather deliberately and replied to Solution's question. "We received a report from a certain establishment that someone had abducted one of their employees. We heard that person illegally supplied some money to a different employee of theirs in exchange. Slave trafficking is prohibited by law... That sounds like a violation, don't you think?"

Staffan's excitement gradually grew, and his tone became increasingly firm, but Solution gave a bored reply. "Oh?"

The visiting pair blinked in surprise. Apparently, they didn't think she'd respond with that attitude, since they were threatening her.

"I leave all bothersome things to Sebas. Sebas, take care of it."

"A-are you sure you're all right with that? You might end up a criminal."

"Oh my, how frightening. Then, Sebas, if it seems like I'm going to end up a criminal, please come tell me." She bid them good day and stood up, beaming. No one called after her as she left the room. That moment proved just how powerful a beautiful woman's smile could be.

Perhaps Solution's beauty had shocked the soldiers—a couple of surprised yelps reached their ears before the sound of the closing door.

"Well then, I will listen to what you have to say on behalf of the young lady." Sebas smiled and sat down opposite the two men.

The smile seemed to discourage Staffan. To shore him up, Succuronte spoke. "Hmm, yes, then we'll have you hear us out. As Mr. Heivish said at the door, our…well, yes, an employee of ours has gone missing. And what do you know? After interrogating one of our men, he admitted to taking money and handing her over. I realized this would count as slave trafficking, which is illegal in the kingdom. I didn't want to believe anyone working at my establishment would do such a thing, but I was forced to charge him with the crime."

"As you should. We cannot permit such injustice!" Staffan pounded the table. "Succuronte here came forward with the slave-trafficking accusation regardless of the impact it might have on his establishment's reputation. He's earned the title of a model citizen!" Staffan sprayed a bit of spit as he pontificated, and Succuronte bowed.

"Thank you, Mr. Heivish."

What is this farce? Sebas thought as he got his brain working. He was sure the two before him were in collusion, which meant they had undoubtedly done a good amount of preparation before coming to attack. His defeat seemed imminent. *So how can I get through this with the least harm caused?*

Conversely, what constituted his victory conditions?

For Sebas, Nazarick's butler, it was to resolve the issue without letting the disturbance snowball any further—protecting Tsuare was not included.

But…

"The claims of the man who said he received money could have been perjurious. Where is he now?"

"He's been arrested on suspicion of slave trafficking and locked up. And after listening to what he said and doing a detailed investigation—"

"We found that you, Mr. Sebas, were the one who purchased my employee."

The man had been arrested and probably told them everything there was to tell. And there was a good chance he was coerced to talk in a way that worked to their advantage.

Sebas wasn't sure if he should pretend he didn't know what they were talking about, lie, or give a proper counterargument.

How would it turn out if I said she wasn't here? How would it turn out if I said she died?

He imagined countless plans, but the probability of them being tricked was low, and they didn't seem like they were going to give up so easily. He decided to ask something he needed to know first.

"But how did you conclude it was me? What's the proof?" That was what Sebas didn't understand. As long as he hadn't left at the scene his name or anything that hinted at his identity, there shouldn't have been any proof. So how did they figure out they should come here? Whenever he went out, he'd been on guard for anyone tailing him. He didn't think there was anyone in this city who could follow him without his realizing.

"The scroll."

A light went on in the back of Sebas's mind.

The scroll I bought at the wizards' guild.

Yes, it was different from normal scrolls, more durably made. Anyone familiar with their appearance would know he'd bought it at the guild. The rest was possible to find out with a little legwork. Someone dressed like a butler holding a scroll would stick out even more.

Still, that didn't prove Tsuare was there. He could insist that she was someone else who just happened to resemble her.

But there would be trouble if the mansion was searched. Namely the issue of having only three people, including Tsuare, living in such a large house.

That I'll just have to accept, Sebas resigned himself.

"…I did take the woman away. That is true. But at the time she was very badly wounded, and her life was in danger, so I had no choice."

"So you admit that you used money to gain custody of her?"

"First, I'd like to speak with that man."

"Unfortunately, that won't be possible. We can't have you two coordinating your stories."

"You can—"

—stand there and listen to us talk, Sebas started to say but closed his mouth.

In the end, this was a setup. Even if he could get to the man, the chance he could turn things to his advantage was low. It was a waste of time to pursue that angle.

"…Isn't it unwise, as a country, to permit the type of work that would give her such horrible wounds all over her body in the first—?"

"The work we do is quite strenuous. Injuries are part of the job. Take a mining job for example—accidents happen. It's like that."

"…I don't think they were those sort of injuries, though…"

"Ha-ha-ha. Well, we're in the hospitality business, and there are all sorts of customers. We're careful, but you know how it is. Anyhow, I understand what you've said. Next time we'll—yes, we'll keep a little closer eye on things."

"A little?"

"Well, you know. Otherwise, it'll start to cost us money. Et cetera." In response to Sebas's question, the corners of Succuronte's lips curled upward in a sneer.

Sebas smiled back.

"—Okay, that's enough." Staffan heaved a sigh—the sigh of a human who was dealing with a fool. "My job is to ascertain whether slave trafficking occurred. Checking on the treatment of employees is someone else's. I can only say that it has no bearing on our current discussion."

"…Then could you direct me to the official who specializes in those matters?"

"…Hmm. I'd really like to, but it's not so simple as that. Sorry, but no one likes someone who sticks their nose in other people's work."

"…Then I'd like to wait until that person can investigate."

Staffan chuckled as if he'd been waiting for him to say that.

Succuronte sneered in a similar manner.

"…Yes, I'd really like to wait as well, but since we've already received the complaint in writing from the establishment, we need to take you in, with force if necessary, and investigate."

In other words, there was no time.

"As things stand, it's clear from the circumstantial evidence that you committed the crime, but the establishment is willing to take a broad-minded approach in settling this. Of course, some compensation will be required. And it will cost a bit to destroy the document that accuses you of slave trafficking."

"What kind of compensation, specifically?"

"Yes, about that. For starters, we'd like you to return our employee. And we'd like you to pay us the money that would have been made if she hadn't been missing."

"I see. How much is that?"

"In gold pieces…hmm. Eh, I'll make it cheap. A hundred. And an additional three hundred as a solatium, for a total of four hundred."

"…That's quite a lot of money. What's the breakdown? How much per day and in what categories?"

"W-wait a moment." Staffan cut into the conversation. "That's not all, Succuronte!"

"Oh, that's right. Since we reported the damage, there is the fee to destroy that document even if we settle the matter privately."

"That's right, Succuronte. It won't do to forget that." Staffan grinned.

"…Seriously?"

"Hmm?"

"Ah, nothing," Sebas murmured with a smile.

"Um, my apologies, Mr. Heivish." Succuronte bowed to Staffan and continued. "One-third of the solatium is considered reasonable for destroying the record, so that comes out to a hundred gold pieces. So the total is five hundred."

"I paid some money when I took her. Will that be deducted?"

"Oh, that's rich. Listen, buddy, if you settle with them, that'll mean you never purchased a slave. In other words, that money never existed—you dropped it somewhere."

So you're telling me to pretend I dropped a hundred gold pieces? Well, you probably have half of it in your pocket as we speak. "…Another issue is that she's not fully healed yet. If you take her now, she might relapse. She could also die, depending on how the treatment goes. I think it's safer to have us take care of her."

A strange twinkle appeared in Succuronte's eye.

When he saw it, Sebas realized he'd made a mistake—now they knew he cared about Tsuare.

"I see, I see. You may be right. If she dies, you'll have to reimburse us with her worth, naturally, but until she's healed, how about lending us the lady of the house?"

"Ohh! That makes sense. If you create a vacancy, you should fill it."

The lust was plain on Staffan's grinning face. He was probably imagining Solution naked.

Sebas's smile disappeared, leaving him expressionless.

Succuronte probably wasn't being serious, but if he found an opening, he would force himself in. Sebas could see that because he'd slipped and revealed his attachment to Tsuare, there was a chance this would blow up even worse.

"…Won't it be problematic if you get too greedy?"

"Don't be ridiculous!" Staffan got red in the face and shouted.

Like the squeal of a pig before being slaughtered, thought Sebas as he silently gazed at the patrol chief.

"What do you mean, 'greedy'?! I'm doing this to uphold the law created through the power of Princess Renner's esteemed will! You call that greed?! How rude can you possibly be?!"

"Now, now, please calm down, Mr. Heivish."

The moment Succuronte chimed in, Staffan immediately quelled his anger. His instantaneous serenity implied that it hadn't been a genuine outburst but just part of the intimidation plan.

What a horrible actor, Sebas whispered in his head.

"But Succuronte…"

"Mr. Heivish, I think we've said everything we can say for now. I'd like to come back the day after tomorrow to hear Sebas's decision. That's fine with you, right, Mr. Sebas?"

"Yes."

With that, the conversation met its end, and Sebas escorted the men to the entryway. He saw them off, and Succuronte, the last one to go, smiled at Sebas with a parting shot. "*Someone* said, 'I owe that former concubine some thanks. I never imagined someone slated for disposal would lay a golden egg.'"

The door closed with a *bang*.

Sebas watched them go as if the door were see-through. There was no particular emotion on his face at all. He had his usual calm expression. But deep in his eyes was something vivid and intense.

Anger.

—No, the emotion couldn't be described with such a simple word as *anger*.

Fury, rage—those terms were more appropriate.

The reason Succuronte had spoken the truth as he left was to inform Sebas that all avenues of escape were blocked and that there was nothing to be done—he was convinced he'd won.

"Solution. Why don't you come out?"

At Sebas's suggestion, she slunk out of the shadows and showed herself. She'd been using an assassin-class skill to melt into the darkness.

"You were listening to our conversation, right?" His question was meant only as confirmation.

Solution nodded, of course. "So what will you do now, Master Sebas?"

Sebas couldn't answer immediately.

In response to his silence, Solution directed a cold gaze his way. "…Shall we turn over that human and be done with it?"

"I don't think that will resolve the issue."

"…And why is that?"

"If we show weakness, they'll come to suck the marrow from our bones. That's the type of humans they are. I don't think handing over Tsuare will fix this. The problem is how they're investigating us and how much they've found out. We entered the capital as merchants, but if they investigate in-depth, that story won't hold water—they'll be able to see through our disguise."

"Then what will you do?"

"I don't know. I think I'd like to take a stroll outside and think about it."

Sebas pushed open the front door and began to walk.

Solution watched in silence as Sebas receded into the distance.

This is so stupid. If he hadn't picked up that human, none of this even would have happened. Of course, it's too late now. What's important is what to do going forward.

As someone working under Sebas, ignoring his orders and acting on her own would be frowned upon, but it seemed worse for her to let things continue the way they were going.

If our littlest sister would come out… There wouldn't be a problem if we could just operate as the Pleïades…

She didn't know what to do.

She was having so much trouble figuring out what to do next that this was probably the most confounded she'd ever been.

Eventually she made up her mind, raised her left hand, and opened it.

A scroll rose from her palm like it had bobbed to the surface of a lake. She'd been keeping the scroll inside her body. Originally, it had been given to her to use for communication in case of an impending crisis. At this point, due to Demiurge's research, their prospects for low-tier scroll creation were fine, but back when Solution was dispatched, they hadn't been, so this Message scroll was designated for emergency use only. She judged that this was a situation in which she should use it.

She unrolled the scroll and unleashed the spell it contained. The item scattered to pieces that turned to ashes. Before they could fall to the ground, they had completely disappeared.

As the spell took effect, Solution sensed herself connecting to the other person with something that felt like string and spoke. "Lord Ainz, are you there?"

"Solution…? What in the world is it? If you're contacting me, it must be some sort of emergency?"

"Yes." She paused for just a moment. She hesitated due to her loyalty to Sebas, and she wondered if she hadn't simply misunderstood. But her faithfulness to Lord Ainz won over.

And although they should be acting in order to maximize the gains of the Forty-One Supreme Beings, Sebas's current actions could be interpreted as contravening that.

That was why she wanted to get their master's opinion. "It's possible that Sebas is a traitor."

"What? …Agh!! …Er…how could that be? Ahem. Quit joking around, Solution. I won't stand for such claims without proof… Do you have any?"

"Well, I'm not sure it can be called proof, but…"

Chapter 4 Congregated Men

Chapter 4 | Congregated Men

1

3 *Late Fire Moon* (September) 4:01 AM

The exhaustion that had built and built inside Brain hit him all at once, and from the moment he entered Gazef's house, he slept deeply for almost an entire day. When he woke up, he ate a light meal and fell asleep again.

He didn't want to admit it, but the reason he could rest so well inside Gazef's house was that he felt safe. He knew that if Shalltear attacked, that monster would easily defeat even Gazef. But still, the fact that he was at his onetime rival's house, which seemed like the securest place in the world to him, relaxed Brain in a way that allowed for this much unguarded rest.

Light slanted through the shutters onto Brain's face.

The sunlight shone through his eyelids and woke him from a sleep so deep he didn't even dream.

After he opened his eyes, he squinted in the bright sun and held up a hand to block a ray.

Sitting up on the bed, he hurriedly took in his surroundings like a baby mouse. The plain room contained only the bare minimum of furniture. The gear he'd been wearing was piled in one corner.

"So this is the room the captain of the Royal Select offers his guests, huh?" he commented snarkily at the empty room. Relieved no one was around, he stretched. His joints popped audibly, his stiff muscles relaxed, and his circulation improved.

He let out a big yawn.

"…He must have one of his men stay over now and then. This room is probably a letdown…"

The reason nobles lived showy lives wasn't only because they were fond of luxury. It was to keep up appearances.

Likewise, if a rank-and-file soldier's superior lived in a splendidly furnished environment, it would spur him on to apply himself in pursuing promotions.

"Eh, I guess it's none of my business," Brain grumbled. Then he snickered—not at Gazef but at himself.

If he was capable of considering such trivial things, perhaps he had healed a little from the two great shocks his mind had suffered.

He remembered the image of that powerful monster and couldn't keep his hands from shaking.

"Yeah…" The fear clinging to his psyche wouldn't come off so easily.

Shalltear Bloodfallen.

An absolute power that even Brain Unglaus, who had sacrificed everything he had to study the blade, couldn't begin to approach. A monster among monsters possessing all the beauty in the world, or so it seemed. A possessor of true strength.

Just remembering her summoned a fear that permeated his entire body.

As a slave to the terror that the monster would come after him, he'd been on the run in the capital with almost no sleep or rest. He'd kept moving, never getting enough rest, ruled by the worries that she would show up while he was sleeping or slink out of the darkness as he ran down the road at night.

The reason he'd thought to flee to the capital was that if he hid himself in a place with lots of people, he would be harder to find. But he hadn't anticipated that the punishing psychological exhaustion of his severe fugitive lifestyle would find him wishing for death.

He hadn't anticipated running into Gazef, either. Or had the faint hope that Gazef could do something unconsciously pointed his feet in the captain's direction? He didn't know.

He had nothing.

He opened his hands and they contained nothing.

He glanced at the pile of gear in the corner and saw the katana he'd acquired in order to wrench victory from Gazef Stronoff's grip.

But what would be the point in beating him? Now that he knew of a power infinitely greater than them both, what significance did their low-level competitions have?

"Plowing fields...probably would have been more meaningful." As he mocked himself, he sensed someone standing outside the door.

"Unglaus, seems like...you're up?" The voice belonged to the master of the house.

"Yeah, Stronoff. I'm awake."

The door opened wide, and Gazef walked in. He was fully outfitted.

"You really slept, huh? I'm surprised how well you rested!"

"Yeah, thanks for letting me have a good break. I feel bad."

"No worries. But I have to head to the castle for now. When I get back, tell me what happened to you."

"...It's an awful story, though. You might end up like me."

"Still, I can't not hear it. If we talk over drinks, I should be able to handle it... Till then, make yourself at home. If you want some food, just let the help know and they should feed you. And if you're going out into the city... Do you have any money?"

"...No, but if it comes to it, I'll just sell some of my items." He held up his ringed hand so Gazef could see it.

"Are you sure? Those are pretty valuable, aren't they?"

"Yeah, it's fine."

He had obtained them to defeat Gazef in the first place. What purpose was there in treasuring them now that he knew that all his efforts were pointless?

"Well, sometimes you can't sell expensive items so easily, and it might take time for the buyer to get their money together. Take this."

Gazef took out a small cloth pouch. When he put it in Brain's hand, there was a clinking sound of metal on metal.

"…Ah, well, thanks. I'll borrow this, then."

2

3 *Late Fire Moon* (September) 10:31 AM

Sebas walked, wondering what to do about the five men who'd been tailing him ever since he left the house. He wasn't going anywhere in particular. He'd set out with the belief that getting moving would change his mood and help him find a good idea.

After a little while, he saw a crowd of people in the road up ahead.

There were voices that could be described as neither shouts nor laughs and the sound of something being struck. People in the mob were saying things like "He's going to die" and "Maybe we should call a soldier…"

He couldn't see through the throng, but it was clear that some sort of violence was being committed.

Sebas thought he would take a different street, went to change direction, hesitated for just a split second—and then proceeded.

He was heading for the center of the crowd.

"Excuse me." With those two words, he wove his way in. Apparently shocked, in awe of this figure slipping by them with unexpected agility for an elderly man, the people he passed by stiffened.

There seemed to be others trying to reach the middle of the crowd—he could hear voices saying, "Let me through!"—but they struggled, unable to break through the mass of people.

Having propelled himself to the center with no trouble, Sebas learned with his own eyes what was going on.

There were several poorly dressed men kicking something.

Sebas strode silently forward to within arm's length of the group.

"What do you want, old man?" One of the five men realized he was there and loudly challenged him.

"I thought you were making a bit of a racket."

"Are you lookin' for trouble, too?"

The men swiftly surrounded Sebas and revealed what they'd been kicking in the process. Was it a boy? He was lying limply on his side and bleeding from either his nose or his mouth—it was unclear which. Perhaps because he'd been getting kicked for so long, he was unconscious but apparently still alive.

Sebas stared down the men. Their bodies and breath reeked of booze. And their faces were red from something other than exercise.

You're drunk, so you can't keep yourselves from turning violent? "I don't know what started all this, but how about you leave it at that?" Sebas asked with a blank expression.

"Huh?! This kid's food stained my shirt! I'm not about to let him off the hook!" One man pointed to something. Certainly, there was a faint stain on the shirt; however, these men's clothes were all grungy anyway. Considering that, the spot was barely visible.

Sebas looked at the one who seemed like the leader of the five young men—the butler had the senses of a distinguished warrior, so he could pick up differences humans would overlook.

"Hmm...this city isn't very safe."

"Huh?" One of the men felt ignored at Sebas's distant comment and made a noise like he was offended.

"...Leave."

"Huh? What'd ya say, old man?"

"I'll say it again. Leave."

"Why you—!" The leader got red in the face, balled up his fists—and crumpled to the ground.

Many of the surrounding people were shocked—including the other four men.

What Sebas had done was simple. He'd made a fist, struck the man's jaw with pinpoint precision—at a speed on the very edge of human perception—and rattled his brain with a high-velocity hit. He could throw punches faster than humans could perceive, but if he did that he wouldn't be able to scare anyone, so he'd held back.

"Do you still want to fight?" Sebas asked quietly.

His composure and strength had overcome the intoxication clouding their minds, and they all apologized as they backed away several steps.

Sebas felt they were apologizing to the wrong person, but he didn't say anything.

He looked away from the fleeing men carrying their unconscious friend and went to take a step toward the boy, but his foot stopped midway.

What am I doing?

What he needed to do was think of a way to solve his problem. Only an idiot would make more trouble for himself at a time like this. Wasn't the whole reason he was in his current predicament because he'd acted so compassionately without thinking?

I saved him for now. I should be satisfied with that. With those thoughts in his mind, Sebas approached the figure on the ground. He touched the limp, immobile boy's back and poured chi into him. A full-powered infusion would have easily healed him completely, but that would definitely have drawn too much attention.

He stopped at the minimum and pointed at someone when their eyes happened to meet. "…Take this child to the shrine. His breastbone may be broken, so take care when you carry him. Put him on a board and try not to bump him around too much."

When the man nodded at the orders, Sebas set off walking. There was no need to elbow his way through the crowd. The wall of people neatly parted for him.

Right after he left, he sensed that the number of people tailing him had gone up.

There was just one problem—their identity.

The five who had been following him from the mansion had to be Succuronte's henchmen. So who were the two who joined after the incident with the boy?

The sound of the footsteps and stride length indicated adult males, but Sebas had no idea who they might be.

"Well, thinking about it won't get me an answer. I guess I'll…catch them?"

Sebas continued walking, turning down dirtier and dirtier streets. He was still being followed.

"…Are they even trying to hide themselves?" There was no indication they were attempting to conceal their footsteps. *Is it because they don't have that ability, or is there some other reason?* Sebas cocked his head and decided he should simply find out. Once the presence of other people had dwindled, right when Sebas was about to make his move, the hoarse—but still young-sounding—male voice of one of his pursuers called out to him.

"Excuse me!"

3

3 *Late Fire Moon* (September) 10:27 AM

Climb was thinking as he walked back to the castle.

He replayed that morning's session with Gazef in his mind several times, ruminating on what he could have done to put up a better fight. Around the time he decided on some tactics to try if there was a next time, he discovered a crowd of people making some angry shouts. Two soldiers were watching awkwardly from nearby.

From the middle of the crowd, he could hear a ruckus. And it belonged to no normal voices.

Climb took on a firm expression and strode toward the soldiers. "What are you doing?"

The sudden call from behind startled the soldiers, and they turned to look at Climb.

They were equipped with mail and spears. Over the mail shirts, they wore something like a surcoat with the kingdom's coat of arms. It was the typical appearance of a kingdom guard, but these two didn't seem highly trained.

First of all, their physiques were not particularly built. Plus, their beards weren't neatly shaved, and their mail shirts weren't polished, which made them look rather unclean. Overall, they seemed sloppy.

"And you are…?" one of the guards asked in a voice that implied confusion and anger at the sudden call from someone younger than him.

"I'm off-duty," Climb declared, and the man's consternation showed on his face. Probably because an obviously younger boy seemed to be suggesting his rank was higher.

For the time being, the soldier appeared to judge that taking a humble approach would be smart and straightened up. "There seems to be some sort of disturbance."

Climb repressed the urge to reprimand them with an *I got that much!* Unlike the soldiers guarding the castle, the ones patrolling the city were commoners, so they hadn't been through as much training. They were essentially peasants who'd learned to use a weapon.

Climb moved his eyes from the nervous soldiers to the cluster of people. Rather than expecting these two to do something, it would be faster to act himself.

Maybe he was exceeding the authority of his position by sticking his nose in their business, but he wouldn't have been able to explain to his compassionate master if he stood by while people suffered.

"You guys wait here."

Having made up his mind, Climb forced his way into the mass of people without listening for a reply. Even if there was a small gap, he couldn't slip through. No, it would be strange if there were a human who could.

As he desperately elbowed his way through, nearly getting shoved aside, he heard a voice from the center of the crowd.

"…Leave."

"Huh? What'd ya say, old man?"

"I'll say it again. Leave."

"Why you—!"

This is bad.

They were going to lash out again, this time at an old man.

When Climb popped out of the crowd, flushed after frantically pushing his way through, the first thing he saw was an elderly man—and the men surrounding him. There was a child who looked like a tattered rag at their feet.

The elegance of the well-dressed older man indicated he either was a noble or served one. The robust men around him seemed drunk. A glance was all it would take to tell who was in the wrong.

The man who seemed to be the strongest curled his hands into tight fists. The difference between that man and the old one was overwhelming.

He had a stocky body, bulky muscles, and a violent temperament that wouldn't hesitate to shed blood. If he hit the older man, he could easily send him flying. The people around them who realized this released faint screams at the thought of the tragedy about to befall the old man.

Climb was the only one among them who sensed something was off.

Certainly, the other man looked more robust, but Climb had the feeling that the absolute power he sensed belonged to the older one.

That momentary distraction meant he lost his chance to stop the violence. The man balled up his fists—and collapsed.

Surprised voices sounded all around Climb.

The old man had made a fist and whacked the drunk's jaw with terrifying accuracy—at quite a high speed. It was a punch that even Climb, who had trained his eyes to follow fast movements, could only just make out.

"Do you still want to fight?" The old man's deep, quiet voice asked the question.

His composure and sudden display of strength were incredibly sobering for the drunk men. No, even the spectators were overcome by the elderly man's drive. The men had completely lost the will to fight.

"U-uhh, we're sorry." They all apologized as they backed away several steps. Then they picked up their friend from his awkward position on the ground and fled.

Climb didn't feel like pursuing them. Mesmerized by the old man's straight posture, he couldn't move.

His spine was straight as a sword. Any soldier aspired to cut a figure like that.

After touching the boy's back, perhaps palpating to examine him, the old man asked a bystander to take care of him and walked off. The crowd parted in a straight line, creating a path, and no one took their eyes off his back. That was the effect of such poise.

Climb rushed over to the boy on the ground and took out the potion Gazef had given to him during their training session. "Can you drink this?"

There was no response. The boy had lost consciousness completely.

Climb opened the bottle and sprinkled the potion over his body. Many people thought potions were only for drinking, but they worked equally well when they were poured on the target. Such was the extraordinary nature of magic.

As if the boy's skin was drinking it in, the liquid was absorbed into his body. The color returned to his face.

Relieved, Climb nodded once.

The bystanders were just as surprised at the use of such an expensive item as they were at the old man's moves.

Climb had given up a potion, but naturally, he didn't regret it. As long as taxes were being collected from the people, it was his duty as someone subsisting on that money to protect them and keep the peace. If he couldn't do that, he should at least do this.

Since I used a potion on him, he should be fine, but we should still probably take him to the shrine, just in case. When he glanced at the guards standing by, there were three more. They must have shown up late.

The guards who had finally arrived on the scene turned a critical eye on all the people in the area.

Climb spoke to one of the uncomfortable-looking patrolmen. "Take this child to the shrine."

"What in the world…?"

"He was beaten up. I used a healing potion on him, so I think he's okay, but I want you to take him to the shrine just to be sure."

"Right. Understood!"

Climb decided he would leave the rest up to the guards. His work there was done. *A soldier from the castle probably shouldn't stick his nose into other jurisdictions too much.*

"Can I ask you to get the details about what happened from someone who saw the whole thing?"

"Understood."

"Then I'll leave the rest up to you."

The guards were more confident with orders, and after Climb confirmed that they were taking efficient action, he stood up and took off running. He heard one of them call, "Where are you going?!" but he ignored it.

When he got to the street where the old man had turned, he slowed down.

He caught sight of his target right away.

Really, he wanted to call out to him immediately, but he wasn't feeling quite brave enough. He felt an overwhelming amount of pressure, like a thick, invisible wall.

The old man continued walking, turning down dirtier and dirtier streets. Climb continued after him. All the time he was following, he couldn't bring himself to talk to him.

I'm tailing him. Climb despaired at his own conduct. He shouldn't do that no matter how hard it was to talk to someone. *I need to change this situation,* he fretted as he kept walking.

Eventually, about when they'd reached a back alley devoid of human presence, Climb took a few deep breaths and shouted with all the courage he could muster, like a man confessing his feelings to a girl he liked.

"Excuse me!"

The old man whirled around in response to the voice.

His hair was completely white, as was his beard, but his back was straight as the blade of a steel sword. Conspicuous wrinkles in his chiseled features gave him an air of kindness, but his penetrating eyes were like those of a hawk targeting its prey.

He even had the elegance of a great noble.

"Did you need something?" The old man's voice was a bit hoarse but full of a lively, dignified energy.

Climb felt an invisible force pressing in on him, and he swallowed. "U-uh…" Overwhelmed by the power of the old man, he couldn't get proper words out.

Noticing that, the old man relaxed. "Who are you?" His tone was gentle.

Finally, released from that heavy pressure, Climb's throat could work normally. "…My name is Climb, and I'm a soldier here. Thank you for doing what should have been my job." Climb bowed, humble and low.

The old man squinted slightly, thinking, and then seemed to realize what Climb meant with a little "Oh… It was no trouble. I'll be going now."

Climb raised his head and, as the old man clipped the conversation short and started walking off, said, "Please wait. Actually…I'm ashamed to admit it, but I've been following you because—and I hope you'll laugh at my impertinence—if you don't mind, I'd like you to mentor me about that skill you used."

"What…do you mean by that?"

"I'm working very hard to get stronger, so when I saw your incredible movements earlier, I thought it would be great if I could get you to teach me the skill."

The old man looked Climb up and down. "Hmm…let me see your hands." Climb stuck out his hands, and the old man gazed intently at his palms. He couldn't help but feel uneasy. The old man flipped his hands over, glanced at his nails, and then nodded in satisfaction. "They're thick and sturdy—good warrior hands."

The smile and the compliment made Climb feel warm inside. The rush of happiness was on par with the one he felt when Gazef had praised him. "No…I'm barely a soldier."

"No need for modesty… Next, may I see your sword?"

The old man gazed first at the grip, then at the blade, of the sword he was handed. "I see... Is this a spare weapon?"

"How did you know?!"

"So it is, then? There's a dent here."

When he closely examined the place the old man was pointing at, sure enough, the blade had a slight ding in it. It must have struck something in an awkward way during training.

"How embarrassing!" Climb was so mortified he wished he could disappear.

Because Climb was aware of how unskilled he was, he paid an obsessive amount of attention to his weapons to gain even a little bit of an edge. Or at least, up until that moment, he'd thought so.

"I see. I have a rough understanding of your personality now. Hands and weapon are mirrors of a warrior's character. You've made a very favorable impression on me."

Climb, beet red to his ears, looked admiringly at the old man.

What he saw was a gracious, good-natured smile.

"Okay. I'll train you, but just a bit. However"—he stopped Climb before he could thank him—"there is something I want to ask. You said you're a soldier, right? Well, the other day I saved this woman..."

After hearing the old man Sebas's story, Climb was furious. He couldn't hide his disgust at the fact that someone would abuse the emancipation of the slaves Renner had proclaimed and that nothing had even changed yet.

No, that wasn't right. Climb shook his head.

The law prohibited the buying and selling of slaves. However, it wasn't uncommon to have people working off debts in poor conditions. That loophole had become a free-for-all. Actually, it was probably precisely because there was a loophole that the law managed to get enacted at all.

Renner's law is nearly meaningless. The thought flitted across Climb's mind, but he shook it off. What he needed to consider right now was Sebas's circumstances.

He furrowed his brow.

Sebas was at a total disadvantage. Certainly, it would be possible to investigate the terms of the young woman's contract and counterattack, but he couldn't imagine the opposing side wasn't prepared for such a tactic. If they appealed to the law, Sebas would surely lose.

The fact that the other men hadn't already done so had to be because they felt they could rip him off even better some other way.

"Do you happen to know anyone who isn't corrupt who could help me?"

Climb knew only one person. He could say with confidence that there was no noble with more integrity than Renner. He knew she could be trusted.

But he couldn't introduce her.

If these people were capable of skirting the slave-trafficking prohibition, they were sure to have connections within various power structures. Naturally, the nobles they were affiliated with probably had a fair bit of authority. If the princess, a member of the king's faction, invoked state authority to investigate, enact a rescue, and cause losses for the nobles' faction, it could lead to an all-out war.

Exercising authority wasn't such a simple matter. One wrong move could trigger a civil war, especially in a case like their divided kingdom's.

He couldn't let Renner be responsible for the downfall of the state.

Lakyus felt the same way, which was why their earlier conversation had gone as it had. That was why Climb hadn't said anything—no, couldn't say anything.

However Sebas had interpreted his anguished silence, he murmured, "I see," and then offered additional news that shocked Climb. "…From what she told me, there are still others held captive in the building, men and women alike."

What the heck? So does that mean there is another brothel besides the one run by the slave-trafficking org? Or…is it the same one?

"If it's a matter of allowing them to flee somewhere…I would have to ask my master, but she has some land, so maybe they could go there…"

"Would that be possible? …Would you be able to shelter the woman I saved as well?"

"My apologies, Sir Sebas, but I can't promise anything without asking my master. That said, she is a very compassionate person. I think it'll be all right!"

"Hmm! If you have that much faith in your master, she must be a wonderful person."

Climb nodded emphatically. He had a more admirable master than anyone.

"I'm changing the subject here, but if we could prove slave-trafficking activities were taking place at the brothel, what would happen to it? Would even that get covered up?"

"There's a possibility they would be forced to close up shop if we turned in the evidence to the proper authorities... At least, I want to believe the kingdom isn't that corrupt."

"...Understood. Now then, allow me to ask you a different question. Why do you want to get stronger?"

"Huh?" Climb let out a foolish-sounding yelp, caught off guard by the sudden topic change.

"You just said you want me to train you. I've judged that I can trust you, but I want to know the reason you are pursuing power."

Climb squinted as he pondered.

Why do I want to get stronger?

Climb had been abandoned as a child and didn't know either of his parents' faces. In the kingdom, this wasn't such a rare thing. And it wasn't uncommon to die facedown in the mud, either.

It had been Climb's fate to die in such a way in the rain that day.

But instead, he had met the sun. After crawling around in the dirt and the dim his entire existence, he was enthralled by its brilliance.

When he was young, he had admired her, and as he grew, the feeling assumed a stronger form.

Love.

He had to destroy that emotion. A miracle like in the sagas the bards sang would never happen in the real world. Just as no human could reach the sun, Climb's feelings would never reach her—no, he couldn't allow them to.

The woman Climb loved was fated to be another man's wife. There was no way a princess would end up bound to someone like Climb, whose status was lower than a peasant's and whose origins were unknown.

If the king suddenly collapsed and the eldest prince assumed the throne, Renner would surely be married off immediately to one of the great nobles. It had probably already been decided between the prince and the noble. Or it was possible there would be a strategic marriage to someone in a neighboring country.

It was strange that she was of age but had no husband or even a fiancé.

It was a golden moment, and he would have given anything to stop time. If he didn't have to train so much, he would have been able to relish it a little more.

Climb was an ordinary person with no innate ability. Still, thanks to his hard work, he'd managed to get fairly strong as a soldier. So deciding he was satisfied with that, quitting his workouts, and spending a little more time next to Renner would be a better use of his time, wouldn't it?

But…could he really do that?

Climb admired her brilliance. That was no lie nor was it mistaken. It was just a feeling from his heart.

But…

"I'm a man, so…" Climb laughed.

Yes, he wanted to stand next to her. The sun shone up in the sky. A human could never stand next to it. Still, he wanted to climb as high as he could, be someone who could stand even a little closer to her.

He didn't want to be forever looking up at her in admiration.

These were the silly feelings of a boy, but they were good for a boy to have. He wanted to be a man suitable for the woman he admired, even if they would never be together.

It was because he had those feelings that he could endure his friendless life, his difficult warrior path, and the studies that chipped away at his sleeping time.

If anyone wants to laugh at my foolish ideas, let them.

Only a person who had truly loved someone could understand.

•

Sebas squinted as he intently observed the boy, wanting to comprehend the countless meanings contained in the short reply. Then he nodded in satisfaction.

"Based on your reply, I've decided what sort of training to give you."

Climb was about to thank him, but a hand moved out to stop him.

"But I'm sorry to say, it appears you have no innate aptitude. If I were to really commit to training you, it would take a long time, and I don't have that luxury. I'd like to train you in a way that is effective and possible in a short amount of time, but...it's quite intense."

Climb gulped.

Sebas's eyes sent a chill up his spine.

They were the piercing eyes of someone whose power surpassed Gazef's best efforts, as impossible as that seemed. That was why he couldn't answer immediately.

"I'll be blunt: You could die."

He's not kidding. Climb sensed that. He didn't mind dying if it was for Renner's sake, but he definitely didn't want to die for his own selfish reasons.

He wasn't a coward—no, maybe he was.

He swallowed and wavered. For a little while, it was so quiet they could hear a far-off commotion.

"Whether you die or not depends on your spirit... If you have something precious to you, if you have reason to cling to life even if you're brought to your knees, you should be all right."

Wasn't he going to teach me martial arts? Climb began to wonder in the back of his mind, but that wasn't the issue at this point. He considered the meaning of Sebas's words, digested it, and then replied, "I'm ready. Please train me."

"You mean you're confident you won't die?"

Climb shook his head. That wasn't it.

He wanted to cling to life even if it was on his knees—because he always had a reason to.

Having perhaps read these feelings in Climb's eyes, Sebas nodded emphatically. "Understood. Then let's begin the training."

"Here?"

"Yes. It will only take a few minutes. Prepare your weapon."

What in the world are we going to do? Climb drew his sword and faced the unknown with a mixture of apprehension and confusion, as well as a tiny bit of anticipation and curiosity.

The ring of the blade sliding against its sheath echoed in the narrow alley.

Climb pointed the sword at Sebas's eyes, and Sebas stared at him.

"Okay, here I go. Do your best to stay conscious."

And the next moment…

…it was almost like blades of ice had shot out from him in every direction.

Climb had no words.

What was really swirling around Sebas was a killing intent.

A thick, dark presence surged over Climb like a wave, almost enough to crush his heart at that moment. He thought he heard a scream like someone's soul being broken. It could have come from close by or far away, or it could have spurted out of his own mouth.

Tossed on the murderous black torrent, Climb felt his consciousness beginning to white out. There was so much fear that his mind was trying to let go of consciousness to avoid it.

"…Is this how much of a 'man' you are? I'm just getting warmed up."

Sebas's disappointment echoed loudly within Climb's fading awareness.

Those words cut Climb deeper than any blade could. It was enough to make him forget the terror coming at him, even if only for a moment.

Ba-bum. His heart thumped once, loudly.

He exhaled sharply.

He was so scared, wanted to run away. But he desperately stood his ground with tears in his eyes. His hands shook and the tip of his sword wobbled crazily. His mail shirt was making a racket he was shaking so hard.

Still he desperately clenched his jaw to stop his teeth from chattering and tried to withstand his terror of Sebas.

Sebas snorted at Climb's unseemly state and slowly began to ball up his raised right hand. In less than a few blinks, it had become a round fist.

Then one of them slowly began moving back, as if it were being drawn like a bowstring.

Realizing what was about to happen, Climb shook his head, trembling. Sebas, of course, would not entertain his wish.

"Well, then…please die."

Like an arrow released from a fully drawn bow, Sebas's fist zoomed forward with a roar of ripping air.

This is instant death. Climb sensed it in slow motion. His mind was seized by the perfect image of death—an iron ball much taller than he was zooming straight for him at a furious speed. If he shielded himself with his sword, the fist would smash through like it was nothing.

His entire body could no longer move. He was so tense he'd frozen.

There's no way to escape the death I'm facing.

Climb gave up but then got irritated at himself.

If he wasn't going to die for Renner's sake, then why didn't he just give up back then? He should have died shivering all alone in the rain.

He saw Renner's beautiful face.

They say a person's life flashes before their eyes when they're on the brink of death. Supposedly, that's the brain groping through the memories of the person's entire past for a possible way to escape, so Climb found it strange that the last thing he would see was the smile of the master he loved and respected.

Yes, she was smiling.

She hadn't smiled for him when she was young right after she saved him. *When did she start smiling for me?*

He couldn't remember. But he did remember her timidly doing so.

Would that smile become a frown when she heard he'd died? Would thick clouds blot out the sun?

Dammit!

Climb's heart flooded with rage.

His life had been tossed into the street, and she had picked it up. That meant this life was not his. He existed for Renner, to make her even a little happier…

There has to be some way to escape!

The fierce emotion shattered the chains of fear.

His hands moved.

His feet moved.

The eyes he'd been trying to squeeze shut flew open and frantically shifted to the fist rushing at him with incredible speed.

It was like all his body's senses had been sharpened to extremes, as if he could detect the slightest vibration in the air.

It's said there exists a phenomenon known as hysterical strength. It's the unbelievable potential people are able to exhibit in extreme situations because their brain releases the limiter holding back their physical power.

The brain secretes large volumes of hormones, concentrating the mental faculties all for the purpose of survival. Suddenly, the person can process a vast amount of information at high speed in order to discern the appropriate course of action.

Climb entered the realm of the best warriors for a brief moment. But Sebas's attack was still faster. Surely it was already too late. He probably wouldn't have time to dodge the fist. Still, he had to move. There was no way he could give up. He could tell he was moving like a tortoise in this intensely compressed period of time, but he desperately twisted his body.

Then—

Sebas's fist blew by Climb's face. The ensuing wind pulled out a few of his hairs.

A quiet voice reached his ears.

"Congratulations. How does it feel to have conquered the fear of death?"

...

Climb stood there with a dazed expression, not understanding what he'd just been asked.

"How was it? How did it feel to face death? And how does it feel to have overcome it?"

Breathing hard, Climb stared at Sebas with an empty expression, as if he'd lost something. It was like his intent to kill had been nothing more than a lie. Sebas's words sank into his brain, and he finally felt relief flooding him.

As if the violent drive to kill had been propping him up, Climb crumpled to the ground like a marionette whose strings had been cut. Flat on the road, he voraciously sucked fresh air into his lungs.

"...You're lucky you didn't die of shock. It happens sometimes. People become convinced they will actually die and give up on life."

Climb still tasted something bitter in the back of his throat. He was sure it was the taste of death.

"If we repeat this a few times, you should end up able to overcome ordinary fear. We need to be careful, though, because this stimulates your survival instincts. If they grow numb to it, you won't be able to recognize clear danger. You always need situational awareness."

"...F-forgive me, but who or what are you?" Climb gasped from below.

"What do you mean?"

"Th-that killing resolve was not the sort a normal person can project. So what in the world—?"

"For now, let's say I'm just an old man who has confidence in his strength."

Climb couldn't take his eyes off Sebas's smiling face. The expression seemed to be born of kindness, but it also seemed like the fierce grin of one with absolute power far surpassing even Gazef.

A man who might far exceed Gazef, the strongest warrior from any of the nearby nations…

Climb decided his curiosity would be satisfied with that. He didn't think it would be right to press the issue.

Still, the question of who this old man Sebas was lingered stubbornly in his mind. He even wondered if he might be one of the Thirteen Heroes.

"Then I think it's about time to get goi—"

"W-wait! There's something I want to ask you!"

A terrified voice echoed out from behind them, interrupting Sebas.

4

3 *Late Fire Moon* (September) 9:42 AM

Brain left Gazef's house.

He turned around and, thinking ahead to his return, took mental note of what the building looked like. When Gazef had brought him here, he'd been only half-conscious due to his low body temperature, so he didn't really remember it.

The location of Gazef's house he knew because he'd been gathering information on him in order to challenge him to a duel in the future. But that was just secondhand information, and there were slight discrepancies with the truth.

"Psh, there's no sword stuck in the roof." Cursing the information dealer who told him such half-baked rumors, he took a close look at the house.

It was far smaller than the mansions nobles lived in and seemed more like a place for regular citizens with a little extra money. Still, it was more than big enough for Gazef and the elderly couple who served him.

Having memorized the image, Brain set off.

He wasn't going anywhere in particular.

Before, he might have wanted to go hunting for weapons, armor, or magic items but not anymore.

"I wonder what I should do..." His grumbles disappeared into the air.

He thought he wouldn't mind just vanishing somewhere. He was still actually attracted to the idea of dying.

When he searched his heart for what he desired, all he found was a gaping hole. His goal had been completely destroyed. Not even a husk of it remained.

So why...?

Glancing down at his right hand, he saw his katana. Under his shirt there was mail.

He'd been holding his katana so tightly on his way to the capital out of fear. Even though he knew it would have no effect on the monster Shalltear, who repelled his full-strength attacks with a fingernail, he was anxious without it.

So why am I holding it now? I should have been able to leave it behind. Am I still anxious? Brain thought but then shook his head.

No.

But in the end, he couldn't figure out what motivation caused him to bring the sword.

Brain walked along, remembering the way the royal capital was the first time he visited it. Some buildings, like the wizards' guild and the castle, hadn't changed, but he also saw lots of new edifices. As he enjoyed the stroll down memory lane, he came upon a disturbance happening down the road.

He frowned at the commotion. He could sense the bristling sensation of violence from the center of the crowd.

Guess I'll go somewhere else, he thought, but just as he'd turned his feet in a different direction, an old man caught his eye. He was approaching the center of the crowd with such fluid motions he seemed to be gliding.

"…H-huh? What the heck? How does he do that?" The words slipped out of Brain's mouth in spite of himself as he blinked several times. The way the old man moved was just too unbelievable. Brain thought he must have just seen a waking dream or the workings of some kind of magic spell.

Brain probably couldn't do that himself. It was a skill that required a complete grasp of another's consciousness as well as the overall waves of the pushing and shoving crowd.

It was the pinnacle of movement itself.

With zero hesitation, Brain's legs carried him toward the crowd of people.

After pushing and shoving his way through to the center, Brain emerged just in time to see the old man swiftly whack the other man's jaw.

What the heck? Would I even be able to block that? Seems…tricky? Was he manipulating the guy's attention and gaze? Maybe I'm thinking too hard. Still, that punch was clean enough to be included in a training manual. As Brain ruminated on the attack he'd just witnessed, an impressed grunt escaped his lips.

It wasn't as if he'd seen it clearly, and it was extremely difficult to evaluate fistfighters and swordsmen on the same scale. Still, from just that short amount of time, he'd understood that the man was terribly strong.

It's possible he's stronger than me.

Biting his lower lip, he compared the old man's profile to all the strong people he could remember, but there wasn't a match. *Who in the world is this guy?*

A moment later the old man had left the circle of onlookers. A boy walked off after him. As if tempted by the boy's actions, Brain followed behind him.

The old man seemed to have eyes in the back of his head, so Brain couldn't bring himself to trail directly behind him, but he didn't have that worry with the boy. He also shrewdly considered that even if the boy were found out, he would be safe.

As soon as he started after them, he realized there were multiple people shadowing either the old man or the boy, but Brain didn't care.

Eventually the two of them turned down dimmer and dirtier streets. Brain became concerned. It was almost like the man was leading them somewhere.

Just as he started to question if the boy didn't wonder where they were going, he called out to the old man.

Fortunately for Brain, they began having a conversation immediately around a corner, so he hid himself behind it and listened.

To sum up their conversation, the boy wanted lessons from the old man. *There's no way. An old guy that strong would never take this little turd as a disciple.* Comparing their ability levels, Brain figured that if the boy was a pebble, the old man was a huge gem. Their worlds were too far apart. *How sad. How incredibly sad that he can't even see the gap in their abilities. Leave it at that, kid,* Brain whispered silently in his head.

It was meant for the boy, but at the same time he was mocking his foolish old self, who had been convinced he was the strongest.

As he listened—he couldn't have cared less about the brothel—the old man appeared to offer the boy some training this one time. He had no idea what the old man saw in him.

What could it mean? Or am I missing something? Nah, that can't be. That brat has barely any ability as a warrior and next to no potential!

What kind of training would it be? He could hear from his current position, but he couldn't see. Letting his curiosity get the better of him, he moved, concealing his presence, to peek around the corner. That was when—

A horrifying presence pierced his entire body.

He let out a wordless shriek.

His entire body froze.

It was like the breath of a gigantic carnivorous beast. The world was so coated in an overwhelming sense of impending death that he couldn't blink, much less move. He felt like even his heart had stopped.

This presence could have rivaled that of the one Brain believed to be the most powerful in the whole world—Shalltear Bloodfallen's.

Far from *seeming* to stop, a weaker man's heart would probably have actually failed.

His legs shook so hard he fell back onto his butt. *If this is what it's like for me, that kid's probably dead—passed out if he's lucky!*

Scared though he was, Brain crawled into a position from which he could see the two figures, and what he saw was so unbelievable he completely forgot his fear for a split second.

The boy was still standing.

The same fear assailing Brain made the younger man's legs tremble, but he was still standing.

Wh-what the heck? How can that kid still be on his feet?! Brain couldn't understand how the boy could stand if his own legs had humiliatingly given out under the fear.

Does he have a magic item or martial art that protects him from fear? Or is he a talent holder?

Those things weren't completely out of the question, but seeing how helpless he looked, Brain sensed it was something else. It was an impossible conclusion, but it was the only one he could come up with: The boy was stronger than him.

No way! There's just no way that can be true!

He was probably working out, but he wasn't anywhere near big enough. Judging from his footwork and his technique as he'd tailed the old man, Brain didn't think he could have a terrible amount of ability. The boy didn't seem to be made of much, but this outcome said otherwise.

Wh-what is going on? Am I really that weak?

His vision began to blur.

He realized he was crying, but he didn't have the energy to wipe away the tears.

"Wagh, ngh…ngh…" He frantically stifled his sobs, but the tears fell one after the other. "Why…? Why?"

He clenched the dirt beneath him and stood up. Still, he was immobile under the desire to kill pummeling him. It was like his feet were under someone else's control—they were paralyzed. It was all he could do to look up and observe the old man and the boy.

He could see the boy's back.

The boy was still standing.

He was still facing the old man projecting all that bloodthirst. He'd thought the boy was weak, but now he seemed so far beyond him.

"Am I..."

...really this weak?

He was irritated at himself. Even when the killing urge vanished, he could barely stand.

It seemed like the boy and the old man were going to continue their training but, unable to hold himself back any longer, Brain mustered his courage and jumped out from behind the corner. "W-wait!"

In his current state, Brain didn't have the wherewithal to consider that he shouldn't interrupt them or that he should wait for a better moment.

The boy whipped around with a jerk of his shoulders, startled at the panicked voice. If Brain had been in his position, he probably would have reacted the same way.

"First, please accept my heartfelt apology for interrupting you. I couldn't wait."

"...Do you know him, Sir Sebas?"

"No, I do not. So you don't know him, either...?"

They regarded him suspiciously, but he had expected that. "My name is Brain Unglaus. Please allow me to apologize again for interrupting you. My deepest apologies."

He bowed even lower than the first time and sensed the pair shift slightly.

When enough time had passed to properly express his regret, Brain lifted his head. He could tell they were a little less wary of him now.

"And what is it you want?"

At the old man's question, Brain flicked his eyes to the boy.

"What could you possibly want with me?"

It was difficult for Brain, but he asked the puzzled boy, "Why...how... were you able to stand in the face of such murderous pressure?!"

The boy's eyes widened slightly. Because he was holding a neutral expression, even that small of a change implied a large emotional shock.

"I want to know. That was beyond the realm of what a normal person can handle. Dammit—excuse my language—it was beyond what even I could take. But you're different. You did it. You stood. How did you do it? Up against something so powerful?!"

He was so agitated, it slipped into his speech. But he couldn't hold himself back. He'd fled from the overwhelming power of Shalltear Bloodfallen. This boy had stood there when faced with an equal thirst for blood. *Where does the gap come from?*

He just had to know.

Perhaps his intention had gotten through. The boy seemed flustered but still gave the question careful consideration before replying, "…I don't know. I have no idea why I was able to stand my ground in such a murderous storm. But it might have been…because I was thinking about my master."

"…Your master?"

"Yes. I was thinking about the person I serve…and I managed to hang on."

Brain wanted to shout, *There's no way that's all you did!* But the old man began to speak.

"So your loyalty is so great it overcomes fear. Sir Unglaus, people can display unbelievable power if it's for someone they hold dear, like how a mother can lift the beam of a collapsed house to save her child or how a man can hold his wife by one hand if she's about to fall. That is, I believe, human strength. This boy was able to tap into that power. And he's not the only one who can do that. If you have something you could never give up, you can probably display power beyond what you think you have, as well."

Brain couldn't believe it. His thirst for power that he'd thought he could never give up had turned out to be meaningless, hadn't it? He'd easily broken, become frightened, and run away.

His expression had been clouding over, but he snapped back to attention as Sebas continued.

"…When you cultivate something on your own, it's weak—because if you bend, that's the end. If instead, you build something with another person or for someone, you may bend, but you won't break."

Brain wondered, *Do I have anyone like that?*

But he didn't. He'd decided they weren't useful to him and thrown away those relationships. So the things he'd abandoned in his craving for power were actually the most important?

Brain laughed. His whole life was mistake after mistake. And so he ended up grumbling, "I threw them all away. Do you think there's anything I can do about it now?"

"You'll be all right. I don't have any innate ability, and I was able to do it. I'm sure you can do it, Sir Unglaus! It's never too late."

They were the baseless words of a boy. Still, Brain felt some warmth in his heart. "You're kind…and strong… I'm sorry."

The boy answered the sudden apology with a blank expression. He was so strong, but Brain had been looking down on him as just a "turd."

I'm a fool. I'm just such a fool.

"By the way, you wouldn't happen to be the Brain Unglaus who once fought Sir Stronoff, would you?"

"…You know your stuff, huh? Were you watching the fight?"

"Oh no, I didn't see it. I just heard the story from someone who did. They said you were a fantastic swordsman, certainly one of the best in the kingdom. The way you carry yourself, your balanced movements, make me think it's the truth!"

With the pure goodwill weighing heavily on him, Brain stammered out a reply. "…Uhh…th-thank you. I—I don't think of myself like that at all, but to hear you praise me…makes me kind of happy."

"Hmm. Sir Unglaus—" began the old man.

"Sir, just Unglaus is fine. I'm not worthy of being treated with such respect by someone with such strength."

"Very well. My name is Sebas Tian, so please call me Sebas… Now then, would you mind instructing Climb here in swordsmanship? I think it would benefit you as well."

"Oh! Please excuse me! My name is Climb, Sir Unglaus."

"Sir—excuse me—Sebas, won't you be training him? It seemed like you were going to before I interrupted."

"Yes, I had intended to, but we have company, so I think I will deal with them—oh, here they are. It must have taken some time to arm themselves."

A moment later, Brain turned in the direction Sebas was looking.

Three men slowly showed themselves. They wore shirts of mail, and in their hands, protected by thick leather gloves, were their naked blades.

Their mood had already gone beyond hostile and was simply murderous. It was directed at the old man, but it didn't seem like they had a fraction of the mercy necessary to leave any witnesses alive.

Brain was shocked and shouted hoarsely in spite of himself. "Of all the ridiculous—! They felt that bloodlust and still want to come over here? Are they that strong?!"

If that were the case, they each had to be equal to—no, stronger than—Brain. Maybe the reason they were so bad at stealth was because they had specialized so intensely in warrior abilities.

But Sebas dismissed all of Brain's worries. "I only directed that at you two."

"…Huh?" Brain knew he sounded like an idiot.

"For Climb, it was training. For you, it was to smoke you out, or I suppose to discourage you from fighting or taking a hostile stance, since I didn't know who you were and you refused to show yourself. I knew these men were enemies from the beginning, though, so I didn't direct any at them. It would have been problematic if they had gotten scared and run away."

Listening to Sebas's horrifying explanation, Brain gave up on being surprised. The ability to control that much power to exclude targets transcended common sense.

"I—I see. Then you know who they are?"

"I have a guess, but there's no conclusive evidence. So I'm thinking to capture one or two and get some intelligence out of them; however—" Sebas lowered his head. "I do not wish to involve you in these matters. Could I ask you to please get away from here immediately?"

"Before that, I'd like to ask you something. Are they…criminals?" Climb asked.

"…They sure seem like it—the type with something to hide."

Brain's comment saw flames leap into Climb's eyes. "I don't mean to intrude, but I would also like to fight. As a keeper of the peace in the capital, it's only natural for me to protect the people."

It's not like we know that Sebas is representing justice, thought Brain. Sure, compared to the guys who had just shown up, anyone would think Sebas and his mien that practically screamed integrity were in the right, but there was no guarantee. *This kid's so green…*

But he knew how the boy felt.

Comparing a man who would protect a child from a bunch of drunks to these guys, Brain knew which side he would choose. "Not that I think you need reinforcements, Sebas, but I'll be damned if— Er, I mean I'll help out as well."

Brain stood next to Climb. Sebas didn't need assistance—really, there was no point for them to even be there. But Brain figured he would follow Climb's example and try fighting for someone else, choosing the option he wouldn't have taken before. He would protect the boy whose heart was strong but whose skill with the sword wasn't enough to match it.

Brain peered at the weapons the men were holding and furrowed his brow. "They're poisoned…? If they're using something they could end up hurting themselves with, they must have some experience… Could they be assassins?"

The grooved daggers, called mail breakers, glistened with some kind of slimy, abnormal liquid in the depressions. What affirmed Brain's murmured hypothesis were their nimble movements, which prioritized mobility more than a swordsman's would.

"Climb, be careful. Unless you have a magic item that will protect you from poison, consider even a single hit bad news." When one's physical ability was at Brain's level, it was normal to have built up a resistance to the most common poisons, but Climb probably wouldn't be able to withstand anything very potent.

"The reason they're facing us head-on but not immediately attacking is because they're waiting for the other two to flank us, correct? If we have the chance, why don't we just break straight through?" Sebas had purposely spoken just loud enough for their opponents to overhear, and they froze for a moment. They were startled that he'd seen through their plan to surround them.

"That seems like the safest move. It's probably even safer to crush the vanguard first and then take on the ones behind." Brain affirmed Sebas's idea, but then Sebas himself shot it down.

"Oh, but they'd run away if we did that. I'll take the three in front, so could you take on the two coming around?"

Brain confirmed, and Climb nodded yes. This was Sebas's battle. They were just forcing him to allow them to help. Unless Sebas was about to make a fatal error, their role was to act in accordance with his plan.

"Okay, let's go!" Brain told Climb, turning away from the men. He was able to show his open back to the hostile enemies because Sebas was there. Letting Sebas cover him gave him peace of mind, like the protection of a thick castle wall.

"Now then, unfortunately for you gentlemen, I'll be your opponent. Oh, but please don't get distracted by these two."

Brain looked over his shoulder and saw three daggers between the ringed fingers of Sebas's right hand. When he spread his fingers, the daggers the men had thrown at the defenseless Brain and Climb fell to the ground.

The men's will to fight shrank visibly.

No kidding. Anyone would lose the motivation to fight after watching their daggers get caught. Did you finally figure out how strong Sebas is? But it's too late now…

They wouldn't be able to escape this old man, even if they scattered.

"Amazing." Climb moved in line with Brain.

"Yeah. If someone said Sebas was the strongest in the kingdom, I would agree."

"Even stronger than the captain of the Royal Select?"

"Stronoff? Yeah, to be frank, if Gazef and I took Sebas on two to one, we'd still have no chance—oh, here they come."

Two men appeared and circled around the outside. As could be expected, they looked much like the other three. At the sound of a sword being drawn next to him, Brain followed suit.

"The reason one of them isn't hiding in the shadows throwing daggers must be because Sebas was onto them."

An ambush was effective because it was hidden. If it was revealed, all it did was diffuse their muscle. They must have figured that since they'd already been discovered, they had a better chance of victory if they each took one man.

"They have no idea... Climb, I'll take the one on the right. You take the left," he instructed the boy after judging which of their opponents was weaker from his movements. Climb nodded and assumed a stance. His unhesitating manner was that of someone who had been in a life-threatening skirmish before. Brain was relieved he wasn't a battle virgin who had done only training exercises.

Climb should be able to win against this guy...but considering the enemy's coming with poison, it might be a pretty close shave.

Even if Climb had experience in actual combat, Brain couldn't imagine that he had walked a bloody gauntlet that included frequent battles against poisoned weapons. *It might even be his first time.*

Even Brain was overly cautious against monsters who used corrosive acids or deadly poisons. It made it hard to fight at his full potential.

Should I kill this guy right away...and support Climb? Would that actually be good for him? Or would it just mess up his effort to help Sebas? Should I step in and fight for him? No...if it came to that, Sebas would probably save him. If Sebas doesn't seem like he's coming, then should I intervene? I never thought I'd worry about stuff like this...

Brain gave his head a self-conscious scratch with his free hand and stared down his opponent.

"Okay. You're gonna be a human sacrifice to make up for lost time."

Three blows.

Sebas charged, and before the men could react, much less defend, he'd thrown three punches. That was the end of it.

Of course it was. Among all of Nazarick, Sebas was the most skilled in battle, so he could defeat this level of assassin with his pinkie finger. He shifted his eyes from the men crumpling to the ground unconscious, limp like octopuses, and checked on the fight behind him.

Brain was keeping constant pressure on his opponent, so he didn't have to worry about him. The assassin fighting him seemed to be searching for an opportunity to run away, but Brain wouldn't let him, like he was toying with him. No, rather than that, it seemed to Sebas like Brain was trying to remove his own rustiness by testing out various attacks.

Come to think of it, I did hear something about making up for lost time. And he must seem a little distracted because he's worried about Climb and wants to be in a position to help him right away if need be. He appears to be a fairly good person.

Sebas turned from Brain to Climb. *Well, he's probably all right.*

It was an unstable exchange of offense and defense. He was a little concerned about the poison weapon, but it didn't seem like he needed to jump in and save him immediately. It pained him to involve kind people in his problems. But—

If he hadn't told me he wanted to get stronger, I would save him… Real combat is good training. I'll step in if it comes to that.

Sebas stroked his beard as he watched over Climb's fight.

Climb parried a stab with his sword.

His back was drenched with cold sweat. A moment too late and his armor would have been punctured. For a split second, he saw discouragement on his opponent's callous features.

Climb thrust with his sword to put some space between them, but his opponent's quick steps back and forth didn't let him. Climb generally fought by blocking with a shield and then attacking with his sword, so using just a sword was a mentally and physically taxing experience. The poison-drenched blade was also a major source of stress. Since a mail breaker was a stabbing weapon, he knew quite well that he had to worry about only thrusts, but still, the idea that he couldn't get so much as a scratch made his movements more conservative.

He reined in his erratic breathing, a product of his general exhaustion. *He's panting, too. I'm not the only one who's tired.* His opponent's forehead was also slick with sweat. He kept Climb at his mercy with his agile, assassin-like fighting style. That was why if Climb could injure at least one of his limbs, his advantage would be obliterated, and the balance in their abilities would be disrupted.

One blow would decide the battle.

That fact was the true nature of the tension between them. Of course, that's how it always was in a clash between equal powers, but it was magnified in this encounter.

"*Shi!*" With a sharp exhalation, Climb struck. It was a small swing without too much power behind it. He was worried about the potential opening a larger swing would create if its target dodged.

The assassin, who easily avoided the swing, put his hand in his breast pocket. Climb, anticipating the assassin's next attack, kept a close eye on that hand.

When the dagger shot toward him, Climb batted it away with his sword.

He'd been lucky. He'd been able to repel it because he was paying such close attention.

But before he could even sigh in relief, the assassin launched himself, gliding toward him in a low posture.

Crap!

A chill went up his spine.

He had no way to defend against this follow-up. He'd swung too widely when he'd batted away the dagger, perhaps because he was frightened. Since his sword was still in the follow-through, he'd never get it back in time to attack. He wanted to devote all his energy to evading, but the assassin was too quick.

He was cornered. At least he could use his arm as a shield—

Climb had made up his mind when the assassin in front of him suddenly put a hand to his face and leaped aside.

A pebble no bigger than a bean had nailed him right above his left eyelid. Climb had been able to see it with his enhanced consciousness in these extreme circumstances.

He knew even without turning around who had thrown it. As proof, he heard Sebas's voice. "Fear is an important emotion, but you can't let it constrain you. I've been watching for a while, and you're fighting too monotonously. You're not putting enough into it. If you were really going to sacrifice an arm, you would have died. If you're losing on the physical side, then please win with your spirit. Sometimes the mind surpasses the flesh!"

Yes, sir, Climb answered in his head and was surprised to find himself feeling calmer. It wasn't the entirely dependent relief of being rescued but the comfort of having someone watching over him.

He couldn't entirely shake the fear that he might be killed. And yet.

"If...if I die, please tell Princess Renner—tell the princess that I fought bravely."

He let out a long breath and slowly brought his sword back up.

Climb sensed a different kind of light in the assassin's eyes. It had been only a short while, but had they come to understand each other as they risked their lives in this battle?

His opponent, who sensed Climb's determination, also made his own decision.

The assassin charged. It was only natural, but he closed the distance between them in an instant, without a word.

Once his opponent had come into range, Climb brought his sword down. That instant, the assassin jumped back. He'd read the speed of Climb's swing and used himself as a lure to pull off a feint.

But he'd overlooked one thing.

Maybe he'd seen through most of Climb's sword techniques, except one. The one move that Climb had confidence in, his overhead swing, was faster and harder than all his others.

The sword came down on the assassin's shoulder, but the mail shirt stopped it from cutting off his arm. However, it easily snapped the man's clavicle, tearing through his flesh and breaking his scapula.

The assassin flipped as he fell to the ground. He was in so much pain he was drooling, and he let out a soundless howl.

"Magnificent."

Sebas approached from behind Climb and casually kicked the assassin in the stomach.

That was enough for him to go limp, like a doll. He'd probably lost consciousness.

In the corner of his eye, Climb could see Brain, who had already defeated his assassin, raising his hands to celebrate for him.

"Very well, now we'll begin questioning them. If you have anything you'd like to ask, please don't hesitate."

Sebas dragged one of them over and jolted him back to consciousness. Then he put a hand on his forehead.

It took less than two seconds. He didn't even push very hard, but the man's head bent way back and returned like a pendulum.

And with that, the man's eyes had changed. Now they were unfocused, like a drunk's.

Sebas began the inquiry. The assassin, who should have known how to keep his mouth shut, blabbed everything.

Climb found the scene so strange that he asked, "What did you do to him?"

"It's a skill called Puppet Palm... I'm glad it worked."

It was a move Climb had never heard of, but he was more concerned about the leaked information itself.

He was an assassin trained by one of the Six Arms, the strongest members of the Eight Fingers security division, and he had been tailing Sebas in order to kill him.

Brain turned to Climb. "...I don't know much about the Eight Fingers, but they're a pretty big criminal organization, right? They must have some mercenary connections..."

"Yes, that's right. And the Six Arms is a name for the strongest members of the group. I remember hearing that each of them is equal to adamantite rank. I don't know who they all are, of course, since it's an underworld matter."

Apparently, Succuronte, who had shown up at the mansion where Sebas served, was one of the Six Arms and had the nickname "Illusion Maniac." His plan had been to kill Sebas and take his beautiful master back with him to do with her what he wished.

Having heard that much of the man's story, Climb was assailed by chills. The source was Sebas.

He stood up slowly, and Brain asked, "What are you going to do, Sebas?"

"Now I know exactly what to do. First, I'll go get rid of the place at the root of all these problems. He said Succuronte is there, too. It makes sense to brush away the sparks before there's a fire."

His resolute answer made Climb and Brain catch their breaths. If he was going to raid the place, that meant he was confident he could win against people with adamantite-rank ability—the pinnacle of human strength.

Of course, it made sense.

He made swift work of those three assassins even though they were so tough, and Sir Unglaus respects him. Who in the world could Sir Sebas be? Maybe a former adamantite adventurer?

"…And he also said there are still others held captive. We should probably act as soon as possible."

"Aha. If the assassins don't return, they'll know something is amiss, and we won't be able to save the captives if they relocate them," Sebas commented.

Letting time pass would put him at a disadvantage and give his opponents the upper hand. That was Sebas's predicament.

"Okay, my plan is to march in there now. I'm terribly sorry, but I don't intend to change my mind. If you two would please drag these two to a guardhouse…"

"Please wait, Sebas! If it's all right with you, I'd like to go along and teach these bastar—guys a lesson. Only if it's all right with you, of course."

"Me, too. As one who attends Princess Renner, it's a matter of course for me to keep the peace. If any of this country's people are suffering, I'll rescue them with this sword."

"…Unglaus may be able to handle it, but I think it might be a bit dangerous for you."

"I know it'll be dangerous."

"Climb…I think he means you'll be in the way. Well, from Sebas's point of view, we might both be in the way, but…"

"No, no, I didn't mean it like that. I'm just worried about you. I don't want you to be misled into believing I would be able to protect you like I did before."

"I understand."

"You and your master may not get any credit for what we're about to do, you know. There is most likely a more suitable place for you to risk your life."

"Averting my eyes from injustice because it's dangerous would make me a worthless man unfit to serve my master. As much as I can, I would like to reach out my hand and aid those who suffer the way she does." *The way she reached out to me…*

At Climb's steely resolution, Sebas and Brain looked at each other.

"…So you've made up your mind, then."

Climb responded to Sebas with a single nod.

"I see. Then I will say no more. Both of you, please lend me your strength."

Chapter 5   Extinguished Embers, Flying Sparks

Chapter 5 | Extinguished Embers, Flying Sparks

1

3 *Late Fire Moon* (September) 12:07 PM

"The place is behind this door. According to the assassins, there's also an entrance in that building over there." Standing in front of the brothel, near the same door Tsuare had been thrown out of, Sebas pointed to a structure a few doors down. Brain and Climb had been there when he'd acquired the information from the assassin, but they had never been to the brothel before, so they listened deferentially to his explanation.

"Yes, he did say that. This entrance could serve as an escape route, and they have at least two people guarding it. Maybe we should split into two teams. What if you handle the front on your own and Climb and I attack from over there?"

"I have nothing against that. What do you think, Climb?"

"No objections here, either. But Sir Unglaus, what will we do when we get inside? Search together?"

"I'd really like you to start calling me Brain. Sebas, I'd be happy if you'd do the same. As for your question…really, it'd be safer to go together, but we need to search the building as fast as we can while Sebas is keeping them occupied with the head-on attack. There might be secret passageways the assassins didn't know about." Then he softly added, "Sometimes there are hidden corridors that only the leaders know about," as if he was remembering something.

"So you mean we should split up inside?"

"...If we're going in there with an understanding of the danger, we should probably operate in a way that will give us the best results."

Sebas and Climb nodded at Brain's remark.

"Then since you're stronger than me, Sir Un— Brain, do you mind if I ask that you do the search?"

"That sounds good. I'll have you camp at the exit."

Naturally, there was more danger awaiting the one who searched inside the building because of the higher chance he would encounter an enemy. Since Brain's strength far surpassed Climb's, it made sense for him to do it.

"Then we're all set for our final preparations, right?" Sebas asked.

They had discussed a rough strategy on the way over, but there had been certain things they couldn't decide without seeing the place. Now that they'd decided, there were no objections.

Sebas took a step forward toward the thick metal door. Climb would never be able to open it, but before Sebas, it looked as flimsy as a piece of paper.

Only a single man was going to assault the front gate, the most highly guarded area, but there was no need to worry—the one attacking was said by Brain Unglaus to be stronger than him and Gazef Stronoff put together. The only word to describe him was *exceptional*.

"Okay, then. Let's go. For that entrance, according to what the man said, the sign that you're friendly is four knocks in a row. Not that I think you've forgotten it but just in case."

"Thank you." He hadn't forgotten, but Climb thanked Sebas.

"Then I'll be taking prisoners to the extent possible, but if I meet resistance, I'm planning to kill without mercy. Are there any problems with that?"

Sebas was smiling kindly, but Climb's and Brain's spines both froze.

It was an utterly normal approach to the situation, not wrong in any way. They both thought they'd do the same under similar circumstances. What sent the fear creeping up their backs was the sense that Sebas had a dual personality.

An extremely tender gentleman and a hard-boiled warrior... Extremes of both generosity and heartlessness coexisted within him.

If they let him go in without comment, it was possible he'd kill every last person in the place.

Climb nervously addressed him. "We should try to keep needless loss of life to a minimum. We're outnumbered, so some casualties can't be helped, but if there is anyone who seems like one of the Eight Fingers executives, could you please do everything you can to restrain them? If we can catch and interrogate them, we can reduce the harm they can cause in the future."

"I'm no fan of murder. It's not as if I came here to kill everyone, so never you fear."

His gentle smile was a relief to Climb. "Then please excuse me. Shall we get going?"

•

"All right then. Let's annihilate them all at once here to buy some time."

If they crushed this brothel, the thugs would stop interfering with Sebas, at least temporarily. If they were lucky enough to get ahold of top-secret documents, the Eight Fingers might put so much effort into dealing with that, they could very well forget about Tsuare completely.

Worst case, Sebas would buy some time and create a chance for her to escape. Or he might find some better way to handle things.

"There was that kind merchant who reached out to me in E-Rantel. I wonder if I could enlist his help…" Even if Tsuare recovered mentally, she would still probably be happier if she had someone she could trust.

Sebas faced the thick iron door once more. Remembering how Tsuare had been tossed out here before, he touched the massive door of iron-plated wood. A glance was enough to tell that it wouldn't break down easily without some tools.

"I wonder if Climb will be all right." He didn't feel like he needed to worry about Brain Unglaus. Even if Brain fought Succuronte, Sebas felt he had a good chance of winning. But not Climb. Climb had next to none.

He was the one who offered his cooperation in storming the brothel, so he was surely ready for whatever would happen. Still, Sebas thought that losing his good, young life would be a waste.

"I'd like that sort of boy to live a long life…" He voiced a thought appropriate to one who had lived a long time himself. Of course, Sebas had been created elderly, so if one counted the time between his creation and the present, he would actually be younger than Climb.

"I suppose it would be much better for me to be the one to dispose of Succuronte. I hope they don't run into him." Sebas prayed to the Forty-One Supreme Beings for Climb's safety.

If Succuronte was the strongest power in this facility, there was a good chance he would attack Sebas, but if he was acting as someone's bodyguard, he might focus on protecting his charge while trying to escape.

Feeling a bit anxious, Sebas grabbed the knob and turned.

It moved a little, and then his hand stopped. Of course the door of an establishment like this would be locked.

"I'm not very good at picking locks… No way around it. I'll have to pick it my way," Sebas murmured with chagrin and lowered his hips. He drew his right hand back, formed a striking edge with it, and held his left hand forward. It was a collected posture with a core as solid as the trunk of a thousand-year cedar.

"Hup!"

What happened next seemed impossible.

His arm pierced through the iron door—through a hinge, at that. No, that still wasn't all. It thrust farther and farther in, scraping along the wood and metal.

The hinge gave a scream and bid farewell to the wall.

Sebas casually opened the door that had lost all means of resistance.

"What! …The hell?!" Inside was a hallway, and at the end of it, a large bearded man stood outside a half-open door, stupid, wide-eyed, and agape.

"It was rusty, so I took the liberty of using a bit of force to open it. I recommend oiling your hinges," Sebas addressed the man as he closed the door. Well, it would probably be more accurate to say he stood it against the frame.

As the man stood there completely stunned, Sebas moved unreservedly into the building.

"Hey, what's going on?"

"What was that noise?"

From behind the man came other male voices.

But the one looking straight at Sebas didn't respond and addressed the terrifying visitor instead. "Uh...w-welcome?" The utterly bewildered man watched in a daze as Sebas approached him. As an employee in this sort of place, he was probably used to violence. Still, what he just witnessed was beyond the common sense he'd lived with his whole life.

Ignoring his allies' questions, he smiled in an effort to appeal to Sebas. His survival instincts seemed to convince him that flattery would get him furthest. Or perhaps he was desperately trying to assure himself that Sebas was a butler in the service of one of their customers.

The bearded man, cheeks twitching as he forced a grin, was not a pretty sight.

Sebas smiled. It was a kind, gentle expression, but his eyes contained not the slightest hint of goodwill. Their glint was more like the mysterious, bewitching sparkle of a sword.

"Could you move, please?"

Ba-boom. Or maybe, *guh-bang.* A stomach-turning sound.

The robust, fully armed, grown man probably weighed a good 180 pounds. He flew to the side, spinning comically through the air at a speed human eyes could barely register. Then his body smashed into the wall with an impressive watery splat.

The building shook as if it had been pounded by a gigantic fist.

"...Shoot. If I had killed him a bit farther in, he would have made a good barricade. Well, it seems there are others in the back. I'll just be more careful from here on out."

Telling himself he'd better hold back, Sebas stepped around the corpse and continued down the hall.

He opened the door wide, entered the room, and scanned it with elegance. He acted less like he was invading enemy territory and more like he was taking a stroll through an empty house.

Inside were two men.

They were staring speechlessly at the crimson blossom staining the side of the hallway behind him.

It took but a moment for the reek of organs, their contents, and blood to mix with the room's smell of cheap booze one would never find in Nazarick and create a nauseatingly unpleasant aroma.

Sebas consolidated the information he'd gathered from Tsuare and the assassins and tried to recall the layout of the building. Tsuare's memories were in pieces, and she didn't remember much, but she did say the real brothel was underground. The assassins had never been below, so their information wouldn't help him past this point.

He looked at the floor, but he couldn't find the stairs leading down. Perhaps they were ingeniously hidden?

If he couldn't find them himself, he simply needed to ask someone who knew.

"Excuse me. I have a question…"

"Eegh!" One of the men he'd addressed shrieked hoarsely, suggesting the option to fight was already out of his mind. That put Sebas at ease. It seemed like whenever he remembered Tsuare he couldn't hold himself back and ended up doling out instant death.

If they didn't want to fight, breaking both their legs would be plenty.

The trembling men pressed themselves against the wall, trying to get even a little farther away from Sebas. Eyeing them emotionlessly, Sebas smiled with just his lips.

"Eegh!"

Their terror intensified. The smell of ammonia filled the room.

I guess I scared them a little too much. Sebas frowned.

One of the men's eyes rolled, and he crumpled to the ground. The extreme stress had caused him to lose consciousness. The other man looked enviously down at him.

Sebas sighed. "I mentioned I had a question... Actually, I have some business down below. Could you tell me how to get there?"

"...Th-that's..."

Sebas saw the fear in the man's eyes as he hesitated to betray the organization. The assassins had been the same way. It seemed they were afraid of being ejected from the organization. Recalling the behavior of the first man he'd met, the runaway he'd given money, Sebas figured that must mean death.

As the man faltered (Should he say it? Should he not?), Sebas ended his hesitation with a single remark. "There are two mouths here—I don't necessarily have to hear it from yours."

The man's forehead oozed sweat, and he shuddered. "I-i-i-it's over there! There's a trapdoor!"

"Over there?" Now that he knew, he saw scuffs on the floor in the area. "Aha. I thank you. And now your role is done." Sebas smiled, and the man intuited the meaning behind his words. He turned pale and shivered.

Still, he harbored a tiny flame of hope and put it into words. "P-please... don't k-kill me!"

"That won't do."

The room froze at the immediate reply. The man's eyes bulged—the human expression of denial in the face of something unbelievable.

"But I talked, didn't I? C'mon, I'll do anything—just spare me!"

"That's true, but..." Sebas let out a breath that was part sigh and shook his head. "...No."

"You...gotta be kidding me!"

"You can believe I'm joking if you like, but there is only one outcome here."

"...Oh gods..."

Sebas remembered how Tsuare had been when he found her, and his eyes narrowed slightly.

There was no way someone who had contributed to something so horrible had the right to make entreaties to the gods. And to Sebas, the Forty-One Supreme Beings were the gods. He felt like it was an insult to them.

"You reap what you sow." With those words of steel, which cut off the discussion, the man sensed his impending death.

Run? Fight? The moment the choice was thrust upon him, the man unhesitatingly elected to flee.

He knew what would happen if he fought Sebas. If he ran, he had at least a sliver of a possibility of surviving. He was right to act as he did with those calculations, because as a result, his life span lasted a few seconds—no, a few fractions of a second—longer.

He darted for the door, but Sebas caught up to him in an instant and lightly spun him around. A gust of wind rushed around the man's head, and his body collapsed like a rag doll. A sphere whapped against the wall, leaving a bloody splotch, and bounced to the floor.

A beat later, the man's headless neck began flooding the ground with blood.

It was the technique of a god. The roundhouse aimed specifically at the man's head and its unbelievable speed and power were awe-inspiring enough on their own, but the most horrifying part was that the shoe on the foot he'd kicked with remained spotless.

Heels clicking, he approached the man who had fainted and brought a foot down on him. Together with a sound like a dead tree snapping, his body convulsed. After several spasms, it stopped moving completely.

"If you think back on your actions up until now, it was only logical that this would happen, don't you think? But take peace of mind from the fact that you've compensated with your life."

Sebas went to collect the corpses. The bodies were mutilated in ways too horrible to behold, so by lining them up by the stairs, he could scare anyone trying to escape this way and make them think twice. That was the deterrent Sebas had thought up for the case where he wasn't able to destroy the entrance.

After placing the corpses, Sebas stomped the trapdoor.

With the sound of metal fittings breaking, the floor opened up. The broken door made an unexpected racket bouncing and sliding down the sturdily built stairs.

"I see… If I destroy these stairs, then it will be impossible for anyone to escape this way."

•

It wasn't a very big room.

The sparsely furnished space contained a wardrobe and a bed, nothing more.

The bed wasn't a humble affair of straw with a sheet over it but a cotton-stuffed mattress. The frame was well-made, like something a noble might use. But, favoring function over form, it had no decorative elements whatsoever.

On top of it sat a naked man.

He was likely long past middle age. His indolent physique was perhaps the aftermath of an insatiable appetite. Although his face might have been nearly average, it lost a dramatic number of points for the sagging excess flesh on top of it. Anyone who saw him would describe him as a pig-like man. Pigs are by nature clever, charming animals who love beauty. But the image of the pig in this case was the basis of the word's more insulting meaning—dim-witted, greedy, and unsanitary besides.

His name was Staffan Heivish.

He pounded his raised fist down toward the mattress.

The sound of flesh on flesh followed.

An expression of delight appeared on Staffan's sagging face. Along with the sensation of the body warping under his hand, he felt something pleasurable creep up his spine. He shivered.

"Ooh…"

There was sticky red blood clinging to his fist as he slowly brought it up.

Staffan was on top of a naked woman.

Her face was hugely swollen, and here and there, the skin was mottled from internal bleeding. Her nose was crushed, and the blood that had run from it had coagulated there. Her lips and eyelids were seriously inflamed, and her once-pleasing features were now nowhere to be seen. The signs of internal bleeding on her body were not so bad compared to her face. The sheets around the pair were also discolored with blood.

Up until a little while ago, the woman had been desperately holding up her arms to shield her face, but they now flopped limply on the bed. The way her hair was spread out over the sheets made it look like she was floating in water.

"Hey! What's wrong? Done already? Huh?"

It didn't seem like she could possibly be conscious.

Staffan raised his fist and brought it down.

He slammed it into her cheek and the bone beneath it, and pain shot through his hand.

He grimaced.

"Tch! That hurt, bitch!"

In his anger, he hit her again.

The bed creaked, and there was a splorting noise. The woman's skin, swollen like a ball, had popped, and he got blood on his fist. Fresh, thick red blood spattered the sheets, dyeing them crimson.

"…Urgh." The woman no longer moved even when she was struck, and her body barely responded.

This was enough beating to be life-threatening. The reason she was still alive was not because Staffan was going easy on her; it was because the mattress was absorbing some of the shock. If she had been taking these blows on the hard floor, she probably would have died already.

But Staffan wasn't hitting with all his strength because he knew about the effects of the mattress—it was because he knew that even if the woman died, it was not a problem. If he paid a certain amount for the disposal fee, the matter would be considered settled.

In fact, he'd already beaten several women to death at this establishment.

It was possible that thanks to the dent in his pocketbook from those accumulating disposal fees, Staffan might have been unconsciously holding back a little, after all.

Gazing at the woman's body, which didn't so much as twitch, he licked his lips.

This brothel was the best place to satisfy special kinks. In a normal brothel, this sort of thing would never be allowed. Well, maybe it would have been, but Staffan didn't know.

It had been great when there were slaves.

Slaves were assets, so there was a tendency to view those who used them roughly with disdain, in the same way that people earned contempt for spending their fortunes in showy, wasteful ways.

But for Staffan and others with peculiar fetishes, slaves were the quickest way to satisfy their lust. With that avenue taken from him, all Staffan could do was come to a place like this for relief. What would have become of him if he hadn't found out about this?

Unable to bear the desire, he probably would have committed a crime and been imprisoned.

He couldn't thank the noble—his master—enough for introducing him to this brothel. Although in exchange, he had to use his authority to do his master's illicit biddings.

"I'm grateful to you, master."

There was a calm in his eyes. It might have been hard to believe considering his fetish and personality, but toward his master, and only his master, he was truly, deeply grateful.

But...

A flame steadily grew in the pit of his stomach—fury.

The emotion he felt toward the woman responsible for the loss of slaves as an outlet for his desire.

"That little bitch!" His face flushed with rage, and his eyes took on a bloody tinge.

He saw the face of the princess he was supposed to be serving superimposed over the woman he was straddling. He concentrated the irritation building inside him in his fist and hit her.

With the sound of flesh being pounded, fresh blood went flying.

"I wonder how amazing it would feel to crush *her* face..."

He punched the woman's face again and again.

Perhaps it was due to a cut inside her mouth from the impact of his fist on a tooth, but a surprising amount of blood suddenly flooded out of her burst lip.

Now she only twitched when he hit her.

"Phew…" After the flurry of punches, Staffan's chest was heaving. His forehead and body were covered in an oily sheen of sweat.

Staffan looked down at the woman beneath him. She'd gone past looking awful, even half-dead, and was a few steps away from lifeless. She was a puppet with broken strings.

Staffan swallowed audibly.

Nothing aroused him as much as sex with a woman beaten ragged. The more beautiful she was before the beating, the better. Nothing satisfied his sadistic hunger more than destroying beauty.

"How great would it feel to do this to *her?*"

He remembered the haughty face of the mistress of the house he visited earlier. She had a beauty equal to that of the princess, and the princess was said to be the loveliest woman in all the kingdom.

Of course, he knew he'd never get to do anything with a woman like that. The only women who would satisfy his fetish were the ones who had fallen far enough in life to end up in this brothel and were one step from being thrown away.

For a woman that gorgeous, one hell of a noble would have to spend one hell of a fortune to buy her and keep her locked up in his domain so word of the sale wouldn't get out.

"I'd like to hit a woman like that someday…beat her to death."

How fun, how satisfying that would be.

Needless to say, it was an impossible dream.

He glanced at the woman beneath him. Her bare breast was moving faintly up and down. Confirming that, he curled his lips into a nasty smile.

He clutched at her breasts, and they deformed to extremes under his grip.

She didn't react at all. She was no longer in a state where she could register even such excessive pain. The only difference between the woman beneath him and a doll at this point was that she was soft.

But Staffan found this lack of resistance ever so slightly dissatisfying.

Help.
Forgive me.
I'm sorry.
Oh, stop.

He heard the woman's cries again in the back of his mind.
Should I have fucked her while she was still screaming?
Feeling a hint of regret, Staffan continued kneading her chest.

Most of the women who ended up in this brothel were mentally absent, their spirits broken. Considering that, he could say the woman he'd been with today had been on the normal side.

"Was she like that, too?"

The woman he recalled was Tsuare. He didn't want to know what fate the man who'd let her get away had met.

But he couldn't hold back the sneer that came over his face when he thought of the butler he'd met at that mansion earlier.

The woman had been fucked by any number of men, possibly even some women and nonhumans—how could she possibly be worth protecting? It was all he could do to not burst out laughing at how that butler had seemed ready to shell out several hundred gold pieces for her.

"Now that I think of it, that runaway screamed nicely, too." He sifted through his memories and recalled her shrieks. Yes, she'd been fairly normal for someone he'd been with at this brothel.

Staffan grinned and moved to satisfy his animal desire. He grabbed the women's legs and spread them wide. He could see the bones in them, they were so thin, and his hands could wrap completely around them.

He shifted himself into the space of her gaping nether regions.

Then he grasped his member, now hard with desire, and—

He heard a *click*, and the door slowly opened.

"—The hell?!" When Staffan looked toward the door, there was an old man he'd seen somewhere before. He realized immediately who it was: the butler from that mansion.

The old man—Sebas—strode casually into the room, his steps clicking against the floor. His movements were so natural Staffan was speechless.

What is the butler from that mansion doing here? Why is he coming into this room? Faced with a situation he could not account for, his mind went blank.

Sebas stood next to Staffan. After glancing at the woman beneath him, he fixed him with a cold gaze.

"You like hitting?"

"Huh?!"

The strange atmosphere compelled Staffan to stand up and move to grab his clothes.

But Sebas went into action faster than he could.

There was a *smack*, and Staffan's field of vision lurched violently.

A beat later he felt his right cheek growing hot as a throbbing pain spread across it.

He'd been hit—no, in this case *slapped* was the word—he finally realized.

"You pastarrrd. You think you can—"

The smack against his cheek rang out again. And it didn't stop.

Left, right, left, right, left, right, left, right…

"Zdap it!"

Staffan was used to hitting, not being hit, and tears formed in the corners of his eyes.

He brought both hands up to guard his face as he retreated.

Both his cheeks were flushed with stinging pain.

"You pasdawd! You zink you can ged away wizzis?"

Talking made his red, swollen cheeks hurt.

"I can't?"

"Of couwse nod! You idiod! Do you know phoo I am?"

"Merely a fool."

Easily closing the distance Staffan had created, Sebas created the same sound from his cheek. *Smack!*

"Sdap it! Pleazsdap!"

Staffan shielded his cheeks like a child being beaten by a parent.

He liked violence, but the people he'd been hitting had always been helpless. Sebas may have looked like an old man, but Staffan was too scared to hit him. He couldn't strike anyone unless he was absolutely sure they wouldn't strike back.

Perhaps having inferred as much, Sebas seemed to lose interest in him and turned to the woman.

"This is simply awful…"

Staffan slipped past Sebas as he stood next to the woman.

"Idiod!"

His mind was feverish. *What a foolish old man.*

I'll call everyone in this building, and they'll teach him a lesson. He's not going to get off easy after doing all this to me. I'll give him a good dose of fear and suffering.

In the back of his mind was the butler's master, that beautiful woman.

A subordinate's failure is the master's responsibility. I'll have both master and servant take responsibility for this pain. I'll make them understand exactly who he hit!

His flabby stomach jiggled up and down as he jumped out the door.

"Somepodyyy! Issomepody dewre?" he shouted at the top of his lungs.

If he screamed, some employee or another should have come immediately.

But that expectation was betrayed. He realized it when he went into the corridor.

It was completely silent.

Not a soul was there.

Staffan, stark naked, glanced around anxiously.

The peculiar atmosphere in the corridor—the silence—terrified him.

There were doors to either side, but it was only natural that no one would come out of those. The rooms of this establishment, for people with peculiar—or even dangerous—fetishes, were completely soundproof.

But there was no way the employees couldn't hear him.

When he'd been led to this room earlier, he'd seen a number of them. They were all hardy, well-built men who Sebas's old body would be no match for.

"Why awn't you coming?"

"Because they're either dead or unconscious," a quiet voice responded to Staffan's scream.

Flustered, he turned around and saw Sebas standing there with a calm expression.

"It seems like there are a few people in the back, but most of them are asleep."

"D-dad can'd be! Dewre's lods of people!"

"...There were three people who appeared to be employees upstairs. Ten downstairs. Then there were seven others like you."

What is this guy going on about? Staffan's expression asked as he stared at Sebas.

"In any case, there is no one in the vicinity who is able to come to your rescue. Even if the employees have regained consciousness, I crushed their legs and snapped their arms. All they can do is crawl around like inchworms."

Staffan's face registered his surprise. What Sebas was saying shouldn't have been possible, but the oddly quiet atmosphere in the building told him it was true.

"Now then, I don't feel any need to leave you alive. I'll have you die here."

He didn't draw a blade or hold up any other weapon, nothing like that. He approached silently at a leisurely pace. Those utterly normal movements frightened Staffan. It dawned on him that Sebas was serious about killing him.

"Waid! Waid! Led's megh a deal. You won'd wegwed id."

"It's hard to make out what you're saying. A deal I won't regret, you say? I see... I have no interest in that."

"Why awe you doing dis?"

There is no reason for this to be happening to me. Why should I have to be killed? Finally, Staffan's thoughts on the matter reached Sebas.

"...Think about the kinds of things you've done. Do you still not know?"

Staffan reflected on his behavior. *Have I done something wrong?*

Sebas sighed. "I see." As the words left his mouth, his front kick slammed into Staffan's abdomen. "So this is what being unworthy to live looks like."

Several of Staffan's internal organs burst, and an unbelievable amount of pain assailed him. Although one might have expected him to faint and die on the spot, he was somehow still dimly conscious.

It hurts!

It hurts!

It hurts!

He wanted to writhe around screaming, but the pain was so intense he couldn't move.

"Go on and die like that," a cold voice said to him.

He tried to shout, "Save me!" but his throat wouldn't move.

Sweat ran into his eyes, and his vision blurred. Through the haze, he saw Sebas walking away.

Save me!

Save me!

If it's money you want, I'll give it to you—just save me!

There was no longer anyone to respond to his voiceless pleas for help.

Slowly but eventually, Staffan died in the agonizing pain coming from his abdomen.

2

3 Late Fire Moon (September) 12:12 PM

"Climb, I'm going to kill the guys upstairs. We don't have anything to tie them up with, and if they call for help, it'll be a pain. We could knock them out, but as long as there's a chance they'll wake up, it's gonna be dangerous to take control of this place, since we know so little about it… What's wrong?"

"Oh, uh, it's nothing." Climb shook his head and cleared away his anxiety. His heart was pounding as if he'd been sprinting at full speed, but he did his best to ignore it. "Please excuse me. I'm all right now. I can go anytime."

"Are you sure? ...Mm, seems like you got your game face on. You'd been acting a little weird since we got here, but now you look like a warrior. I understand you're nervous. There are powerful enemies here who you can't beat as you are now. But don't worry—I'm here and so is Sebas. You focus on surviving—for the one who keeps you going."

Brain gave Climb a hard pat on the shoulder and, blade already in hand, knocked four times on the door.

Climb gripped his sword tightly.

They heard someone clomping over and the sound of locks turning. Three of them.

The moment the door began to open, Climb acted according to their plan and yanked it as hard as he could.

Brain rushed the man faster than he could raise a puzzled shout. Climb heard the sound of flesh being severed and the thudding of something crumpling to the ground.

He jumped in a moment later.

Ahead of him, Brain was cutting down their second opponent. There was one other man in the room, with a short sword and leather armor. Climb closed the distance between them in one swoop.

"Wha—?! What's with you, ya little shit?!" The man panicked and tried to stab Climb with his short sword, but Climb parried it easily. Then he brought his sword down from overhead in one swift motion.

The man tried to block it with his short blade, but it was certainly not going to take the weight of Climb's entire body in that heavy blow. Climb's sword knocked away his opponent's weapon, sliced into his shoulder, and came out near the base of his neck.

As the fallen man groaned in pain, a profusion of blood spread across the floor, so much that one might wonder where it had all come from. The body jerked and twitched before lying still in death.

Judging it to be a fatal blow, Climb kept his momentum and forged ahead into the room while still on guard. There were no enemies lurking to bring their swords down on him. He heard Brain racing up the stairs to the second floor behind him.

All that was in the room was commonplace furniture. After confirming that, Climb ran into the next room.

One minute later...

Having inspected their respective floors and determined there were no other enemies, Climb and Brain met up at the entrance.

"I took a look around the first floor, but I didn't get a sense anyone was there."

"The same for the second floor. There weren't even any beds, so no one spends the night here... There must be a secret passageway to the place where people sleep."

"Did you find it? I doubt it would be on the second floor, but..."

"Nah, I didn't see anything that looked like a trapdoor. But if what you said is right, then it's down here."

Climb and Brain exchanged glances and then examined the room.

Climb didn't have any thief skills, so he couldn't discover a hidden door by glancing around. If he'd had a fine powder like flour and some time to thoroughly search, he could have found the door by sprinkling it around and blowing. The powder would have collected in the door's crack and made it easier to find. But he didn't have any powder, and he didn't have any time to scatter it. So he took some magic items from his pochette.

They were small handbells he'd received from Gagaran of the Blue Roses. "It's dangerous to go adventuring without a thief, but sometimes you just have to. At times like those, having these will make a big difference," she'd said to him. He considered the pictures drawn on the outer surfaces of the three bells and chose the one he needed. It was called the Bell of Secret Door Detection.

As Brain watched him with intense interest, he rang it once. A clear tone audible to only the owner of the item echoed throughout the room.

Responding to the bell, one corner of the floor began to glow a pale blue. It blinked as if to say, *Here's the trapdoor.*

"Wow, that's a handy item. Everything I have is for making me stronger or to use in combat."

"Isn't that normal for a warrior, though?"

"A warrior..."

Climb moved away from Brain and his wry grin, remembered the location of the reaction, and took a spin around the rest of the room. The effect of the item's magic lasted only a set amount of time. He needed to investigate as thoroughly as possible before it wore off. He circled the area, but there was nothing besides the first spot.

All they had to do now was open the trapdoor and sneak inside, but Climb squinted at it. Then he sighed and took his bells back out.

This time he chose one with a different picture on it and rang it like the other one.

The tone was similar to the first's but different: the Bell of Trap Removal.

He was being very careful. Climb didn't have the ability to detect and disable traps, nor did he have any means to escape one were he to get caught. If they'd had a caster with them, they could treat him if he got hit with paralysis or poison, but he and Brain were only two warriors. Climb once heard that there was a martial art that granted temporary immunity to poison, but he didn't know it, and he didn't have an antidote. He had to consider himself out of commission if he got a bad status.

A case like that called for using a magic item without hesitation, even if it could be used only a limited number of times per day.

There came a heavy *clunk* from behind the trapdoor.

Climb stuck his sword in the door's gap and pried it open.

One big corner of the wooden floor came up and clapped down onto the other side. There was a crossbow attached to the underside of the door. The tip of its quarrel shone in the light, reflecting it in a strange way different from the way plain metal would.

Climb changed positions and stared at the crossbow.

A highly viscous liquid was slathered on the tip of the bolt. It was almost certainly poisoned.

If they had carelessly opened the door, they'd have been shot with poison.

Exhaling with a bit of relief, Climb tried to see if he could take the crossbow off the door. Unfortunately, it was attached pretty well, and he would have needed tools to remove it.

Giving up on that, he peered past the door.

A fairly steep staircase led down, but he couldn't see where, due to the angle. The stairs and their surroundings were solidly built out of stone.

"So what are you going to do? Wait here?"

"I'm not very good at indoor combat. If possible, I'd like to go down and take up a position in a more spacious area where it would be easier to fight, if there is one."

"In a one-on-one fight, it's to your advantage to wait at the top of the stairs, but if you end up fighting here, I might not be able to hear the commotion from farther down. And if reinforcements show up... Yeah, maybe we should skip that idea. Wanna go together, then?"

"Yes, please."

"I'll go in front. Follow me, but keep a little distance."

"Understood. And about that item I used to remove the trap, I can use it up to three times per day but not in a row. I have to leave thirty minutes before I can use it again, so we can't rely on it."

"Gotcha. We'll be as careful as possible. If you notice anything, let me know."

With that, Brain stepped down into the staircase. Climb followed behind him.

Brain descended step by step, tapping each one with his katana first, just in case. At the bottom of the stairs, the floor was well-laid with cobbles, and the walls were also fortified with stone.

Several feet ahead they could see a wooden door with iron reinforcements. Brain didn't really think there would be more than the crossbow booby-trapping this emergency escape route, but he'd heard too many stories about heavily armored warriors being rendered helpless by a single pitfall. He definitely had to avoid that.

It was only a short distance, but Brain took his time, stepping cautiously, to reach the door.

Climb stood by at the bottom of the stairs so he wouldn't get caught up in an accident if there was one.

First, Brain poked at the door with his sword. After a few times, he seemed to make up his mind, grabbed the doorknob…and turned it. Then he stopped moving.

Climb was worried something had happened when Brain turned around and said pathetically, "…It's locked."

Of course it was. It made sense for the door to be locked.

"Do you have any way to open it? If not, we can break it down, but…"

"I do, actually. One moment."

Climb rang the third handbell at the door.

They heard the faint noise of the latch opening by the power of the Bell of Unlocking.

Brain turned the knob and opened the door slightly to peek inside. "There's no one here. I'll go in first."

Climb entered after Brain.

It was a large room.

Around the edges along the walls were cages and wooden boxes big enough to fit a person inside. Was it a storage room? It seemed a little too big for what was there.

Across the room was a door without a lock. Climb strained his ears and heard some noises like a faraway commotion.

Brain turned around and asked Climb, "How about here? It fits the bill for space…but you might end up having to fight multiple enemies at once."

"If a group shows up, I'll open the entrance door and fight near the stairs."

"Okay. I'm gonna take a quick look and be right back. Don't die, Climb!"

"I won't. You be careful, too."

"Do you mind if I borrow those items?"

"Of course not. I'm sorry I didn't offer." Climb handed all three bells over to Brain, and Brain tucked them into a pouch on his belt.

Then with a proper warrior-like bravery on his face, Brain said, "Okay, I'm going in," and advanced deeper into the brothel.

Climb, on his own now, looked around the room. First, he checked to make sure there was no one hiding in the shadows of the wooden boxes and no secret passageways. It was only a warrior's search in the end, but it didn't seem like there were any hidden doors. Next, he examined the countless containers.

If possible, he wanted to acquire some information about other Eight Fingers facilities besides this one. If there were smuggled or otherwise illegal goods here, that would be great. Of course, a general search would be done after they'd occupied the building, but he figured he should investigate as well as he could on his own first.

There were large boxes and small ones, but he decided to approach the largest. It was probably almost seven feet to a side.

He inspected it to make sure it wasn't booby-trapped. Of course, like before, Climb had no searching abilities, so he couldn't even begin to pretend to be a thief.

He put his ear to the box and listened.

He didn't think anything was shut inside it, but there was no telling what could happen in an underworld place like this. It was possible they were smuggling some kind of animal.

Unsurprisingly, he didn't hear anything. Next, he moved to take off the lid.

It didn't open.

It wouldn't budge.

He scanned for something like a crowbar or a poker, but from his cursory investigation, it didn't seem like there were any tools like that in the room.

"Oh well…"

He tried the next box, which was about three feet to a side.

This one opened with no trouble. There were all sorts of clothes inside, from simple sack dresses to garments fit for the daughters of nobles.

"What's all this? Is there something hidden under all these clothes...? Doesn't look like it. Is it spare clothing? This is like a laborer's outfit, and here's a maid uniform... What the heck is this?"

Climb racked his brain, unable to figure out what all the clothes could be for. He picked up a piece, and it seemed utterly normal. If crime was involved in some way, the only thing he could think of was that they might be stolen, but that wasn't evidence that would let them take out the brothel.

Deciding to leave alone things he didn't understand, he moved on to the next box, which was as big as the first. Then a loud *bang* suddenly echoed throughout the room.

There was no way. He'd searched every corner and made sure there was no one. Then he came upon a realization: *What if someone using Invisibility was here from the very start?*

Climb shivered at the thought and whirled to face the direction the noise had come from—the unopened seven-foot box. One side was flush against the wall. The side opposite that had come off.

The exposed contents were not cargo but two men. In the back was a tunnel. What should have been a wall was actually a hole. The wooden box, of course, connected to a secret passageway.

Climb blinked furiously in genuine surprise as the two men came out.

An unpleasant sweat ran down his back.

One of the men fit Sebas's description perfectly. His name was Succuronte. He was their biggest obstacle in this infiltration mission as well as their prime candidate for capture.

One of the Six Arms, who were equivalent to adamantite-rank adventurers... Grasping a drawn blade, the enemy Climb had no chance of defeating narrowed his eyes and said, "We knew from Alarm there was an invader, so we came through the secret passageway specifically to not bump into them... I guess we should have made some other way out?"

"Well, there's nothing we can do about it now," the man behind him answered in a high-pitched voice.

"Hmm? I've seen this kid somewhere before."

"Considering our circumstances, I'm going to be angry if you tell me you slept with him."

"Oh, come on, Succuronte. That couldn't be it. But I do believe he's the little pet of the female who pisses me off more than any other in the world."

"Oh? So he serves the princess?"

Succuronte flicked his eyes over Climb from top to bottom as if he were lapping him up.

The eyes of the man behind him were filled with unsettling lust, but Succuronte was estimating Climb's strength as a warrior or, perhaps, like a snake, trying to judge whether this prey would fit in his mouth.

The man in back licked his lips and said to Succuronte, "I want to take him with us. What do you think?"

A chill went up Climb's spine, and he felt a twinge in his anus. *Ugh, this guy's...*

"It'll cost extra."

Disregarding Climb's mental screams, Succuronte turned to face him. There had never been any openings, but now Climb was beset by the feeling he was facing a solid fortress.

Succuronte took a purposeful stride forward.

Climb took a step back from the encroaching pressure.

Perhaps this was obvious, but a fight between two clearly different powers never lasted very long. Still, Climb would have to make it happen.

If I maintain a defensive posture and focus all my efforts on blocking, I should be able to buy time till one of the others gets here.

But there was something he had to do first.

He took a deep breath.

"Heeeeelp!!!" he screamed at the top of his lungs, using up every last bit of air inside them.

Winning the battle on his own was not victory. Victory meant capturing both these men. Or to put it another way, losing either of these powerful men and their presumably ample intelligence ultimately meant a loss.

So what reason could there be for hesitating to call for help?

Succuronte's face grew stern.

The scream gave his opponents an urgent need to finish the battle in a short amount of time. It was extremely likely that they'd pull out the big guns.

Climb continued observing their every movement.

"Coccodor, it seems it will be a bit troublesome to bring him with us. We need to settle this before he gets backup."

"Huh? You're one of the Six Arms, aren't you? You can't even knock out one little brat? The title 'Illusion Maniac' weeps!"

"Well, if you're going to put it that way… I'll do what I can, but please remember that as long as you escape, we win."

Climb continued to stare down Succuronte, trying to figure out why he was called Illusion Maniac. He wouldn't have a nickname that had nothing to do with his abilities. So if Climb could figure out the reason for the nickname, he might get a clue about what kind of abilities he could use. Unfortunately, there was nothing he could learn from his appearance or equipment.

He knew he was at a disadvantage, but he roared to encourage himself. "I'm protecting this door with my life! As long as I'm still standing, neither of you will leave this room!"

"We'll know if that's true or not soon enough—when you're shamefully flat on the floor."

Succuronte slowly brought his sword up.

Huh?! Climb did a double take—because the sword flickered. It wasn't some kind of trick. The strange phenomenon ended right away, but he definitely hadn't been seeing things.

It must be some kind of martial art…

Perhaps it had something to do with being an "illusion maniac." In that case, he was probably already using some kind of power. Climb wasn't off his guard, but he did need to bring it up a notch.

Succuronte charged, brandishing his sword overhead.

His technique didn't seem worthy of an adamantite-rank adventurer. It was a little sloppier than Climb's. Climb held his sword up to block, in line with the trajectory of the incoming blade, but a creeping sensation made him jump to the side.

Suddenly a sharp pain ran across his flank, and he was knocked back. "Kha! Guh!"

He staggered into the wall behind him. He didn't have time to figure out what had happened. Succuronte was already right in front of him.

He was raising his sword again like last time. Climb held his blade up to protect his head and did a diving roll to the left.

A sharp pain ran across his upper right arm.

Coming out of his nimble roll, he swung his sword behind him without bothering to look.

He sliced air.

Realizing there wouldn't be a follow-up attack, he held his right arm and turned around. Succuronte was running for the door that led to the stairs while keeping one eye on him. Climb ignored the man's attempt to open the door and instead focused on Coccodor. He had a hunch that this would be enough to stop Succuronte, who was responsible for Coccodor's security—and he was right.

Succuronte's hands stopped. He took up a position between Coccodor and Climb and clicked his tongue in frustration. Then he looked at the exit, Climb, and Coccodor in turn and grimaced. "We're trapped! You'll have to excuse me. I'm killing this boy here."

"You can't be serious! He'll be a great asset against that little bitch if we keep him alive."

"He tricked me. Taking up a position to protect the door, saying he'd protect it with his life...that was all part of his plan. This little brat...messed with my head!"

Yes! He bought it. So I guess they don't know what's going on outside this room. Now they can't run.

With only one escort, it was a bad plan to run while Climb was still alive and able to fight. And if Climb had friends upstairs, they'd be caught in between. For the same reason, Succuronte couldn't let Coccodor run on his own before finishing the boy off.

When Climb had immediately abandoned the door he would suppos-edly protect with his life and made a move toward Coccodor, Succuronte fell for the bluff. Now he was probably convinced someone was waiting on the other side to catch them in a pincer attack and capture Coccodor.

He had to have judged that the only way to escape safely was to take out Climb now. Of course, that was assuming he wasn't aware of conditions outside the room. If he knew the truth, he would open the door and run away.

Climb, having won his bet, raised his sword against Succuronte's growing desire to kill. "Ngh!" He had to bear the pain in his side and right upper arm. He might have had a few broken bones, but he was lucky he could still move. No, if that pervert weren't lusting after him, he probably would have been killed. Wearing a mail shirt wasn't enough to completely block a slice.

But what is that attack, anyway? Is he swinging again really fast? I don't think that's it, but then what could it be? Gazef's face flickered across the back of Climb's mind.

Gazef Stronoff's original martial art, Sixfold Slash of Light, was six attacks at once. So was this some lesser version of that, like a Twofold Slash of Light?

But in that case, Succuronte's art was a weird one where the first attack was normal speed and the second was superfast.

It doesn't match up. If I can figure out what kind of attack it is, I should be able to do something about it... All I know is that a defensive battle is not going to go very well. Guess I should attack?

Climb swallowed hard and broke into a run. His gaze moved from Succuronte to Coccodor.

Succuronte's face warped like he'd bitten down on something bitter.

When you're acting as security, you hate it when the one under your protection gets targeted, even if it's merely as a threat. I'm the same way, so I know how it goes. Executing a tactic he'd hate to have to deal with himself, he closed in. *A maniac of illusions... I can imagine... Well, maybe his name is misleading...but it's worth testing.*

Once in range, he brought down his sword, but Succuronte unsurprisingly deflected it easily. Climb braced through the shock and struck again. He wasn't swinging from overhead, so there wasn't a ton of power behind it, but it was still enough.

Succuronte's blade deflected his again, and Climb took some distance with a satisfied nod. "It's an illusion, not a martial art!"

He'd felt something off the moment his sword was deflected. It felt like the block occurred a little bit in front of the blade he could see.

"Your whole right arm is an illusion. The real arm and sword are invisible!"

In other words, the sword he'd blocked had been an illusion, and the real one had cut into his flesh.

Any hint of emotion disappeared from Succuronte's face, and he began to speak in a flat voice. "...That's right. It's nothing more than the combination of a spell that can make parts of things invisible and a spell that causes hallucinations. I'm an illusionist and a fencer. It's a lame trick once you know the secret, right? You can laugh."

There was no way he could laugh. Sure, putting it into words made it sound so simple he wondered why he hadn't thought of it, but there was nothing scarier than an invisible sword in combat where one hit could mean death. And being able to only half see through it was as confusing as it sounded.

"Since I diversified my abilities, I might be less of a warrior than you, but..." Succuronte flourished his sword. But was that even really his arm? It was entirely possible that this was an illusion and his real arm had a dagger out and was waiting for the right time to throw.

The dread of illusion set in, and Climb broke out in a cold sweat.

"Illusionists can only use spells that belong to the illusion tree of arcane magic. In the upper tiers, some illusion attacks fool the brain to death...but I haven't gotten there yet."

"That seems fishy. What proof do I have that's true?"

"Right." Succuronte laughed. "Well, you don't need to believe me. Anyhow, what was I trying to say? Oh yeah. Because of that, I can't cast strengthening spells on myself and I can't cast weakening spells on you. But can you tell the difference between illusion and reality?"

As he finished speaking, Succuronte split into multiple Succurontes. "Multiple Vision!"

One would think the real one was in the center, but there was no guarantee of that.

Why did I give time to a caster?! It *was* Climb's goal to buy time, but giving a caster leeway to cast support spells was too dangerous.

Climb screamed a battle cry, used an art to boost his abilities and perception, and closed the gap between him and Succuronte all at once.

"Scintillating Scotoma!"

"Ugh!"

It was like a part of his field of vision had gone missing; however, the effect disappeared immediately. Apparently, he had successfully resisted the spell.

Charging forward, he swung his sword to mow down all the Succurontes at once, but only one of them was in range. To get them all, he'd have to be fighting at extremely close quarters. Climb wouldn't be able to get enough momentum behind the blade at that distance.

The unlucky Succuronte fell to the side in halves, but no blood spurted out, and the sword moved smoothly through him.

"Better luck next time!"

A chill slithered up from Climb's bowels. He was suddenly hot near his throat. He brought his left hand up to protect the hot area.

A sharp pain coursed through his hand, and he felt the awful sensation of fresh blood soaking his clothes. If he hadn't sensed the killing urge, if he had hesitated to sacrifice his hand, his throat would have been slashed. Relieved to be alive, he gritted his teeth against the pain and swept his blade sideways.

Again, it met no resistance and slashed only air.

It can't go on like this. Realizing that, Climb switched arts and used Evasion as he backed away. His field of vision contained the two remaining Succurontes raising their swords at the same time. Knowing that both blades were illusions, he focused all his attention in his ears.

The mail shirt he was wearing and the beating of his heart made a racket. Right now the only things he wanted to hear were the sounds of the man in front of him.

No… No… There!

It was definitely not the sound of a sword being brought down. The faint sound of something slicing through wind was approaching his face from an empty space in front of him.

He rushed to turn his head, and along with the searing sensation that streaked across his cheek, he felt his flesh being painfully torn off. A hot liquid flowed down his cheek and ran down his neck.

"There's a fifty percent chance!"

Spitting the blood that had welled up in his mouth, Climb bet all he had on a single attack.

Because he'd used it as a shield earlier, his left arm was pure agony from the wrist down. It was possible the nerves had been severed, so he wasn't even sure his fingers would work right. Still, if he could line them up, he could grip the hilt of his sword.

An explosion of pain coursed through him, and he grit his teeth. But his left hand moved and gripped the hilt. The limb probably felt swollen only because of the excruciating injury.

He grasped his sword tightly with both hands, mustered all the strength he could find, and brought the blade down from overhead.

Blood spurted. He felt the blade cut into something hard, and the sticky red sprayed up like a fountain. It seemed he'd nailed the real one this time.

Apparently, he'd hit a vital point, and Succuronte thudded to the floor. Climb couldn't believe he'd won against someone said to be adamantite equivalent, but it was definitely true that the man was lying on the floor. He suppressed the joy welling up inside him and returned Coccodor's stare.

It didn't seem like he had the will to run away.

Perhaps because Climb had relaxed a bit, the pain in his cheek and left hand was enough to make him feel sick. "I can't…quite call this victory."

Taking Succuronte prisoner would have been best, but it had been impossible for him. Still, if he could capture a man escaping with the protection and assistance of the Six Arms, they should be able to get plenty of intelligence.

As he stepped forward to capture him, Climb felt something was off in the man's expression. He seemed too composed.

Why?

At that moment, a searing sensation ripped through his abdomen.

The tension drained from his body all at once, leaving him limp as a puppet. His vision went black for a moment, and when he came to, he was on the floor. He couldn't understand what had happened. A pain filled his abdomen, like a burning iron rod had been shoved into his stomach, and he exhaled roughly. All he could see was the floor, but then a pair of legs entered his field of vision.

"Unfortunately for you, I can't let you win."

Climb strained to look up, and what he saw was a nearly unscathed Succuronte.

"Fox Sleep. It's an illusion for after you get injured. That hurt! You probably thought you'd finished me off, right?" His finger traced a straight line across his chest. It was the path Climb's sword had followed.

Climb's breath was coming short and rough. He could feel the blood flowing from his abdomen, soaking into his mail shirt and clothes.

I'm going to die.

Pain was tearing at his consciousness, but he frantically held on before he lost it.

If I black out, I'll die for sure.

But even if he stayed conscious, it was only a matter of time, and the probability Succuronte would finish him off was extremely high.

He'd done battle with a man on par with an adamantite-rank adventurer. He'd probably even put up a good fight. There was nothing left to do now but give up. It meant the gap in their strength was indisputable.

But he couldn't give up.

There was no way he could give up.

Climb clenched his teeth so hard it seemed like they would break.

He couldn't stand to allow someone to die, or die himself, without Renner's permission.

"Kugh! Gngh…gyngh…g…g…" Groaning and grinding his teeth, he steeled himself, although he'd almost lost to the intense pain.

I can't die yet. There's no way I can die yet.

He desperately remembered Renner. He wanted to go home to her today like always…

"We don't have time for this, so I'm gonna go ahead and finish you off. Later." Succuronte turned his sword on the groaning boy.

His prey was fatally wounded and death was only a matter of time, but Succuronte had the feeling it would be better to finish him off here once and for all.

"…Hey, why don't we take him with us?"

"Please, Coccodor, no. There's a good chance this brat has friends on the other side of that door. And even if we take him with us, he'll die before we get to a safe place. Please give it up."

"Then let's at least bring his head. We can arrange it with some flowers and send it to that female brat."

"Okay, okay. I guess that's fi— Uh, whoa!" Succuronte leaped aside.

The boy had flashed his sword.

For a boy on the edge of death, it was a sharp, steady swing.

Succuronte had been gazing at his pitiful prey and its frantic resistance with contempt, but now his eyes widened.

The boy leaned on his sword and stood up.

That should have been impossible.

Succuronte had killed more people than he could count on his fingers, and in his estimation, that blow should have been fatal. The boy should not have been able to stand.

But the scene before his eyes betrayed the knowledge born of his experience oh so easily.

"H-how can you stand?"

He felt sick to his stomach. The boy was practically an undead.

Before his pale face and the long string of drool hanging down from it, Succuronte could only think he had ceased to be human.

"I ca…di…ye… I…nee…retur…avor…to…cess…R…ner…"

Faced with those strangely twinkling eyes, Succuronte caught his breath for a moment. He was afraid. He was frightened of this boy who had done the impossible.

The boy staggered, and Succuronte returned to himself. What washed over him at that moment was shame.

He couldn't believe he, one of the Six Arms, had been afraid of a lesser opponent.

"You half-dead trash! Die already!" Succuronte charged. He was sure the boy would die if he stabbed him.

But he was taking him too lightly.

Certainly, the total gap between them was overwhelmingly obvious. However, Succuronte was an illusionist and a fencer, while Climb was a warrior. In terms of pure combat ability, Climb was no weaker than Succuronte—more than a match for him, in fact. It was only because of magic that Climb was at a disadvantage. Without magic protection, Succuronte was the weaker of the two.

His blade descended with a roar, followed by a shrill *clang*.

The reason it had been possible to block the boy's overhead swing was because his movements on the brink of death were sluggish.

A cold sweat ran down Succuronte's face.

His opponent was nearly dead. That thought had distracted him, clouded his vision, but now his eyes popped open. As a fencer, he'd trained to evade his opponents' attacks; the reason he blocked the boy's strike with his sword was because it was that extraordinary.

That was not the attack of a person on the verge of death. Those words flitted across Succuronte's mind in his panic. *No, his sword is actually moving faster than when he wasn't hurt!*

"What the heck? What's with this kid?"

He was standing in another realm of combat. It wasn't impossible, but Succuronte had never seen someone like that in real life.

It felt more like something had come undone.

"What's going on? Are you using a magic item? A martial art?" His voice was distraught. He was cornered, unsure who was superior anymore.

What had happened to Climb? It's simple.

Thanks to Sebas's training, his sense of self-preservation was confused. His determination to live overlapped with the death he'd seen before him in Sebas's training, and his brain's limiter had come off in the same way as then to unleash hysterical strength.

The training had consisted of being shown only one move, but without it, he would have died here and now, helpless.

A hard blow sent Succuronte flying.

The shock of slamming into the floor traveled through his back and rocked his stomach. His orichalcum mail shirt absorbed some of the impact, but even so, the wind was knocked from his lungs and he couldn't breathe for a moment.

What happened? As the one who'd received the blow, Succuronte couldn't understand, but to Coccodor, who was standing to the side, it was obvious.

He'd been kicked.

The moment his overhead swing had been blocked, the boy had unleashed a kick at Succuronte.

Still not sure what had happened, Succuronte hurried to his feet. For fencers, who pride themselves on their agility, lying on the ground was the same as being in the jaws of death.

"Shit! This kid uses his feet! That's not very soldierly! If he would fight by the rules…!" Succuronte whined with a click of his tongue as he rolled and rushed to steady himself.

This wasn't the fighting cultivated by soldier training; that dirty style made this feel like a battle with an adventurer. So he couldn't underestimate him.

Succuronte began to feel anxious.

He thought at first that it'd be an easy win, that he'd be able to kill this little brat no problem. But now he felt that confidence ebbing.

Now on his feet, he saw the dangerous-seeming boy slowly crumple to the ground and held his breath.

From the boy's complexion, it looked like the previous exchange had expended the rest of his life. No, that was exactly what had happened. He'd exhibited the power of a candle flaring the moment before it goes out.

But now so much as a light push would probably kill him.

Succuronte felt slightly relieved to see that, but confusion and rage soon overtook him at the fact that he, one of the Six Arms, the strongest members of the Eight Fingers, could feel this cornered by a single soldier. At the fact that he'd worried at all. But now the fight was decided. All that was left was to kill him and escape.

But—

"I'll have you stop right there."

It seemed like he'd made it just in time.

Climb lay on the floor, his face clammy with sweat and paler than white. Nevertheless, he was still alive. But the wound in his abdomen was fatal, so he'd die if there was any delay in getting him treatment.

With no sense of relief, Brain charged into the room.

There were two men there. One seemed entirely incapable of fighting.

"Don't worry about that shady guy. Just kill the kid!"

"He'll charge and kill me instantly if I do that. He isn't like that brat. I can't win against him unless I focus and fight with all my might. If I let my guard down for an instant or get even a little distracted, it'll be over."

Brain understood that the one who'd replied was Succuronte. He *did* fit the description he'd heard. The warrior could have deduced the man's identity from his double and blood-splattered sword alone, but now he knew for sure.

Brain walked briskly forward without a word, drawing his katana and striking in one fluid motion, but Succuronte had already jumped away. The sword sliced through nothing but air. Brain had swung it only to get him away from Climb anyway. He stepped over the fallen boy and took up a position protecting him.

"Climb, are you okay? Do you have any healing items?" he asked quickly, with no time to lose. If he didn't have something, they'd need to come up with another plan as soon as possible.

"Agh," he panted. "Y...ye...s."

Brain glanced down and saw that Climb's hand had let go of his sword and was moving. "Okay," he answered, feeling deeply relieved. Then he turned a severe stare on Succuronte. "Starting now, I'm your opponent. I'll be taking revenge for him."

"Given the katana, I guess I shouldn't be surprised you'd be so confident. Those rarely find their way this far north... I've never even heard of one in the kingdom. Can I ask your name?"

Brain didn't feel like answering.

He and Climb had the same objective—they were comrades. With Climb half-dead, how could he answer a question like that as if nothing had happened...? Brain suddenly wondered to himself, *Was I always like this?*

Hadn't he abandoned everything besides growing stronger with a sword? He cocked his head slightly and laughed to himself. *Ohhh, I see.*

His heart, his dreams, his goals, his livelihood, his very way of life—it had all been broken by the monster Shalltear Bloodfallen. The boy called Climb must have wedged himself into those cracks the moment he'd earned Brain's admiration for being able to withstand the mysterious Sebas's brutal intent to kill when Brain himself couldn't, despite being weaker. He'd seen the brilliance of this young soldier who had something he did not.

He stood in front of Climb and exchanged glares with Succuronte. *Can I get Climb to see the same thing in me as I saw in him that time?*

His old self would have burst out laughing, saying, *You've gone soft.*

He used to think that bearing the burden of another made a warrior weak. He'd thought warriors needed to be sharp.

But now he understood.

"This is another way to live... I get it, Gazef...but I may never make it to where you are."

"Did you not hear me? How about I ask you again? What's your name?"

"Sorry. I don't think it'll matter if I tell you, but sure, I'll answer... I'm Brain Unglaus."

Succuronte's eyes opened wide. "What?! *The* Brain Unglaus?"

"No way! That's him?! He's not impersonating him?"

"No, Coccodor, there's no doubt about it. A valuable weapon shows a warrior's rank. If he's really who he says he is, a katana makes sense."

Brain grinned bitterly. "The fact that most of the people I've met today know who I am...might have made my old self happy. But now I can't really say I care." Succuronte's smile of goodwill confused him, but his questions were cleared up immediately.

"Hey, Unglaus! Why don't we quit fighting? A man of your caliber should be one of us. How about it? Want to join? I'm sure you'd be able to be one of the Six Arms. I can tell you're that strong by looking at you. You're the same as us. You want power, right? I can see it in your eyes."

"...Well, you're not wrong."

"In that case, the Eight Fingers isn't a bad gig. For people with strength, it's the best place to be! You can even get your hands on powerful magic items. Check out my orichalcum mail shirt! My mythril sword! My rings! My clothes! My boots! They're all magic! So, Brain Unglaus, join us—be one of the Six Arms with me!"

"...Is that all? Sounds lame."

Succuronte's face froze at Brain's unbelievably cold, insulting answer.

"What?"

"You didn't hear me? I said that a bunch of guys with nothing but strength doesn't sound like such a great group."

"Y-you bastard! ...H-hmph. If that's what you think, then you must not be so tough, either!"

"You're right. I don't think I'm strong. Not someone like me who's seen a real monster." Brain took pity on the frog sitting comfortably in his well, thinking he was powerful, and gave him a genuinely compassionate warning. "And that goes for you, too. We may be about equal—which is why I'll warn you. We're not that great at all." Brain turned to check over his shoulder on Climb, who had just finished drinking a potion. "And I've learned something. Strength for someone else's sake surpasses the strength of one alone." Brain smiled. It was a friendly, pleasant smile. "Maybe it's only sunk in a little, but I know."

"I have no idea what you're talking about… It's too bad, Unglaus. I can't believe I have to kill the genius swordsman who once gave Stronoff a run for his money."

"I wonder if you can really kill me, swinging your sword only for yourself."

"Yeah, I can. I can kill you without breaking a sweat. I'm gonna kill you, and then I'm gonna kill that brat lying on the floor. I'm not playing anymore, and I'm not holding back. I'm going all out."

Without taking his eyes off Succuronte, who had begun casting a spell, he cautioned Climb when he sensed movement behind him. "Don't move, Climb. You're not fully healed, right?"

The movement stopped.

Brain smiled and, with the same surprise he'd felt at himself earlier, said, "Leave the rest to me."

"Thanks."

Brain smiled instead of responding and sheathed his sword. As he lowered his hips, he flipped his sword and sheath upside down.

"Please be careful. Succuronte uses illusions. Not everything you see will be real."

"Hrm… That does make him a tricky opponent…but that's fine."

Brain silently, motionlessly watched Succuronte. At some point, five images of him had appeared. Not only that, they appeared to contain magic sparks, shrouded in something like mantles of shadow.

He had no idea what kind of spells those were.

"Thanks for the prep time! Give a caster a little time and they can become even stronger than a warrior. Your defeat is certain, Unglaus!"

"Yeah, don't mention it. Now that I talked with my friend here, I know for sure that I'm not gonna lose!"

"Shut your mouth! You didn't move because you're protecting that brat? How nice of you."

He heard Climb shift on the floor.

The boy must have felt bad for giving their enemy time to cast. And that was why Brain announced, loud enough for Climb to hear, "One hit."

"What?!"

"I said I'm finishing this in one hit, Succuronte."

"Just try it!"

Succuronte charged at Brain with his afterimages trailing behind him.

He came into range, and Brain turned around, calmly showing Succuronte his defenseless back. Then at a godly speed, he attacked over Climb, drawing his sword with a flash into space, where there was no one.

There was a crash, and the walls shook.

Climb, from the floor, and Coccodor turned toward the source of the noise.

It was Succuronte. His body was on the ground, not so much as twitching. His sword lay nearby.

Brain's single blow had knocked Succuronte back, slamming him into the wall with unbelievable momentum. If he hadn't struck him with the back of his blade, he surely would have been cut in half, even with his orichalcum mail. Or so one might think after witnessing such a blow.

"…It doesn't matter if an opponent is invisible, my martial art Domain can still detect them. Using auditory illusions to draw my attention forward while attacking from the rear… That's a great plan, but it wasn't going to work on me. And it was stupid of him to go for you, too. He was probably going to kill you and then say, 'See, you couldn't protect him,' but he diverted too much attention from me to target you. Did he forget who he was fighting?" Brain smiled at Climb. "See? One hit!"

"Magnificent."

Another voice's "Magnificent" overlapped with Climb's. The two of them were taken by surprise—it was Sebas's voice, but that wasn't what shocked them. They were startled at the direction it came from for a reason.

They both looked to where Coccodor had been standing and found Sebas with Coccodor crumpled up on the ground.

"When did you get here?!" Brain asked.

Sebas answered calmly. "Just now. It seems like you didn't notice because you were both so focused on Succuronte."

"Oh, I see…," Brain answered, but he didn't really think it could be possible. *I was using Domain! It covers a small area, but if he ran in a straight line in front of me, he should have been in it. But I didn't detect him…? The only one who could move like that so far was Shalltear Bloodfallen! I thought so when I felt that killing intent before, but is he on that monster's level? Who is this guy?!*

"I went ahead and saved all the prisoners. Also, apologies to Climb, but several people put up quite a bit of resistance, so I was forced to kill them. Please forgive me…but I guess I should heal him before I say all that."

Sebas went over and put his hand to Climb's abdomen. It was only for a moment. He'd barely touched him when he was already pulling away. But the effects were dramatic. Even with the potion, Climb's face had been pale, but color returned immediately.

"You healed me… So you're a priest?"

"No, I didn't heal you with the power of the gods. I poured chi into you."

"A monk! I see, that makes sense." Now Brain understood why Sebas didn't have any armor or weapons, and he gave him an affirming smile.

"What are you two planning on doing now?"

"…I've come this far. I'll stay with you till this is finished."

"Well, first I'm going to run to a guardhouse, explain what's happened here, and see if we can get some soldiers to help us. I'd like you to hold the fort down here while I do that. But it's possible that reinforcements from the Eight Fingers will come."

"That sounds fine to me. But could you leave me out of your explanation? I originally came to this country for business, so I'd rather not poke my head any further into its underworld."

"It's fine to mention me if you want. You can tell them Stronoff will vouch for me."

"Ah. Understood."

3

3 Late Fire Moon (September) 7:05 PM

Climb finally returned to the castle as night began falling on the royal capital.

His wounds were completely healed, but his body was utterly exhausted. Partly from the battle, but all the things they'd had to coordinate had taken a lot of time, too. In the end, the reason things went well wasn't because Climb was the princess's servant but because the guards' fear of the Eight Fingers made them indecisive. A particularly major issue was who would report the incident.

There was an extremely good chance, not just a vague worry, that the Eight Fingers would kill those responsible for this as examples. For that reason, they'd had a soldier deliver to Princess Renner a piece of paper with a summary of what had occurred and gotten her permission to list her and Climb as joint reporters.

Of course, there were downsides to this plan, but there were at least two benefits.

One, naturally, was that it would be good for Renner's reputation.

Having her personal attendant spearhead the exposure of an organization that sullied their country, whose members were doing something as awful as slave trafficking, would earn some recognition for a princess who rarely left the palace.

The second was that it would shield Sebas and the woman he was protecting, who had been exploited by the brothel.

They didn't seem to want attention, so by taking responsibility for the incident, Climb could conceal them from the retribution of the Eight Fingers.

I was practically useless during the raid, so I should at least do this much…

Brain had said he would explain everything to Gazef himself so Climb didn't have to worry about it.

With all those things floating around in his head, he knocked on Renner's door.

Really, he had permission to enter without knocking, but it was late, so he modestly refrained. One time she'd been dressed in light silk…

She understood his reasons.

Before he heard her response, he sniffed himself.

He had wiped himself down, but his nose was accustomed to the smell of blood, so he couldn't be sure if he'd gotten rid of it or not. He had no business entering the princess's room like this, but he urgently needed to tell her of the day's events from his own mouth.

The most pressing issue was the women who had been held at the Eight Fingers facility. They'd been entrusted to a guardhouse for the time being, but they needed to be moved somewhere safe in the next few days. Also, some of them were injured, so they would need a priest or someone else who could cast healing magic.

Princess Renner is so kind, I'm sure she'll lend a hand to these suffering people.

It pained him in many ways to cause trouble for his master. He found himself wishing impertinent things. *If only I were stronger… The reason I have such a wonderful master, the reason I'm able to live the way I do—it's all thanks to her… Huh? No response?*

He didn't hear anything like permission to enter.

There was no night guard in front of her door, and she was usually still awake at this time. *Did she go to sleep without alerting her guard?*

Climb knocked again.

This time he heard a faint voice granting him entry, so he went in, relieved. The first thing he needed to do was obvious. "I'm sorry I'm late."

He bowed crisply.

"I was worried!" Her voice contained distinct anger. That was surprising. Climb's master was almost never angry. Even if someone insulted her, he'd never seen her get upset. She must have been truly worried.

Enduring the heat creeping into the corners of his eyes, he kept his head down and repeated his apology.

"I was really worried! I thought maybe the Eight Fingers had made the first move and done something to you... So what in the world happened? I got your brief report, but can you give me the details?"

Climb started to talk as he stood, but Renner invited him to sit in his usual spot. Steam rose from the tea she poured out of her Warm Bottle into a cup set in front of him.

Thanking her, he raised the perfectly hot tea to his mouth and drank.

He told her everything that had happened. Of course he did—there were people he was depending on her to help.

"So what did you think when you saw them?" Renner's first question after hearing his explanation was a strange one. But since she had asked, he had to answer.

"I felt sorry for them. I thought if I were only stronger, I could have saved them from having to suffer so much."

"I see... So you pitied them."

"Yes."

"I see. You're so kind, Climb."

"Princess Renner, if you ever need someone to guard them, I'm prepared to go at any time."

"...If it comes up, please do. More importantly, I should tell you: Tomorrow or the next day at the latest, we're going to attack the Eight Fingers facilities listed on the parchment that Lakyus brought. With this raid on the brothel, the more time that goes by, the stricter their security will become."

"My apologies! I've acted imprudently!"

"No, don't worry about it. You made up my mind for me. Besides, I think very highly of your actions. We captured Succuronte, one of the Six Arms, and Coccodor, chief of the slave-trafficking division. That has to have shaken them to their foundations. That's why I want to hit them again now." Renner threw an adorable punch with zero speed and strength. "One more punch before the news leaves the capital!"

"Understood! I'll go immediately to rest up for tomorrow."

"Thanks. It's going to be a big day. Take care."

Climb left her room. She sensed the smell of blood abate somewhat.

"It must have been tough for you, Climb. Now, then…"

Draining the rest of her lukewarm tea, Renner stood up. Her goal was a handbell. It was a magic item that rang its linked mate in the next room when she jingled it. She brought to mind the face of the maid standing by in the next room and smiled coldly, thinking how lucky it was that she was the one on duty today.

"Oh, right, what expression should I make?" She stood before the mirror wobbling her cheeks up and down between her hands. She was human, so it wasn't as if she could change her face by doing that. It was more like an autosuggestion.

She pulled her hands away and smiled.

"No. This is the smile I make when I see someone as the princess…" She imitated the expression and then smiled again. After trying out several different smiles, a pure, innocent one appeared on her face. "This'll be best."

Her preparations complete, she rang the bell.

A maid promptly knocked on the door and entered.

"I have a favor to ask. Could you boil some water for me?"

"Of course, Princess Renner." She curtsied and smiled at Renner. "What is it? You seem in high spirits. Did something good happen?"

Now that the fish had bitten her hook, the princess smiled happily. "Oh, it's amazing! Climb's done the most amazing thing!" She talked like a little girl, an appropriately stupid tone for someone blabbing important information.

"That's wonderful." This maid wasn't a fan of Climb, and although she tried to cleverly hide the fact, her true feelings came through.

*   *   *

I'll kill her.
I'll kill this woman, too.
*I'll kill everyone who looks down on **my** Climb.*

Renner didn't show that she'd noticed—because right now she was a naive princess. She wasn't supposed to be perceptive enough to catch on to people's malice, and she forgave the maid's rudeness. That was the kind of simple-headed—ditzy—princess she played.

"Yes! It's just amazing! Climb beat up some really bad guys! And he freed some people who were held captive and left them somewhere…at one of the guardhouses. Now we can punish the nobles who were working with the bad guys!"

"Is that so? Quite amazing. I'd expect nothing less from your Climb. Will you tell me more details about his amazing feats?"

Renner poured her poison into this idiot, who didn't suspect anything because she thought the princess was a fool.

Renner held everything in the palm of her hand. She would get what she wanted.

3 Late Fire Moon (September) 10:10 PM

A mysterious group had melted into the dark of night.

Each of them was outfitted differently. They didn't seem at all like soldiers. They most closely resembled adventurers.

Standing at the head of the group was a brawny man. Next was a delicate man and a woman dressed in light silk. Then there was a figure in a robe and, at the end of the line, someone in full plate armor.

The group was peering through an open door into a space engulfed in darkness. There was no sign of any human presence. No matter where they looked, it didn't seem like there was anyone around.

That was strange. Certainly, all the goods inside the brothel had been carried out and taken to a guardhouse. But just because there was nothing left inside didn't mean there shouldn't be someone on lookout. And near the entrance on the empty street, they could see the fire of the night watch burning brightly.

The reason there was no one around regardless was because they had used their authority to keep the soldiers away temporarily.

The boulder-like man in front—Zero—cast a stern look at the fallen brothel and snarled in a hateful, low voice, "How idiotic. I suppose we'll have to apologize to Coccodor. We lent him Succuronte of the Six Arms, and the place went down this easily. And on the same day we dispatched him...what a laugh."

Zero sent a sharp glance over his shoulder at the snickering.

Keenly familiar with Zero's personality, the silk-clad woman quickly spoke. "Oh, uhh, so then, what should we do, boss? Should we kill Succuronte, since he's been caught? We can't send brute muscle as long as he's at a guardhouse, so we'd have to borrow some assassins from a different division... What should we do?"

"Not that. He's a handy fellow. I'll ask the count to have him released today... That'll cost a fortune. Draw up a list of things the count likes."

"What should we do about Coccodor?" the slight, delicate man asked.

"He can use his own connections. If he asks, we can pull some strings as an apology. What happened to the customer list? Do we know if the guards got ahold of it?"

"Haven't heard anything like that. Rather, there aren't any details yet." The dark voice from beneath the robe carried a spine-chilling, hollow echo, as if it were emanating from an open grave.

"I'd really like to get our hands on that list. We could blackmail so many people."

"Don't be stupid. We'll look even more suspicious if we get it. They'll think the whole thing was our plan. If we find the list, we should hide it in a safe place and then return it to Coccodor later when we apologize. Besides, they write in a code that can't be cracked so easily, so we wouldn't be able to use it anyhow."

The delicate man shrugged at Zero's remark and said, "Anyhow, we'll go in and figure that out later. If it's there, it's probably in a hidden safe... Still, this is crazy. How did they make this hole? Doesn't seem like a weapon... Magic?"

"A fist."

Everyone's eyes gathered on Zero. He repeated himself.

"A fist? What a guy!"

"Don't be stupid. This is nothing." Zero interrupted the woman's admiring words, steadied his breath, and struck at the door with his hand. His fist pierced the iron as if it were ripping through paper. He slowly withdrew it to reveal a hole like the one Sebas had made.

The delicate man opened his mouth in astonishment. "We can't have you being the standard, boss... Anyhow, he's strong enough to punch through an iron-reinforced door and take out Succuronte, one of the Six Arms, albeit the weakest one. I suppose we should consider this a fairly powerful enemy?"

"What are you saying? Just because Succuronte lost doesn't mean the enemy is strong." The voice under the hood scoffed. "Once you see through his illusions, his abilities can't measure up to ours. He's tough in a fight where he is clearly superior, but against someone at the same level or where he is even slightly inferior, defeat is inevitable. I believe you all knew that."

Someone laughed quietly in agreement with that opinion, ridiculing the less powerful man.

"So keeping that in mind, I'll ask the question: What should we do? Stay out of it? Even if we confront this, I can't imagine the benefits can balance out the losses," the hooded figure continued.

"Don't be stupid." The irrepressible anger was showing through here and there in Zero's speech.

"If we don't make the guy who attacked the brothel into an example by killing him, it'll be bad for our reputation. Now's no time to think about losses. The Six Arms need to move together to kill the raider. Undead King, Davernoch." The figure in the robe thrust out a hand. The hand, which was not that of a living thing, contained an orb that gave off a strange aura representing the owner's emotions.

"Spatial Slash, Peshurian." The figure in full plate armor who had been silent up until now pounded his fist against his chest with a violent *clang*.

"Dancing Scimitars, Edström." The woman dressed in light silk gave an elegant bow, and the golden bangles on her arms jangled.

"Thousand Kills, Marmvist." The delicate man clicked his heels together.

"And me, Fighting Ogre, Zero!"

Everyone around Zero nodded in agreement or maybe understanding.

"First, let's bail out Succuronte and the other captives and get info from them. Once that's done…get together some guys who can perform torture. We'll show the raiders what a hell this world can be. We'll make them regret the foolish things they've done!"

3 *Late Fire Moon* (September) 5:42 PM

By the time Sebas finished everything and returned to the mansion, the sun was already going down.

Climb will protect women who were being held captive. Succuronte and the place's manager have been arrested. Things are probably a mess on their end, so perhaps we've bought some time.

So what to do about Tsuare? He thought it would be best to take her somewhere safe, but as far as he knew, no such place existed. Sebas was worrying about all these things when he reached the mansion.

His hand stopped as he went to open the door. Someone was standing immediately behind it. The presence was Solution's, but he couldn't tell why she was right inside.

Some kind of emergency?

With some trepidation, Sebas opened the door. What he found was so unexpected, he froze.

"Welcome back, Master Sebas."

It was Solution in her maid uniform.

A chill went up Sebas's spine.

She was supposed to be acting the part of a merchant's daughter. A human who knew nothing—Tsuare—was in the house, and she was wearing her maid uniform. That meant either she didn't need to act anymore or there was some reason she needed to wear her maid uniform.

In the former case, it meant something had happened to Tsuare. In the latter…

"Master Sebas, Lord Ainz is waiting for you inside."

Registering what Solution's quiet voice had said, Sebas's heart skipped a beat.

Sebas was unfazed before a powerful enemy or a guardian-rank being, but a visit from his master made him nervous.

"Wh-why…?" His tongue tangled on the word.

Solution only looked at him. "Master Sebas, Lord Ainz is waiting."

Her attitude told him she had nothing else to say, and he followed after her.

His footsteps were as heavy as those of a man being led to the guillotine.

OVERLORD
Character Profiles

Character 17

SEBAS TIAN

GROTESQUE

Butler of steel

Position —— Butler of the Great Tomb of Nazarick

Residence —— One of the servants' rooms on the ninth level

Alignment —— Extreme good (Karma points: 300)

Race Levels —— Unknown

Class Levels —— Monk ———————————— 10 lv

Martial King ———————— 10 lv

Striker ————————————— 5 lv

Internal Chi Master ———— 15 lv

External Chi Master ——— 5 lv

Etc.

[Race levels] + [Class levels]	100 levels
● Race levels	Class levels ●
25 acquired total	75 acquired total

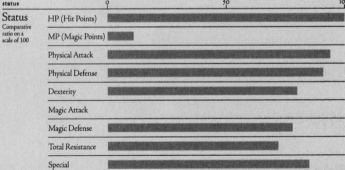

status		0	50	100
Status Comparative ratio on a scale of 100	HP (Hit Points)			
	MP (Magic Points)			
	Physical Attack			
	Physical Defense			
	Dexterity			
	Magic Attack			
	Magic Defense			
	Total Resistance			
	Special			

Character 18

SOLUTION EPSILON (ε)

GROTESQUE

Prison of Dissolution

Position —— Combat maid of the
Great Tomb of Nazarick

Residence —— One of the servants' rooms
on the ninth level

Alignment —— Evil (Karma points: -400)

Race Levels —— Shoggoth —————— 10 lv

Ubbo-Sathla —————— 10 lv

Class Levels —— Assassin —————— 2 lv

Poison Maker —————— 4 lv

Master Assassin —————— 1 lv

Etc.

[Race levels] + [Class levels] —————— 57 levels
● Race levels   Class levels ●
45 acquired total   12 acquired total

status	0	50	100
Status Comparative ratio on a scale of 100			
HP (Hit Points)			
MP (Magic Points)			
Physical Attack			
Physical Defense			
Dexterity			
Magic Attack			
Magic Defense			
Total Resistance			
Special			

Character **19**

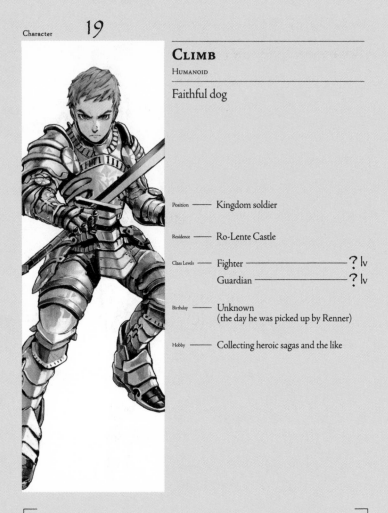

CLIMB

HUMANOID

Faithful dog

Position ——— Kingdom soldier

Residence ——— Ro-Lente Castle

Class Levels ——— Fighter ———————————— **?** lv
          Guardian ——————————— **?** lv

Birthday ——— Unknown
          (the day he was picked up by Renner)

Hobby ——— Collecting heroic sagas and the like

{ personal character }

A boy found by the Golden Princess, Renner. He wears the pure-white plate armor given him by Renner and carries a broadsword and shield. He's a hot-blooded, hardworking boy and has pledged absolute loyalty to the princess. Thus, in order to be useful to her, he never misses a day of training with his sword. However, despite his hard work, he never had any aptitude to begin with, which frustrates him. Partially because of the special treatment he gets from Renner, he's not close to anyone besides her.

Character 20

RENNER THEIERE CHARDELON RYLE VAISELF

HUMANOID

The Golden Princess

Position ——— Princess

Residence ——— Ro-Lente Castle

Class Levels ——— Princess (ordinary) ——————— **?** lv
Actress (ordinary) ——————— **?** lv

Birthday ——— 7 Early Fire Moon

Hobby ——— Staring at Climb

{ personal character }

Long, pale blond hair and eyes like sapphires. The princess of the Re-Estize Kingdom is so beautiful she is known as the Golden Princess. There is no shortage of stories about her beauty, such as how every bard without exception sings songs of her. Plus, she's not only beautiful, but she also values both her country and its people and attempts to display her abilities in the political arena as well, such as when she abolished the slave trade. She's compassionate, gentle—a shining example of a princess—however...

Character   **21**

GAZEF STRONOFF
HUMANOID

The strongest warrior in the kingdom

Position ——— Captain of the Warrior Select

Residence ——— The royal capital

Class Levels ——— Fighter ————————————— **?** lv
Mercenary ————————— **?** lv
Champion ————————— **?** lv
Etc.

Birthday ——— 21 Mid-Earth Moon

Hobby ——— Saving money

{   personal character   }

Known for being the greatest warrior not only in the kingdom but also
in the surrounding region as well. His upstanding reputation precedes
him domestically and internationally, though he is not well-liked by
nobles. Born a peasant, he became one of the king's retainers after defeating
Brain in the finals of a royal tournament. Since then, he has worked for
the king and is more loyal to him than the average subject. He's a genius
with a sword but has yet to earn a place in the realm of heroes. He has
southern blood in him, which is evident in the color of his hair and eyes.

BRAIN UNGLAUS
HUMANOID

Seeker of might

Position ——— None

Residence ——— None

Class Levels ——— Genius Fighter ——————— **?** lv

Sword Master ——————— **?** lv

Sword Saint ——————— **?** lv

Etc.

Birthday ——— 10 Mid-Wind Moon

Hobby ——— Drilling with his katana
(and getting stronger in general)

{ personal character }

A genius with a sword. Extremely greedy with regard to one thing and that is getting stronger. His strength is on par with Gazef, the strongest in the kingdom. He sees the captain of the Royal Select as his rival so he took on a great deal of itinerant training. But when he battled Shalltear, he witnessed strength beyond what he'd ever imagined. He lost all his drive when faced with the reality that there were heights one could never reach with hard work and became a shell of his former self. Surprisingly, he enjoys shopping, but that's because he likes looking for items that will make him stronger.

Afterword

It's Kugane Maruyama, the author. *Overlord* is already five volumes long. Allow me to express my gratitude to everyone who has been reading all this way. Thank you.

Now then, Volumes 5 and 6 are a pair, part one and two, so do we even really need an afterword? is what I asked my editor, but she said there might be people who are looking forward to it, so please write one. Are there… people who…look forward to this? Or, like, is it possible to look forward to an afterword? Nnngh, are people expecting the impossible, like, "Hey, say something interesting!"?

Is there anything fun to say…? I don't have anything to talk about except for the fact that while working on books five and six I didn't leave the house at all on weekends or holidays from August till the end of November because I was so busy.

And book six has a deluxe edition with a drama CD like the fourth one did, so that made it even more intense.

This is what it's like to lead a double life as an author!

Hmm, this isn't a fun story at all. It's more likely to crush everyone's dreams.

* * *

Let's switch subjects.

I'm still updating the web version of *Overlord*, but book six will be about 90 percent new writing.

It was always my plan to add material when turning the web novel into a book. This next volume will be the fruit of that endeavor.

I've already finished writing it, so unless there are any issues, it should be out at the end of January 2014. I'll see you again in the afterword there.

From here on out, I'll turn to thank-yous.

To so-bin for the illustrations, Code Design Studio for the design, Osako for the proofreading, F——ta for editing, and everyone involved in producing *Overlord*, thank you. And Honey, thanks for everything.

And to all of you who picked up the book, really, thank you!

KUGANE MARUYAMA
December 2013

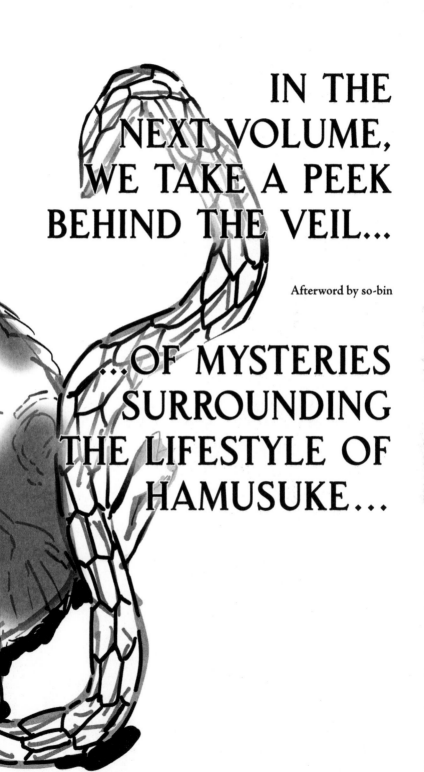

IN THE
NEXT VOLUME,
WE TAKE A PEEK
BEHIND THE VEIL...

Afterword by so-bin

...OF MYSTERIES
SURROUNDING
THE LIFESTYLE OF
HAMUSUKE...

Profile

Author Profile ——————————Kugane Maruyama

He began writing novels, and as a result his life is even more sedentary, so he's developed a very fatty midriff. It's not because he's planning to hibernate for the winter, so he is giving real consideration to going on a diet.

Illustrator Profile ——————— so-bin

Has recently been chided by everyone for being "too skinny" and is feeling sad, so decided to set a new goal for 2014 to put on weight.

THE **SIX ARMS**—THE STRONGEST COMBAT UNIT OF THE EIGHT FINGERS, THE UNDERWORLD ORGANIZATION LURKING IN THE KINGDOM—IS ON THE MOVE. INTERCEPTING THEM ARE THE ADAMANTITE-RANK ADVENTURERS **THE BLUE ROSES.**

Then a mysterious great demon, Jaldabaoth, wriggles himself into the middle of their battle.

The fierce struggle will wrap the royal capital in flames in Volume

Volume
Six

OVERLORD
Volume 6: The Men of the Kingdom (Part II)

Kugane Maruyama | Illustration by so-bin

Coming soon from YEN ON !